AMBASSADOR 5: BLUE DIAMOND SKY

PATTY JANSEN

GET FREE EBOOKS

Visit pattyjansen.com
or scan the QR code below with your phone to get four series starter
ebooks for free!

DID YOU KNOW?

Ambassador 5 is also available in audio. Visit https://pattyjansen.com
to find out more.

1

———

THE GUN WAS a thing of beauty, a marvel of engineering.

It was the latest *Deysha* model, produced on Asto, the most heavy-duty weapon I was allowed to have on a regular civil permit. Thayu had selected it for me, had ordered it and had personally travelled into town to take delivery of it at the Exchange.

She had come back to the apartment carrying a big box that drew envious glances from young Deyu and Reida.

She had set the box on the table in the living room and opened the lid. She had unpacked the box—with a foam mould and packaging material inside—and everyone in my association had come into the room and watched, drooling, as she took the shimmering, virgin weapon out of its packaging. Everyone, that was, except me.

I'd been out at some meeting and only heard about the drooling bit when she brought me the weapon, in a dedicated arm bracket, while we sat at the table at dinner.

Eirani looked askance at it while unloading her tray onto the table —her opinion about guns was pretty much in line with mine—but didn't dare ask a top-level spy, two former members of the Chief Coordinator's guards and the other trained members of my association to remove it from the table. She knew enough by now that she would be booed out of the room. So we ate with this shimmering, smooth, high-tech, deadly thing next to my plate. I barely dared touch it. The feel of it in my hands was sort of comfortable, but the comfort was overruled by the overwhelming fear that I'd accidentally hit a wrong button and kill someone.

I needed to learn to use it, Thayu had assured me.

So after dinner I went with Veyada to the shooting range. He taught me all the tricks and technological whizzbangery that made it almost impossible to miss—at least so he said—and we kept visiting the range every day until I learned how to use the technology to actually hit the target, at least most of the time.

Clearly, the natural talent I had displayed in the past for hitting stuff—like murderous opponents—evaporated quickly when I was not under threat of being killed and the world was not about to explode.

The problem was, Veyada said, that I was enjoying myself too much. Trying to hit a shooting target was strangely stress-relieving, and there had been plenty of stress in my life recently. It was as if my brain was telling me to take it easy and treat this as a game. Which, Veyada kept telling me, it was not. Guns kill people, blah, blah, blah. I'd heard him repeat his spiel so many times before, to Reida, to Deyu, to anyone who wanted to hear it, and even some people who didn't. Veyada took guns seriously. There were severe consequences to guns being used. People died. One got into legal situations. All reasons why I'd preferred not to carry one. Dog, meet tail.

But eventually, I mastered enough skill that Veyada judged it safe to take my skills into the wild. We were going on a trip. A hunting trip.

In the marshlands where the Barresh delta opened into the sea lived colonies of flying fish that were good eating. Local Pengali fishermen would catch them by throwing a stone in the water to scare the fish and scoop up the ones that broke the surface with a large butterfly net. One could also shoot them. They were extremely good target practice, Veyada said, because it required one to be fast and accurate.

Besides, he had developed a taste for fish.

We were to go for a few days, just myself, Thayu and Veyada. Nicha had his son to look after, Sheydu was running a course about explosives for the benefit of the Barresh guards, and Deyu and Reida were training with her. We weren't going anywhere that required security, so even Evi and Telaris could stay behind. I'd given both of them permission to take time off, hoping they would use it to visit their family on Indrahui even though I was unsure how many of their family were still alive. That subject was fraught with painful history, so the brothers preferred to keep silent about it.

We packed all the camping gear, including the tent, because the wet season was on the verge of breaking. Thayu rented a boat. No, we didn't need a driver. She knew how to operate a boat.

I took my surfboard out of the storage room downstairs and hauled it to the jetty, under the curious gazes of many. Eirani was most disturbed when she saw that our gear didn't include food. I told her that the concept of a "hunting trip" was that you caught your own. But what about if you don't catch any, was her concern. For her, food was something you bought at the markets.

Veyada added, "If he misses too many times, we'll be eating lily bulbs. Serves him right."

We set out from the *gamra* island on a bright sunny morning. Already, big billowing banks of clouds were building on the top of the escarpment. They were still white, but soon they would turn dark and be big enough to roll off the escarpment and sweep over the delta with lightning, thunder and sheets of driving rain. We'd already had a bad pre-season storm a few days ago, which toppled trees and lifted one of my beach chairs off the balcony, depositing it in the garden downstairs. Such storms would become more frequent. It was probably one of the last stretch of days in the year that this trip would be nice, or even possible.

Thayu steered the boat in a southwesterly direction. The powerful jet engine propelled us away from the island at high speed, skimming over the water, wind in our hair. I had forgotten just how nice it was be out here, and remembered with a pang that I had promised to take Raanu surfing.

I hadn't heard from Raanu for a while. When I asked, Ezhya had told me that his daughter was busy with tutoring. I thought it was more likely that his security had disabled the account that she had used to contact me. I had a vision of her lying on her stomach on her bed, with her chin propped up in her hands, contemplating ways to circumvent her father's security and write political letters to important leaders.

Tutoring, my arse.

Raanu was becoming a stubborn and smart young lady.

Maybe I should send her a message to check that she was all right, and let her know I hadn't forgotten her and that the trip was still on.

Soon, Barresh and the *gamra* island had disappeared in the haze that hung low over the water, and we were surrounded by nothing but reeds and channels and copses of megon trees, their trunks rising, ghostlike, from the water. We had a small break at a couple of small islands on which stood the ancient ruins of one of the early settlements in the area. Apparently the building had been a type of school, a few hundred years ago, but the roof had long since fallen in, and the walls had crumbled and were overgrown with moss, creepers and other weeds. The ruins housed a large colony of meili, bat-like creatures that also lived in the city in great quantities. They built nests out of a mixture of mud and tree gum that hardened like concrete. The nest itself looked like a little shelf and was set against a vertical surface, like a tree trunk, a rock face or a wall, in a place that was always in shadow.

We walked into an open space that once must have been a hall, where these nests encrusted an entire wall, each of the little shelves with a furry, wide-eyed and slightly alarmed, squawking, bickering occupant. It was a living wall that reminded me of the walls covered in moving plants in the aquifers around Athyl.

In the late afternoon, we arrived at the long sand spit that separated the brackish water delta from the ocean.

The sand was white, the ocean brilliant turquoise, the waves perfect and glassy. A few offshore islands protruded from the ocean like giant humpbacked whales. The breeze carried the tang of ocean water, laden with humidity.

The spit was narrow in some places, but in others it was wider and sometimes even housed copses of rainforest. We chose a beach next to such a patch of forest, because where there was forest, there was always a fresh water upwelling. We did carry a solar water distiller, but it was easier to just scoop the water for cooking and drinking out of a well.

We set up camp on the edge of the forest in the shade of the trees. We gathered up shells and tubers. The big storm a few days ago had dislodged a lot of lily bulbs which had washed up on the inner shore of the sand spit. We didn't even need to go out to collect them. Since it was almost dusk, the tide was out, and we ventured onto the exposed sand to dig up sand worms.

Veyada turned out to be quite deft at camp cooking, and the meal, shared on the warm sand in the cooling night with the sound of waves crashing on the shore in the background, was one of the more memorable I'd recently shared.

The hunting started the next day. Our main quarry lived where the current in the mouth of the delta was strong. We went out there in the boat. Thayu operated the engine—and it was going full blast. An hour or two after sunrise, the tide was going out like blazes, and with the added current of storm water still finding its way to the ocean, the outlet was a churning mass of water. Veyada threw scraps from last night's meal in the water to attract the fish, and then threw rocks and bits of wood in the places where the fish came to feed.

With each projectile hitting the water, at least two or three silvery glittering winged fish would take to the air.

I stood in the bow with my gun, hitting most of them at their highest point before they fell back into the water.

Thayu would then steer the boat so that Veyada could use the net to scoop the fish out when it floated past.

We had collected half a bucket full of fish when a big maw opened up under the surface and sucked in a fish before Veyada got it.

"Uh-oh. I think we've got an eel," Thayu said.

Veyada squinted at the water. "Looks like it. Might be time to head back."

"Yup. The engine probably needs a recharge, too."

We had no intention of becoming fodder for a twenty-metre-long marsh serpent; and killing it, even if we wanted to, was generally frowned upon by local Pengali and keihu people, so we let the boat drift back to the sand spit, where Thayu went about setting up the solar recharge for the boat's engine, and Veyada and I cleaned and gutted the fish.

We set up the solar water cooker—since one could not make fires in Barresh—and went to collect water from a pristine spring in the middle of the patch of forest, where a bunch of eared lizards squealed their alarm and took off into the greenery.

In the afternoon, I paddled my surfboard out into the ocean and caught glassy waves in the turquoise sea. Thayu watched me from the beach. She later had a try of it, too. Since visiting New Zealand with me, she had been determined to learn how to swim. Surfing, however, was a completely different skill that involved understanding waves.

We cooked our fish and ate so much of it that I thought I'd burst.

The next day went pretty much like the previous, with an added bit of hanky-panky in the clear pool in the forest that Veyada pretended not to notice.

On the last morning before packing up, I went for a last surf. Veyada had said he's spotted some beisili offshore when walking to the forest to get water at sunrise. As soon as I'd paddled past the surf, I could see that they were still there: there were at least four giant looming light-grey blobs in the water. Occasionally they would lift a flipper into the air, or poke their head on a swanlike neck up to have a curious glance at me with a sharp blue eye. I approached carefully.

Beisili could be a bit stroppy, particularly at this time of the year, but the younger ones were often curious and would sometimes come right up to the beach. It was a family group: two adults, probably sisters since they were light grey, with young that measured about the length of the surfboard excluding their long neck. The word "plesiosaur" best described them.

One of them even came so close that I could almost touch it— although we were always warned not to do this. Their skin was really rough and could cause cuts. They were also full of sea growths that stung and caused skin irritation. This particular one was young enough not to have developed the rough, sea-growth-encrusted ridges on its back or the top of its head. The eye, too, had not yet assumed the adult cobalt-blue hue. It was still dark grey.

The group eventually moved on and it was time for me to go, too. Go back home and face all kinds of boring problems.

There was a bit of current so I let myself drift to the beach that was closest and rode the board all the way to the sand. I stepped into the surf with a feeling of melancholy. I loved coming here, and should really do so more often, but there never seemed to be any time.

I picked up the board, and then—

Something had washed up on the high-tide line: an empty clear jar sat on the sand that was otherwise unmarked even by footsteps. Why was it that every beach anywhere in the universe where people lived always seemed to be fouled by rubbish? It should be put in the bin where it belonged.

I picked up the jar, tucked it in between my board and my side and walked back to the camp where Veyada had breakfast ready and Thayu had made a start on packing away the camping gear.

"What have you got there?" Thayu asked.

"I get so annoyed when people throw out rubbish." I dumped my board at the high tide line. The jar fell, too, bounced and rolled over the sand back towards the water.

While I ran after it I noticed that there was something inside. I stopped it rolling into the water with my foot, picked it up and turned it over. Inside was a sheet of paper.

I unscrewed the lid. It came off easily, meaning that the jar hadn't been in the water for long. Seawater on Ceren was even more corrosive than on Earth, laced with more salts, which tended to gum up every surface.

The paper inside was a bit moist but otherwise clean. Not overgrown with black mould either, and in the warm weather that would happen within days.

Printed on the front of the waxed paper was some sort of schedule. I'd seen these sheets distributed in town for those few Pengali who didn't have or refused to buy readers. Schedules like this were available for channel ferry and train timetables, and were usually kept in a holder mounted on the wall at a station entrance or ferry stop.

The paper was only printed on one side. On the back someone had scrawled, HELP in big capital letters.

In Isla.

What the hell. . . ?

The letters were awkward and ugly, written with what looked like a piece of brightly coloured, sulphur-encrusted rock like one could find near the hot springs.

Underneath the text, there was a clumsy drawing: a curved line meeting another curved line, and an arrow pointing towards a half circle.

"What is it?" Thayu asked.

I showed her the back of the wrapper. She frowned. "What is the point of that?"

"It's a message in a bottle. A long time ago on Earth when people first started to navigate the oceans, a ship would sometimes run aground or storms would smash it against the rocks. The story goes that people who survived these ship wrecks used to throw a bottle in the water so that other people could come and rescue them."

She frowned. "But the current might take the bottle to a place where there are no people."

"Yes."

"And even if it does float in the right direction, it might take a very long time."

"Yes. This was before any form of long-distance communication existed."

Her frown deepened, as if she couldn't imagine such a thing. "But the people could be long dead by the time anyone found them."

"Yes. But sending a physical message by land was the only way to contact another person."

Now she looked at the jar. "So, is this such a thing? Why would anyone use it while we have so much better communication? Is this real or a joke?"

"That is the question, isn't it?"

"What does it mean? That is writing, isn't it?"

"It says 'Help'. I don't know what any of those other scrawls mean. There's an arrow here, but I have no idea what the other things are."

Thayu squinted at the paper. She shook her head. "What do they mean, help?"

I spread my hands. "That's the big question."

Veyada said, "My big question would be: why is it written in Isla?"

Well, yes, that, too.

Thayu said, "Someone trying to pull a prank? Trying to see how far a jar will float? This could have been lying here for years."

Veyada shook his head. "The paper would be covered in mould and the lid would have been gummed shut with salt and growths. It's recent."

"I agree," I said.

"And I still don't see why it should be in Isla."

No, he was right. But I had no idea either. It was very, very strange.

2

———————

I **PUT THE JAR** with our packs in the boat and then spent the entire way back to Barresh thinking about how this jar would have ended up where I found it.

It just didn't make any sense.

Barresh was the biggest settlement on the entire west coast of the continent and definitely the only one where people from Earth would live or even visit.

For someone to write a message in Isla expecting someone who could understand it to find it was . . . ludicrous. The person who wrote the message would be . . .

A tourist who didn't know any local languages? Highly unlikely. It was hard enough to get a permit to travel here, and expensive enough to use the Exchange, that people who travelled to other worlds usually did so for a very good reason. They were very few, but they all had family or business interests on other worlds, which meant that they had at least some knowledge of other languages. Enough to write "Help" in Coldi.

Playing a trick? I couldn't see what purpose it would serve. Pranks only worked if someone else appreciated it and could laugh at it.

Children playing? I could understand that. There were people from Earth with families in Barresh, and their kids could have been playing pirates or something. But then for the jar to have washed out of the city, out of the delta onto the ocean side of the sand bar was a real stretch.

On the other hand, the only other settlements along the coast were Pengali villages, and they had no need for storage jars and even less need for ferry timetables and absolutely no need for notes written in Isla.

And there was that storm that had washed a lot of rubbish out of the city, when it was so windy that many trees had fallen over, and so much water fell that the council had to open the locks that drained water out of the canals into the marshland.

So, had it been left somewhere by children and then washed out to sea after the rain?

Maybe. I'd have to investigate it.

We arrived at the *gamra* island.

Thayu steered the boat to the jetty. Two keihu youngsters from the downstairs kitchen and domestic staff had come to meet us with a trolley. They took the tent, cooking gear and large items, like the surfboard, that we handed to them from the boat.

We carried our weapons and personal packs, and I rescued the jar before it got put on the trolley.

It was quiet on the quay and in the building. We'd been able to plan the trip because the assembly wasn't sitting and many delegates were visiting their home worlds. When sessions resumed, we would be gearing up for the election for Chief Delegate, so many delegates needed to consult with authorities back home. They wanted to show the people at home that the delegate they would be voting for was the best choice.

Not that the race was terribly heated.

Soon after getting the Aghyrian ship to leave, I'd managed to get the assembly to vote Marin Federza as temporary Chief Delegate. His instatement had heralded such an industrious, quiet, scandal-free period that no one had felt the need to stand against him. Not that no one would change their mind at the last moment, but for now, things were quiet and under control.

I was happy to see that Evi and Telaris were not at the door. It was quiet in the hall of my apartment, too. The boys hadn't yet returned with our luggage, because they had to wait for the lift.

I couldn't see Eirani, but I spotted the shimmer of a projection in the hub, so I went in there.

Devlin sat at the control bench, looking at a projection of a block of text. His eyes moved as he read and he didn't seem to have noticed that I'd come in.

"Anything going on?" I asked.

He started. "Oh, Muri, you're back."

"Yes, we just came in. Is anything the matter?" I hadn't liked that look on his face as he read, before he noticed me.

"In a way, yes. There has been a breach of security. This is a report from the Exchange for a check they did on our systems. I got it just now. They're saying that we're fine with the hub up here, but the downstairs office is compromised."

"What? How? The databases?"

"I don't know yet."

Communication was almost always compromised. That came with Coldi and their loyalty networks. Occasionally *gamra* employed a new head of security who was not Coldi and who suddenly "noticed" all these lines of communication everywhere and would ring unnecessary alarm bells. Devlin had enough experience not to flip out when that happened anymore. The annoying part about it was that the breaches alway took us away from things we should be doing instead.

We simply *had* to deal with it.

Bugger.

I sat down on the bench next to him. By the look of things, he'd been sitting there for a while, having gathered a collection of empty cups around him. Since when did he drink *manazhu*?

"I'm sorry," he said when he noticed me looking at the cups. "I tried some and I liked it. I'll buy some more when it runs out."

"That's not necessary. I'll gladly have a drinking partner. Has Eirani seen you drinking it yet?"

"She has."

"The look on her face would have been something. Pity I missed that."

He laughed. Then his face turned serious again. "This report says that someone installed bugs in our communication system downstairs. They came through some external newsletter advertising archiving services. We're always getting those types of newsletters. You know, the ones from businesses hoping to sell their services."

I nodded. *Gamra* was big business in town, the most important source of income after agriculture, and there were always hopefuls wanting to sell their services to diplomats with deep pockets. They would send elaborate and sometimes quite garish messages.

"Don't we have measures to prevent infection from outside?"

"Yes, but it bypassed our scans. Apparently the newsletter contained a bug that was only activated when it was transferred to a less-secure directory and it went from there."

"What does it do?" I rubbed my eyes. It was a rude shock to deal with this kind of crap immediately after walking in from a relaxing trip. I was having trouble getting my brain to engage.

"They're working on that. They'll report back when they've completed their analysis."

"Who else is affected?"

"A few people, but mainly us. I think they targeted us because we ran out of storage space when you were gone."

"That's a while ago, and how would they know about that? It's not exactly a thing you talk about with other people."

"People know, that's all I can say. Also, if your business is storage and archiving, you would have ways of knowing."

"I guess." I scratched my head. "Another option could be that this has been going on for a long time and it's a remnant of some of Renkati's systems that were left in this apartment. People in town would know about this and would know how to access it."

He gave me a disturbed look. "But didn't *gamra* security check the entire apartment?"

A voice came out of the darkness, "*Gamra* security is utter crap. I've been saying so for ages." That was Sheydu, and yes, she had been saying this for ages.

"Hello, Sheydu. I hope you had a nice break, too."

She gave me the evil eye. Sheydu did not have breaks. Sheydu was always right. And yes, after spending some time with her, I was coming around to her point of view.

I looked at the document that Devlin had on the projector in front of him. It was a dry report that stated exactly in which directories foreign material had been discovered. It was mostly communication from the office: our contact lists, our logged conversations from the office and anything that people had sent us that we hadn't yet moved to the system upstairs. The list contained nothing too damaging as yet, mainly operational stuff that I didn't always see the need to protect, but that *was* protected, as per *gamra* protocol.

"What is the status of our *gamra* directory's security?"

"I've checked and moved all the classified material to a separate encrypted area. I've not yet found anything suspicious."

"That doesn't mean it's not there," Sheydu said.

That area contained highly sensitive information in relation to Asto, and hundreds of other things that at the very least I would be uncomfortable sharing with people for whom it was not intended.

I sighed, forcing my brain out of its holiday mode.

"All right, show me what you've done and found out so far."

Devlin showed me the offending document, a nondescript solicitation to let the sender of the document take care of archiving. It was definitely a local, keihu-run business. Only in Barresh did people have this irrational prejudice against using company names. Maybe one day a long time ago, when Barresh had been a frontier town and everyone knew one another, business names were not necessary, but that time had long passed, and the tendency of keihu business owners not to name their companies was one of the most annoying features of the local scene.

The advertisement touted in bright letters CHEAPER THAN *GAMRA* ARCHIVES. The bright and screaming text irritated me. That alone should be a red flag never to use this joint. It even irritated me that some people engaged the services of these types of fly-by-night operators. There was not *that* much money to be saved, delegations got very generous stipends and all of the official services were fully integrated. The document contained a little jiggly graphic of a clock counting down—presumably to when the SPECIAL OFFER finished—and it was this thing that contained the offending bit of code. It apparently opened a communication channel when called from the outside.

Devlin couldn't yet tell me whether anyone had already used the channel, much less what they would have been looking for. He'd let me know when he found out.

———

With that, I left the room. I went into the bedroom where Eirani had already unpacked all my things, taken them to the laundry and put them in the wardrobes or the storage downstairs. Thayu would insist that I went armed everywhere, but I drew the line at wearing a weapon inside my own house. I unclipped the gun bracket from my arm and put it on the cabinet next to the wall, next to the jar with the piece of paper that Eirani had set there.

I picked it up and turned it over, so that the piece of waxed paper inside rolled around.

When I was a little boy, my grandfather on his farm in the Bay of Islands used to tell me that things were never as simple as they looked or as difficult as they appeared to be. He would also say that problems were like band-aids: once you lifted a corner, it was easier to get the rest off.

I was looking at firmly stuck plaster with this one.

I was just getting my *gamra* blues out of the wardrobe when the door rattled open and Thayu came in. She frowned. "What are you doing with those?" She nodded at the blue shirt in my hands.

"I'm going to see Melissa after dinner."

"Do you still think that message could be serious?"

"I don't know what to think. I don't want to discount that it could be serious. I don't want to be blamed for not taking something seriously when I should have, and that some person died because I didn't do anything."

"If they're really in trouble they'll be dead already anyway."

"I love your optimism."

"Have you seen the teeth on the beisili? They'll just nibble at anyone unable to get away quickly enough. It's their breeding season, too, so they'll be aggressive."

"But the person didn't necessarily have to enter the water."

"Tell me how to go anywhere on the coast without getting in the water. They attack boats, too. Some of those island have no fresh water. If this person is anywhere further down the coast, the Thousand Islands tribe will have killed them off."

"You *are* on a roll today."

"Yes. If you want to die, eels are better than beisili or hostile

Pengali with poison darts. The eels will eat you in one go. No long days of agonising pain involved."

"Thay'!"

"I'm just being realistic. *If* someone got lost out there and found it necessary to use this . . . archaic form of communication, they would already have been dead even before the moment you first took that piece of paper out of the jar this morning."

There was a sound at the door, and Nicha came in, carrying his son. Little Ayshada looked around with wide-open eyes, taking everything in. He gave a squeal when he saw Thayu, and Nicha handed him to his sister.

Thayu bounced him on her arm. He laughed loudly and then she tickled him, which caused him to make even more noise. Yes, I knew she wanted a child and, despite telling me that there was no hurry, I had to do something about that sooner rather than later.

"How was the fishing?" Nicha asked me.

"It was good," I said, and went into a description of what we caught and ate.

Nicha pulled a face. He did not like fish. Like most Coldi, he was mostly vegetarian. He ate eggs and worms and snails and crayfish from Asto, but that was as far as his meat-eating went.

Thayu said, "I heard a bit of an issue developed here with the security while we were away."

"Yeah," Nicha scratched his head. "Not sure what all the fuss is about, but we'll let *gamra* security do their thing and we'll hear about it soon enough. We seem to be getting one of these breaches at least twice a year." He nodded at the blue shirt that I still held in my hands. "You look like you're going somewhere."

"I'm going to see Melissa."

"That's an odd choice for a first visit after a trip."

I showed him the jar and told him where we found it. As Thayu and Veyada had done, he frowned deeply, and, like them, he had no idea how that jar would have gotten there. "Maybe you can map the currents," he said. "That way you can figure out how the jar would have fetched up where it did."

"I'm thinking that the storm would have had quite a bit to do with how far it was carried."

He nodded. "What would Melissa know about it?"

"Nothing, but she might be able to shed any light on exactly who from Earth is here, who is likely to have written that note or who has kids old enough to play pirates, so that I can take it there, establish what happened and we can all get on with our lives."

"Fair enough. Do you want me to come?" Nicha asked.

"I think I'll get better responses out of Melissa if I go by myself." For someone having grown up with a Coldi stepfather, she was surprisingly distrustful discussing human subjects with anyone not from Earth.

Eirani called for dinner in the hall.

I left the shirt on the bed, deciding not to risk spilling food on it —that cobalt blue showed every little speck of grease.

We had a quick dinner at which Deyu and Reida were also present. They appeared to have been recruited to help Devlin with his directory checks. Deyu had proven herself quite good with systems, and her keenness to put in the effort to learn was fast outstripping Reida's swagger and bravado.

When we finished, I went to change. I didn't know why I always felt that to see Melissa I needed to dress up. Maybe it was because she constantly challenged me and that, because she was a journalist, I never felt quite relaxed when talking to her. She *said* she no longer worked for Flash Newspoint, but I bet if she saw a story worth money, she'd contact them in a heartbeat.

I decided to go all out and even strapped the gun bracket back on.

Thayu liked it, probably a sign that Melissa wouldn't, which was the effect I was going for: this is official business, this will be logged and archived for future reference.

How good were we all becoming at the "cover my arse" attitude.

3

———————

THESE DAYS, Melissa lived on the other side of the island, not far from the station.

I walked there with Thayu and Nicha, through the leafy courtyards, shaded underpasses and service areas with shops selling basic things and also with plenty of eating houses, although none were busy.

Melissa's apartment was quite small, the type for single, minor delegates. Sometimes I considered that if everything had gone to plan when I first came here, Nicha and I would have shared an apartment like hers; we'd have gone quietly about our business and spent lots of time attending assembly meetings, cooking our own food, writing our own correspondence and cleaning our own house.

Instead I'd been shunted into one of the largest, most expensive and prestigious apartments on the island—at least at the time it felt like I'd been shunted, with no means to pay the rent and the salaries of more than twenty staff, and even less of an idea what to do with them.

There had been a mistake in allocating the apartment to me, I insisted back then, but now I often wondered how much of a mistake it had really been and how much it was due to machinations by Ezhya and Marin Federza.

Because being put up in that apartment—that no one wanted because it was bugged to within an inch of its life by nonverifiable off-island sources—had spurred me into being much more than a minor diplomat. It had forced me into trying to prove that I was worthy of it, and as a result, money had materialised in the form of a heavy stipend paid by Ezhya.

These days I owned the apartment and paid the staff. I had even hired more.

Had I not been put in the apartment, I would have been like Melissa, and I wondered what distinguished me from Melissa in that I'd gotten these tremendous opportunities and she was just allowed to do her job.

I could never get my head around it. What did Ezhya see in me?

Thayu snorted. Of course she had been following my thoughts through the feeder.

"You are the first non-Coldi with a Coldi association and you're still asking that question?"

"But everyone can do what I've done."

"Maybe, but they haven't." That was her standard response to that argument. I knew it, I had heard it all before and was still afraid that one day I was going to wake up to find that it had all been a dream.

We arrived at the building. Thayu and Nicha had agreed to stay outside and I climbed the side stairs to the top floor. From here, I could see Thayu hanging around "inconspicuously" on one of the quayside benches, looking very much like a guard hanging around and waiting. Nicha was down there, too, although he'd been talking about getting something to drink.

I knocked on the door.

It was opened a moment later by a tiny woman with flaming red hair. She was a member of the Kedrasi delegation, her name was Taysin Katara Yelak, and she was Melissa's housemate.

"Oh, Delegate!" She bowed. "Good evening. How can I help you?" She wore a grey kaftan with blue stripes. A *very* junior delegate to *gamra*.

"I'd like to see Melissa."

"Come in."

She preceded me through a hallway to the apartment's living room. The entire far wall was made of glass. Most of the view was taken up by water, dark and black at this time of the day, with the city lit up in a string of lights. A train zoomed in the direction of the city, its headlights just lighting a small section of rails in front of it.

"That is a very pretty view," I said.

"Oh, hello Cory." Melissa spoke Isla. She sat in an armchair by the window, studying something on her reader. I hadn't seen her because it was very dark in the room. She put the reader down and got up, flicking a lever on the wall next to her.

A pearl light came on. To mitigate the pearl light's natural zombielike pale green glow, she had concocted a little lampshade of wire and yellow foil.

"Does the Delegate want some tea?" Taysin asked in Coldi.

"That would be nice, thank you."

These days, few people spoke this formally to me. Most knew that I didn't like it, and being affiliated with Coldi people reduced the need for formality in general.

"Sit down." Melissa gestured at the couch, and I sat down. Her gaze wandered to the gun in the bracket on my arm.

"Wow, you've really gone all out." Again in Isla.

"I'm allowed to have it." The Isla words felt odd on my tongue, somehow *wrong* for this place.

"I didn't think you were that keen on weapons."

"I am not, but they've saved my butt often enough for me to appreciate their existence."

"Granted." Another shifty look at the gun. "Did you get training in using it?"

"It feels like I've done little else lately. I've just come back from a hunting trip. We went to the sand bar for a few days."

"Oh, then you missed all of the scandal."

My heart jumped. "Scandal?" Had I been too quick in judging Marin Federza's administration scandal-free?

"There was a major security breach of the *gamra* island's systems. Your office was one of the most heavily affected. Haven't you heard that yet?"

"Oh, that. Yes, I heard about it. Those sorts of mishaps happen every few months. It goes with the territory of mixing a Coldi loyalty system with *gamra* security requirements. It's annoying when it happens, but it isn't the first time and won't be the last. Security fixes it and then we move on."

"Except this involved links going off world. It's a highly organised operation."

"What do you mean? Who gave you that information? The Exchange hasn't released any statements. I doubt they know exactly who it is—"

"Oh, they know. They just don't want to say."

"Was your office affected, too?"

"I don't *have* an office with twenty people."

"Your data, then?"

"No, but—"

"Then how do you know what's going on?"

"It's not *that* hard to tell, is it?"

"Well, I could think of a whole bunch of people who would like to get their hands on what goes on in my office, but I have no evidence that anyone got their hands on anything of importance. In fact, the culprits were probably commercial data miners after low-grade commercial resellable databases, but if the Exchange finds differently, I'm happy to listen. I'm happy to listen to you, too, if you can cite a credible source."

She glared at me, and I glared back.

Predictably, she had no credible source. A "hunch", she had called it several times in the past. At times like this, she remained far too much of a gutter press journalist out to find sensationalist stories. Annoyingly, too, her hunches had proven right more often than not.

"If the Exchange knew of any high-level plot behind a security breach, rest assured that some of the people in my association would know about it. As far as I can see, it was done by a commercial company, who would have had some clever people working for them and happened to luck upon a routine that attacked the *gamra* security walls from an angle that the programmers hadn't considered. This company sells archives and archive space. Likely, they will sell databases of low-level information, and in the next year or so, I will receive a bunch of solicitations from companies wanting to sell my household bed sheets, because the domestic database shows that we replace ours every four years or something. There is much more money to be made doing that than there is with the high-profile spying."

"Well, I hope you're right. I don't trust everything the Exchange says."

"I can see no reason for the Exchange to lie."

"No reason? To protect itself? Not to have to admit that it did something wrong?"

I saw in my mind an image of Yetaris Damaru standing in front of a room full of important *gamra* people telling them that the system had gone completely down, and he had no idea where one of their key leaders was. I could not imagine that man lying deliberately, ever. But I wasn't going to argue that with Melissa, because I'd be "too naive" and "bought out by the people in power" and once we went into that territory, there was no end to it.

"Melissa, all I can ask is this: If you have any information that I don't have, present it to the *gamra* assembly at the next sitting. If it can't wait, take it to security."

Meanwhile, it would be a good move for her to ditch the conspiracy-theorist, gutter-press mentality, but that was another discussion I'd made the mistake of having with her, and one I wasn't going to repeat.

She continued giving me a pointed look. I shouldn't let myself get so worked up over her attitude. If there was a real issue, we'd find out.

"Anyway, whatever is happening, someone will sort it out. That's not why I'm here." I sipped from my tea. It was fragrant and hot.

"Why are you here then?"

I set down my tea, rummaged in my bag and put the jar on the table.

Melissa frowned at it and then at me. "Whatever is that?"

"You tell me."

She picked up the jar, unclipped the lid and took out the piece of paper. Her frown deepened. "Help? What sort of joke is this? Did this get left on your doorstep or something?"

"No. I found it." I told her about our trip and the location where I had found the jar.

"That is . . . odd. Really, really, really odd."

"It is, and I need your help in trying to decide what to make of it. I'm not taking it one hundred percent seriously, but I don't want to dismiss it either. Just in case it's a real cry for help."

She nodded and turned the jar over. "It's a locally made thing. I've seen these jars in restaurants for storing pickles and things. And locally made paper. It's a train or ferry schedule."

The waxy surface wasn't very good for writing either.

"Ferry. This is for the service from the eastern side of the main island to the back of the council building." Melissa shook her head and snorted. "If whoever wrote this would really want help, then they might have been a little bit more specific about where they are."

"Unless they don't know that either."

Now her expression looked disturbed. She stared at the jar, shaking her head.

"This is why I'm here: before I dismiss this as a really strange prank of some kind—and to be frank I can't see how anyone could pull off something like this—who are the people who could have written this note and are any of them missing? Who are the people from Earth in town?"

"Not many, but I'll give you a list." Melissa picked up her reader.

I was almost ashamed that I didn't know the Earth people in Barresh. I only ever spoke to Melissa. There were a few others I would see in passing on the streets or at events, but the only other person I'd spent significant time talking to was my predecessor Seymour Kershaw, who had become a member of Amoro Renkati and who had been killed at the assembly for trying to kill Ezhya Palayi.

Weren't we supposed to have an Earth Society or something like that? One with monthly social meetings at which Earth foods were served and we watched old movies?

"So, here are the Earth people." Melissa had pulled up a short list on her reader. "There's you and me, and Huang Le and his family—" Le was a bit of a celebrity on Earth because he held the honour of owning the first-ever interplanetary Chinese restaurant. "There is Benton Leck at the History Centre." He was an older academic who was well-integrated in the local population. "Then there is Clovis Keneally and Juanita Rey." They were a retired couple, a bit eccentric.

I felt ashamed. I knew these people. I never saw them or made an effort to help them or even to check if they were all right.

Melissa flicked to another page. "Oh, and Jasper Carlson."

I'd heard that name a few times even if I hadn't met the man. He was a merchant of some kind and had a reputation of being a recluse. I wasn't sure what he sold but he had a warehouse and shop in town, and of all the Earth people in Barresh, was probably the one who had been here the longest.

"Do any of them have children?"

"Huang Le does. He has a boy and a girl. They're about ten or twelve."

I guessed she was speaking in Earth years, because in Ceren years, that would make them adults, and I didn't think that was what she meant.

"Would the kids have been playing pirates or something?"

"I don't know. You would have to ask him."

"I presume these people sometimes get visitors from Earth."

"Maybe. I don't know. I'm not aware that anyone has any visitors right now. The Exchange would be able to tell you." That same Exchange she didn't trust. If anything, travel data was the type of thing that I could see being manipulated for the purpose of circumventing arduous, and expensive, administrative processes to bring visitors or partners across.

"Would any of these people contact you if they had visitors?"

"Sometimes they do, but it's not a formal requirement. A few months ago, Huang Le's brother visited. He wanted to investigate the possibility of exporting Chinese foodstuffs, seeing as his brother's restaurant is so popular here. He came to me because he wanted make sure that everything he did was above the table. I've heard that Huang Le is looking into training chefs and opening a second restaurant on the *gamra* island."

Hmmm, so even the locals liked their Chinese food, huh? "Can I have that list of names?"

"Sure."

My comm pinged when it received the document. I glanced down the short list. First was Huang Le with his wife Fifi, and their children Matara and Peris. Both were keihu names, so they must have been born here.

The next person on the list was Benton Leck, age sixty-three, Earth years of course. "Leck is not married?"

"He has a partner who lives with him."

"A local?" I guessed.

"Mirani."

The next entry was Clovis Keneally. "Does he have any business interests in town or anything or does he live off retirement income only?"

"Who? Clovis? Oh, he has lots of income. He owns shops and other businesses. He was smart enough to use all of his retirement capital to buy Trader credits before he came here, and we all know what happened with them. They're quite rich."

" 'They' refers to him and Juanita?"

"Yup. They own investments all over town and manage it all from their house. They live on the northern shore of the main island." One of the "new rich" areas in town.

"Do they get a lot of visitors?"

"Sometimes. I don't really know." Melissa shook her head. "They stick to themselves, mind their own business. I honestly don't know much about most of these people. I've never met Benton Leck. These people don't want to have social gatherings."

"They probably hate each other's guts."

Melissa laughed. "Have you met Jasper Carlson?"

"No, I haven't."

"I have. He's probably the reason why they don't want to have a little Earth club and meetings with cups of tea. He's a strange, suspicious, divisive, vindictive character."

"Do you think this note could be in some way related to their disagreements and vindictiveness?"

"Maybe. Look, I'm stabbing in the dark as much as you are."

"All right, then. Appreciate your honesty." It was always worth quizzing Melissa on those subjects about which she did not have conspiracy theories.

I picked up the wrapper and put it back in the jar. "Yet someone wrote this note. Probably because there was nothing else to write with. I need to make sure that there isn't someone out there in real trouble. I'd love to dismiss this, but I can't."

Melissa nodded.

"I'm going to visit all the people on this list."

"I was afraid you'd say that. Most of these people don't want anyone gawking. They're not here to represent Earth. They're here to get away from it."

———

"Visit all these people? Why don't you ask her to do it?" Thayu asked me when we walked back through leafy avenues of the *gamra* island. "After all, she is the representative."

The evening was warm and the air laced with the humidity of the approaching wet season. All around us, people sat eating at outdoor eateries or lounged on benches or balconies.

"Melissa represents Earth at the assembly. She's not running a diplomatic post."

"You're not, either."

"No, but I'm the one who found the jar. I should probably get to know these people better, anyway. I'm not comfortable that I hardly know any of the people on that list. Coldi on Earth have the registry. There's a similar registry here in Barresh. Coldi can always rely on others to help them in time of need. These people have . . . nothing. Any of them could disappear tomorrow and I would never find out about it unless someone told me."

"Coldi have a registry because we're Coldi, and we have loyalty networks. Indrahui don't have a registry."

"No but if Evi or Telaris were in trouble, related somehow to Indrahui, their folks would help them."

Thayu spread her hands and let them sink again. "So, it's like a 'back to your roots' kind of thing?"

I didn't know what to say to that. People often said to me that I was more Coldi than some Coldi, or they accused me of trying to be Coldi. I was much more fluent in Coldi than Isla. I dressed Coldi. I'd had my face treated so that I no longer grew facial hair. I was the head of a Coldi-style association and, a little while ago, Thayu and I had visited the Aghyrian geneticist Lilona Shrakar in her office in town to discuss possible gene modification for me that would effectively turn me Coldi.

Was visiting these Earth people a "back to my roots" thing?

Was it a last-chance, "Let's see if these people are really so bad" thing?

After all, I'd not been interested in any of these people for all the years I'd lived in Barresh. If I'd been a true diplomat representing Earth, I'd have given parties at my apartment for all of them. Seymour Kershaw used to do this.

Instead, I'd moved into a top floor apartment with a whole bunch of Coldi and never even contacted any of them.

No wonder those stories about me did the rounds.

I sighed. I didn't really want to discuss what I was. Half the time, I didn't know either. "It's a peace of mind thing. I'd like to think if there is someone out there in trouble, I've done all I could to help, just because I'd like to be a decent person. I also think that because I can read the message and I know Barresh, I'm in a good position to help. It's really got nothing to do with my personal situation."

"Good."

We walked silently for a bit, and then she added, "I'm happy that you believe that."

Because, clearly, she didn't.

4

—————

W E WALKED HOME over the leafy boulevards of the *gamra* island. The night air was warm, not as humid as it would be later on, and filled with the squawks of meili in the trees and the rattling of ringgit that had taken up residence in the planter boxes, especially where there were fountains or ponds.

It was quite odd for the nightlife to be so prevalent here, and a sign of how quiet the island was when the assembly was not in sitting.

The question of what it was that made me human, and whether or not you could transition from being human to being Coldi or something else, and if so, whether I had already done this, was one that bothered me at times. Most of the time, I simply made my decisions and acted as I thought was right, and as was right for the situation and the people around me.

Then someone would accuse me of being a Coldi pawn, or would say, "But you're one of them now." These remarks could be made in jest, but often there was a passive-aggressive sentiment to them that belied the speaker's deeper intentions, which seemed to be to shame me into acting my part, or to express jealousy about my interactions with a type of successful people they realised they would never understand.

And sometimes, when that happened, I lay staring at the ceiling at night, wondering if I was human and if so, should there be any loyalty to my fellow humans associated with that fact, because I had to admit I didn't feel any whatsoever.

Of course I loved my father, but I was no longer in contact with any of my cousins, had very few human friends on Earth, and when I visited, I referred to Amarru at the Exchange. I no longer took orders from Nations of Earth politicians, and considered even Margarethe Ollund a foreign head of state in need of advice and protection from the, for her, strange customs at *gamra*.

On the other hand, I was the only non-Coldi person to have visited Asto, I belonged to the Domiri clan—and Asha kept telling me that we should have an official induction ceremony, which would require me to travel to Asto again—and Ezhya had made it clear that he would use his special powers to free a spot for me to live on Asto, if that proved necessary. Several times, I had chosen my loyalty to him over my position.

Did all this make me less human?

We came home to the unusual sight of Deyu and Reida standing at the door. During our camping trip, Evi and Telaris had indeed gone to visit their family. Apparently their mother had reached an auspicious milestone, although no one was quite sure whether "Freedom of Care" simply meant that Evi and Telaris' much younger brother had left home, or whether it referred to those horrible "life debts" that bound poorer Indrahui people to their financial masters.

I went to the bedroom to change out of my formal gear, and to take off the gun, and rejoined Thayu in the living room, where Nicha had also turned up. Thayu had filled him in on my discussion with Melissa, of which she had followed a good deal through the feeder. Her increasing knowledge of Isla scared me sometimes.

Nicha was saying, "So he wants to go and visit all these people? Isn't that what Melissa is for? Don't we have better things to do?"

"It's not her task," I said, sitting down on the couch. "When I held that job, they explicitly told me so. I was not to render services for the benefit of individuals, even with regards to their safety."

"And you broke that rule straight away."

"I did, but they broke their promises to me, too. Anyway, this is not relevant. Melissa has far fewer resources than we do, and what is the harm in visiting these people and just asking them if anyone they know is missing?"

"With you, it's never just asking," Thayu said.

"I've got some time. Neither of you need to get involved if you don't want to."

"You wish. Those projects of yours in which you don't want us involved are the most dangerous of all."

"Then do get involved. I don't care. I don't want later accusations that I should have done something instead of letting someone else sort it out. That's not my style."

And that, I realised as soon as the words were out of my mouth, was a very Coldi leader thing to say.

Screw this. Why did it even matter what boxes I ticked?

I sat back and looked out the window. Out there, over the marshlands beyond the horizon was the ocean. A big bank of clouds was silhouetted against the last rays of daylight, and the occasional flash of lightning flickered inside the billowing masses.

The wet season was coming. If anyone was in trouble out there, we had mere days to mount a search. And I was going to find out if that was necessary.

I told my association at breakfast that I planned to go into town that morning. Thayu and Nicha looked at each other, knew what I was doing, and as one insisted on coming. I guess I should have known that would happen and, to be honest, I was secretly glad that they wanted to. They didn't always understand why I wanted to do things, but they always came around to accepting that some things were important to me.

They also promised to honour my request that they stay outside while I visited the people, even if both felt it necessary to remind me that Earth people had such strange habits.

We travelled to town in the train, and even it was much less busy than usual.

Huang Le's restaurant was in one of the new buildings in the market square these days, although he had moved a few times since I had come to Barresh. He had obtained a permit to grow Chinese vegetables in a special closed-system glasshouse at the back of his shop that was approved by quarantine. The glasshouse was a novelty in town, seeing as Barresh had a tropical climate and glasshouses were rarely a necessity. When you walked past, you would often see people looking over the wall at Huang Le's wife pottering between the rows of tables. Someone had even put a crate next to the wall so that little children could see over the top.

The restaurant part of his business was small, with the tables crowded together to fit in as many paying customers as possible.

The shop was still dark, and a young keihu woman was mopping the floor. We greeted her and went to the counter at the back, where there was light and where Huang Le and his wife were cutting up vegetables.

Huang Le glanced up at me. "We don't open until midday." There was no *Good Morning, Delegate* and definitely no formal Coldi pronouns.

"I'm not here for lunch. I'd like to ask a question."

"Yeah. Ask away." His keihu was almost flawless. He was one of the few people I knew to manage the noun inflections well enough to be inseparable from a local. My keihu wasn't half as good, so I switched to Coldi. "My question is kind of long."

"Is it?" He gathered a bunch of heads of bok choi and chopped the bottoms off with a vicious *thwack* of his giant knife. "I got food to cook, dishes to put out, plants to water. I don't have all day to be answering your questions." His Coldi wasn't bad either, although not quite up there with his keihu.

"I understand that, but it's important, and it won't take terribly long."

He snorted and dropped his knife, pushed aside part of the counter and came into the shop. "Make it quick, then."

He was a much shorter man than I, who appeared to have taken to the local habit of long lunches and looked the part. He wore a loose kaftan with the sleeves tied up above his elbows and an apron. He'd been sweating so much that the moisture seeped through the fabric.

He yelled something in Chinese to his wife, and she responded.

He led me to a table at the edge of the terrace area separated from the restaurant next door by a row of planter boxes.

We sat down, and his wife brought us two glasses of chilled juice. Huang Le downed half of his, wiping sweat off his face. Was he more affected by the heat than most of us, or did he neglect to take adaptation medicine?

A couple of boys in their early teenage years peeked over the shop counter. Two were keihu, but the third had straight dark hair and Asian eyes. They giggled and left again.

"Your son?" I asked.

"Now, what are you here for?"

Straight to business. Shut up, Delegate, stop wasting my time.

I took the jar out of the carry case that also contained my reader, and put it on the middle of the table. I told him where we'd found it. I unclipped the lid and showed him the piece of waxed paper.

He turned it over, raised his eyebrows at the timetable and snorted. "I guess someone's ferry took a long time arriving, so he took a ringgit jar and a timetable, because that was all he had, and sent a message in a bottle, but he neglected to write where he actually was, because he didn't have a pencil. This seems like a child's trick to me. I think you've been had."

"I wish I could laugh at it, but I have to discount all possibilities. Do your children play with these . . . ringgit jars?"

"They're for the kitchen, to stop the damn pests coming in and eating stuff. Like the beans, they love the beans, and the flour, too, but we keep it in the cooler. But the herbs, yes, we'll use the ringgit jars for the herbs."

His wife called out something in Chinese from the back of the shop, holding up a glass jar similar to the one I had found, containing ochre-red powder.

"See, there you go. Ringgit jars. Doesn't your fancy kitchen use any?"

"To be honest, I'm not sure." I didn't think they did. Ringgit infestation didn't seem to be as much of a problem at the *gamra* island as it was in town. I'd heard people say that it was because of the lack of drainage tunnels where the crustacean-like creatures liked to breed.

"But to get back to your question, if I catch my children playing with stuff from the shop, I'll teach them a lesson they won't forget in a hurry. Not saying that they wouldn't find a jar somewhere. It's amazing the rubbish people leave everywhere."

"Yeah." Where there were people, there was rubbish. Sad truth.

"Anyway, my children couldn't have done this."

"Could I ask them?"

I could see that he was starting to refuse, but then he snorted. He yelled something in Chinese to his wife, who walked out the shop's back door, and yelled something in Chinese that echoed through the house.

A bit later, two children came into the shop. The boy, Peris, was the one I'd seen before. The girl Matara looked much younger. Despite having Asian faces, both looked more keihu than human. They wore keihu clothing and had keihu hairstyles, especially the girl, who sported a typical keihu stepwise haircut with big chunks of hair in different lengths and thin plaits at the front.

Huang Le said in keihu, "This is Mr Wilson from *gamra*. He wants to show you something."

The children looked at me with wide eyes.

I asked, "Do you speak Isla?"

No reaction.

"Coldi?"

No reaction.

"They only speak the language of their home," Huang Le said.

Which, clearly, was keihu. There was nothing for it: I had to tell my story in halting keihu, no doubt committing crimes against grammar along the way.

The children listened to my story, with their faces impassive, their dark eyes going over the piece of waxed paper on the table between us.

The boy shook his head when I finished speaking. He said in perfect keihu, "We wouldn't do that sort of thing. Daddy would get very angry with us."

Huang Le gave a self-satisfied smile.

The girl squinted at the paper. "What does it say, anyway?"

The realisation sunk in: these kids could never have written this, because they didn't speak, write or read Isla.

"Thank you for letting me ask them," I said to Huang Le. "They can go now."

"Go help your mother," he said in keihu. The children scurried off.

"No one else in town has children?"

"None that would write in Isla on a ferry timetable, put it in a jar and throw it in the water."

"You haven't done this?"

He snorted. "What do you take me for? Do I look like I need help?"

"Do you know anyone who might have gone out there?"

"Who writes Isla? No."

"Anyone who has visitors?"

"No, you're at the wrong address here. I don't know of anyone who goes out there. I buy my fish from the Pengali."

"You're not missing anyone? Do you know of anyone who went fishing, or—"

"I don't know anyone else from Earth except those people you already mentioned. I'm sorry, but I really can't help you. I try to stay away from Earth." He laughed, not in an amused way. "I came out here to get away from other people and their silly rules. Do you want me to spell out for you all the rules that we need to follow to have a menu in most of the cities on Earth that are worth living in? We need to cater to all diets. We can't include foods that can lead to allergic reactions. We can't use prawns, peanuts or peanut oil, certain spices, eggs—" He counted on his fingers. "If we want to serve those, we need approval and accreditation. That's all very well if you're a big business and have lots of restaurants, but for a single family, it's ridiculous. They killed the best restaurants, that's what."

———

I rejoined Thayu and Nicha around the corner not much later. They appeared to have had a much more relaxing and enjoyable chat with a Barresh town guard about the subject of guns. Nicha clapped the man on the shoulder as the guard announced that he was going to continue with his work.

"Find out anything?" Thayu asked, although she must have known from my feeder input that I hadn't.

"Not really." If we'd been on Earth, I might have thought Huang Le brusque and uncooperative, but he hadn't said anything that warranted that harsh a judgement. It had been his . . . attitude that disturbed me most. He was probably just busy, and I had never shown any interest in him, so that probably explained why he was reluctant to cooperate with me as if he were my best friend. Maybe he'd had an illegal visitor or two. Who knew?

The next person on my list was Benton Leck.

Out of all the people from Earth in the city of Barresh, I was most familiar with him.

When he wasn't working for the History Centre, which was part of the Barresh Council and with which he was affiliated as an academic, he had his own history investigation business. This type of activity was a keihu thing where one could pay someone to investigate into the history of a family of interest, most commonly for the purpose of marriage or business.

The keihu families preferred to use non-keihu for this type of research, lest their competitors find out any juicy bits that came up, so there were a couple of these "Family Historians" in town, some Damarcian, some Kedrasi.

Leck sometimes came to the *gamra* island. He had been a historian for universities on Earth before coming to Barresh on a research project funded by Nations of Earth. He had never left.

Unfortunately, Benton Leck was away on business. His assistant, a middle-aged keihu woman, met us in his office, which was reminiscent of the old-style historic libraries on Earth, with shelves of musty documents, archives and a few documentation screens along the walls.

"He has gone to Miran to consult the library," she told us. "But do come back when he returns."

I asked her if her boss had any visitors from Earth, and she said he did not. Visitors were rare, she said, because it was so expensive.

I guess I knew about that. As far as I knew, Benton Leck was the one who most frequently visited Earth. I presumed his work paid for it.

After having assured that I'd come back when her boss returned, I left again.

Thayu and Nicha were waiting in the downstairs foyer.

"Let's go to the Exchange while we're here," I said before Thayu could ask me anything. I was sure she already knew that this visit hadn't delivered any useful information either.

I was fast getting grumpy about this goose chase and, yes, it was my idea and, no, I hadn't expected information to just be waiting for me. I had expected . . . I don't know . . . a little more solidarity, a bit of help?

Not only did these people not know anything, I felt they were fundamentally uninterested in me and my jar.

We traversed the building complex through the maze of passages and courtyards until we came out at the front entrance's foyer, where the broad marble staircase led up to the front part of the building that housed the Exchange.

Up there, at the counter, a friendly woman told me that they had no records of any people from Earth visiting in the past few weeks. Benton Leck had indeed gone to Miran, they showed me. The list of offworld visits by Earth people this year was very short—even shorter when you took me and my association off—and the list of Earth people visiting Barresh was even shorter.

Huang Le's brother was on it, Melissa's sister, and even Margarethe Ollund's visit was still on the front page. How long ago was *that*?

So I'd drawn another blank.

5

––––––––––

THE VISIT TO CLOVIS and Juanita took us along the northeastern tram loop. The tramline split off from the northwestern—hospital—line and described an M-shaped path along the northeastern shore of the island. It was a part of the train network that I very rarely used, a section of town that had been rebuilt not long before I came to Barresh. The houses were modern, the streets quiet, and the business premises that were dotted throughout the residential areas of the rest of the city were virtually absent. This was the height of modern Barresh suburbia.

New rich, they called this area, because any of the old rich families lived in the mansions behind the council buildings. Many people who lived in this area had made their wealth off their contracts providing services to *gamra* or the rapidly growing city as a result of *gamra*'s presence.

A short walk from the station brought us to Clovis and Juanita's house, a low, single-storey, fairly simple-looking building with wide verandas, a sloping roof—as opposed to the flat roofs with glass domes of most of the established families' houses—and a neatly-maintained garden that featured a lawn—that had to be a local novelty!—and clipped hedges. When we entered the gate, I half expected a dog to come bounding towards us, but quarantine would make that impossible.

"Wow," Thayu said.

"Yes," Nicha agreed. "This is different." He glanced at the neighbouring house, a blocky structure with two floors and extensive metal latticework and coloured glass windows that characterised the keihu building style.

Clovis' house looked, I realised, like something out of old movies in which people from various countries in Europe moved to countries in Africa to become landowners. Colonial, that was the word.

"Hello?" a woman called from the veranda, in Isla. "Why, Mr Wilson, is that you? Welcome to our house. Come up here."

"We'll wait here," Thayu said, nodding at a garden bench with an overhanging trellis heavy with a creeping plant with trumpet-like, pink flowers.

They sat down in the shade, and I went up to the house.

As soon as I stepped onto the veranda, I understood why the house had no second floor: Juanita sat in a wheelchair.

She was probably in her early seventies, Earth years, had long grey hair that hung loose over her broad, fleshy shoulders. She wore a wide dress with bright patterns in purple, pink and mustard that didn't fully disguise the fact that she enjoyed her food. Both her legs stopped at the knee.

I did my utmost best not to stare, and felt deeply ashamed for never seeking these people out. They could have used some help.

She held out a fleshy hand and I shook it, Earth style. Her eyes glittered with mirth.

"And what is the lofty occasion that you come off the island to visit us?"

"I'm sorry to disturb you. I have a question for both of you."

"Oh—it's all right. Don't bother with the formalities. Let's go inside."

She waved her hand and a young Pengali woman resolved from the shadows. I hadn't noticed her before because she wore no shirt and the skin on her shoulders and arms was marked with big pigment blotches, a bit like the markings on a giraffe. This made her well camouflaged against the background of the shelf next to the door, which contained pots and hats and boots and gardening things. Her patterns were very unusual. I was only familiar with the stripes and the spots. I wasn't aware there were other varieties.

The Pengali woman wheeled Juanita's chair into the house, negotiating a screen door without any trouble. I followed them, looking at the Pengali's black-and-white banded tail.

"We got visitors," Juanita announced when we entered the kitchen.

An elderly man sat at the kitchen table, writing by hand in a thick book. His hair was white and his face red, tanned but blotched with darker and lighter pigment patches. I guessed he was half his wife's width, his arms protruding like sticks from the too-wide sleeves of a locally made felt kaftan.

He closed the book and pushed it aside. "Oh. Mr Wilson. What an honour to have you here. Would you like some tea?"

I said I would, and we made some small talk while the Pengali woman drew hot water from the inlet and busied herself with the teapot. I asked him how business was going and he talked a bit about the storm and how one of his businesses was a building company which had received several calls for help to replace broken sheds and leaking roofs.

"And all your ferries that washed out into the marshland," Juanita said.

"Oh, that wasn't so bad," Clovis said.

"Not bad? With all the damage we had, and two whole days of reduced services? And all the people you had to pay to get them back into the channels?"

Clovis shrugged. "It happens."

Juanita spread her fleshy hands and rolled her eyes at me. " 'It happens,' he says. Mr Wilson, you should have heard him *when* it happened. It was the end of the world. He spent a whole day out there himself and got himself covered in bites of all those horrible little creatures. I told him to leave it to the young guys, but no, the customer always comes first and we have to be seen to serve the customer—"

"Darling, please, I'm sure Mr Wilson is not here to talk about that."

No, apparently Mr Wilson was not.

The Pengali woman put the teapot on the kitchen table.

Clovis turned to her and said something. He spoke Pengali. I had never heard a non-Pengali person speak Pengali. It was a complicated, intricate language with many nuances. It sounded . . . odd to hear him speak it. Quite well, too.

The woman picked the teapot back up and carried it out the other door into the kitchen. Clovis pushed his partner's wheelchair, and I followed to the back veranda, where a set of benches and chairs surrounded a low table.

The back of the yard sloped down to the edge of the island. Being close to midday, and dry season, a good section of beach and adjacent reed beds were exposed, but behind the reed beds was the channel that took a lot of the water that came off the Mirani highlands to the ocean. It was the same channel where we had been fishing and where, around the corner on the beach, I had found the jar.

We sat down.

The Pengali woman poured us tea, and then left after Juanita said something to her, also in Pengali.

"She's a good girl," Clovis said when the screen door had fallen shut after her black and white banded tail. "I don't care much that you think this is all very colonial."

"I don't think—"

"Oh, yes, you do, I can see it in your face. We're like the white plantation owners in Africa, teaching the natives manners, bringing *religion* to them, by God." He sighed and shook his head.

"We're providing a service, Mr Wilson," Juanita said. "These young people come here from the tribes and they want to work in town, but they don't have the slightest clue about all the shenanigans that unscrupulous city employers and apartment owners try to pull on them. They get ripped off left, right and centre, and get forced to work for starvation wages, or for food and accommodation only. So we offer them a job when they first arrive, so that we can teach them to avoid those traps."

Hmm . . . as far as I knew the patronage system was alive and well in Barresh. The large keihu households brought their entire extended family and staff, Pengali included, into those huge mansions, and they all lived there like a mini-village. This part of Barresh still had a large barter economy. Not only was it crass to advertise too much, it was considered tacky to charge fellow keihu. People had "accounts", but few transactions ever saw anything that could be described as money.

But I left the subject. I was not an expert on Barresh society, and it was indeed not why I had come here.

I took the jar from my bag put it on the table and took the piece of paper out.

Clovis had to go and get his glasses to look at it. While we waited, and Juanita chatted about the Pengali youngsters and where they'd gone on to find jobs—because she didn't seem to be able to shut up— I couldn't stop glancing at the fast-churning water that flowed past the house. One only needed to throw a jar in there and it would float all the way to the ocean at a steady clip.

Clovis came back with a pair of white-framed glasses on his nose. Wow, I hadn't seen any of those for ages. Those were fashionable on Earth when I was a teenager.

He studied the jar. "This is not old," was the first thing he said. He knew how fast mould could grow inside a warm bottle.

"No, it isn't." I went on to explain where I had found it.

"All the way out on the sand bar?"

"It could have been washed out of the city with the storm."

"What were you doing there?"

"Surfing, fishing."

"Fishing? It's Thousand Islands tribe territory. You need a permit to fish."

"Not on the sand bar." That was what Veyada said. "I know the islands, for sure, are Thousand Islands territory."

Smart one, Mr Wilson; the name kind of gave it away.

"Did you pass the yellow buoy on the way out?"

"There's a flight beacon just before you get to the sand bar. It's a big yellow thing."

"That's it. That's the tribal land boundary."

"It's a flight beacon."

"It's that, too, but it is in that position to indicate the boundary."

I stared at him. Well, there you go, Mr Wilson. Surprises lurk in the smallest corners.

"Did you come here to learn something about the Pengali?"

I said, "No, I wanted to ask a question. Do you get any visitors from Earth?"

"Who wants to visit us?" Clovis said, snorting. "We got no friends left, and if we die, none of our money will be worth anything on Earth, so the relatives don't come either."

Juanita shook her head. "And if they do, they're not getting anything. I'll tell them that after I deducted contributions normal people would have given their wheelchair-bound relatives, there wasn't much left of their inheritance, so I've given it to people who will appreciate it more than they do. I wish I could see their faces when they're all gathered in the solicitor's office."

"Would either of you have any clue about how that piece of paper got where I found it?"

Clovis pulled a face and shook his head.

Juanita spread her hands. "Someone trying to play a practical joke?"

"I could believe that if it was left on my doorstep or found on the *gamra* island, but no one knew that I was going to visit that beach. We didn't even know ourselves. There is no one out there."

"That's what you say, but as soon as you go past that buoy, you're being watched. Mark my word."

"You're suggesting that the *Pengali* would play a practical joke?"

"I'm not. I'm just disputing that there is no one there."

"But who has written this? That is what I'm interested to hear."

"I truly have no idea, Mr Wilson."

"No," Juanita said. "It's no one we know from here. But sometimes people have illegal visitors."

"Which of the people have illegal visitors? Do you know any cases?"

Her cheeks flushed. "Oh, people. It happens a lot. I mean people from all over. I know that the Tamerians came in that way, and I've heard of other cases."

"I don't think that's relevant, dear," Clovis said, his voice sharp.

"Mr Wilson wanted to know how it could happen. That's how. That's all. I don't actually know of any cases where people from Earth came in that way. What would I know, sitting here in a wheelchair all day—"

"Dear, Mr Wilson wants to know about *this particular* case."

Juanita's face grew even redder. She looked down.

"I'm sorry, my partner gets a bit carried away sometimes. We don't have any concrete evidence."

"But you do have suspicions?"

"One always has to have suspicions, but that's more to do with business."

"Benton Leck?"

"God, no. That man is a saint."

"Huang Le?"

"He's too busy with his food. He might get the occasional illegal cook, but nothing major."

"Jasper Carlson?"

He said nothing. His mouth twitched. Eventually, he said, "I don't like that man. That's all I'll say about it. It's not relevant to your question. I don't know who has written this. I truly have no idea and that's the truth."

I left the house not much later, feeling queasy with the tea. I went down the veranda and through the meticulously kept garden to where Thayu and Nicha sat on two garden benches that faced each other. Well, Thayu sat reading. Nicha lay on his back, with his feet on the armrest and his hands behind his head. He was asleep.

"Hmm, you took your time," Thayu said.

Nicha gasped and sat up.

His sister laughed.

"Don't laugh. Babies are exhausting."

"How did it go?" Thayu asked me.

"Don't ask. I've had enough tea to last me a lifetime. Not the best quality either."

While we made our way back to the station, I filled them in on my visit and how Clovis and Juanita firmly believed they were why the Pengali didn't get exploited more often.

"They mean well," I said. "But I honestly don't think they understand how Pengali society works. They're trying to push it into human boxes with human descriptors."

It was as Melissa had said: all these people had broken with their former lives on Earth in a way I had not. It was disturbing, Huang Le trying to be keihu, Clovis and Juanita trying to "help" the Pengali—who truly did not need help, but that aside. Did they look at me in the same way, as trying to be Coldi?

I pushed that uncomfortable thought away.

I was learning lots, but none of the things I wanted to learn.

The last person on my list was Jasper Carlson, the man everyone professed to hate.

Visiting him required getting back to the station, catching the tram into town and then changing to the southern train line that zoomed over the water along the much more densely populated suburbs where the stations were at the water's edge.

In the older parts of the city, business premises were always mixed with residential ones. In any one street, you could find eating-houses, warehouses, shops and offices.

I had learned that Jasper Carlson lived in the caretaker's apartment attached to a warehouse which he used for his business.

The door to the warehouse was shut and when I knocked, it was opened by a male keihu assistant of middle age.

Yes, his boss was there, but he was busy and about to go out. Could I please come back later? I spotted Jasper at the back of the warehouse, on the steps that led into the office: a tall man with long black hair which he wore in a ponytail. Melissa had not made any concessions to local styles in her appearance. Clovis had dressed very much like my grandfather had done in New Zealand. Huang Le acted keihu but had made no great effort in changing his appearance, either. But this man looked . . . Damarcian perhaps. Not from Earth at any rate.

I spoke up so that he could hear us. "Tell your boss that if he has a moment I would like to know if he's had any visitors from Earth."

A voice called from the back of the shed, "Tell Mr Wilson that it's none of his business."

I yelled back at him, "Good afternoon to you, too, Mr Carlson."

There was the sound of footsteps down the stairs and the shuffling as Jasper Carlson came to the door. Scratch the Damarcian; he could have passed for a keihu man, with sleek dark hair and olive skin, if it weren't for his nose, which was narrow and grooveless. He was probably on the slight side of normal for a keihu man, too.

"What do you want?" He stuck his chin in the air.

He glared at me as I explained the situation, which, with all the practice I'd had today, I could do in a couple of sentences. I showed him the jar.

He didn't reply immediately. He frowned at the jar. His mouth worked.

Eventually he said, "Am I supposed to know who the sender of this . . . thing is?"

"No. I'm only wondering if anyone you know has gone missing?"

"If I knew that someone had gone missing, sending us messages in a bottle, the first thing I would do is to tell the guards about it, wouldn't I?"

———

"I suggest you forget about it," Thayu said on the way back in the train. "Someone played a prank. No one wants to talk to you about it, even if they may know what happened—"

"They don't know what happened."

"Well, that's pretty much the same. They don't want your help or your involvement. And they don't want you to know who did it."

"That's not the same thing. They may not *want* my help or involvement, but that doesn't mean I shouldn't be told. If any of them played a prank, and got a bunch of Pengali to carry this message out there to keep me busy, then why not fess up and apologise?" I spread my hands.

Thayu sighed. "These people make you grumpy. I hate it when you're grumpy."

"Yeah," Nicha said. "Whatever they're up to, it's not worth it. We've got stuff to do. You've done what you can. It's not your job."

I turned the jar over in my hands.

They were right, but I didn't like unsolved mysteries.

6

—————

O**N THE WAY** home in the train, I tried very hard to forget about the note in the jar.

But I wasn't quite ready to discount it completely, so I set the jar on the corner of my desk in my office, just in case I needed it, or I got some inspiration, or a visitor saw it and remembered having seen it before, and went on with the rest of my work.

After lunch, I went to find Devlin in the hub. He had sent me a long list of documents and directories that I needed to check, to decide what level of security they needed.

The prospect of spending the whole afternoon doing this annoyed me, and after the morning's waste of time, I was easy to annoy. I asked him, "Why don't we just hire storage space and put all of it in the highest security? This sort of thing keeps happening, and we keep wasting time on it."

"You have just answered your own question, Muri. This keeps happening. It keeps happening because people make mistakes or become smarter at cracking secure processes. Or they get access through some loyalty chain. These things change all the time. People slip up, people get smarter. If we put everything under one level, no matter how high, they'd crack that and have access to everything. Nothing is unbreakable. And working with highly encrypted information is extremely laborious. You would quickly find it annoying."

As in: *You have no patience, Muri.* Right. I got the message.

Someone order an emergency truckload of fucking patience for me.

I guess he was right, but these constant security breaches were an annoying side effect of having one foot in a society that operated with levels of security and needs-to-know and one in a society that relied on openness of all records.

So I went through my umpteenth security reshuffle. I absolutely fucking hated this with a passion of ten thousand flaming supernovae.

Not only that, it had to be done soon so that we were fully operational before all the delegates returned to the assembly for the elections. I was sure I would have to do some lobbying in favour of Marin Federza and I would be under intense scrutiny for not breaking any rules about giving candidates unfair advantages or disadvantages through information being leaked from my correspondence. That meant having a secure system.

Great. Just great.

What was worse, I had to tell Thayu that we had to postpone our next meeting with Lilona Shrakar until after the elections because of this stupid situation.

"I'm extremely sorry about it, but if the assembly smells blood, and finds out that we're conducting business with the main candidate's partner, they'd turn us out on the street."

Thayu nodded, but I could see the pain on her face. I knew how much she'd been looking forward to that visit.

Lilona had taken all of the medical knowledge from the Aghyrian ship, and was going to report to us what she would need to develop a treatment that would make me genetically compatible with Thayu. I still wasn't sure what to think about it. It seemed the sort of thing that you went to talk to your parents about before you did it. *Hey, Dad, I'm going to change my genes so that I may look different, act differently and may essentially no longer be the same person.*

The thought gave me the shivers.

But I promised her, and she was upset about the delay, even if she didn't show it.

So my punishment was to sit in my office and sort files. And I grew increasingly annoyed at the number of times that I'd done this previously, and knew that we couldn't cordon sensitive information off from my Coldi networks. And so this problem was going to rear its ugly head again and again. Seriously, for fuck's sake, as if I had nothing better to do.

And I also couldn't help thinking about Melissa and her conspiracy theories, and so when I got *really* bored, and I couldn't stand the sight of one more directory list, I looked up the company that had been responsible for sending us the infected message to see if I could poke them with a really sharp stick.

Gamra security would have investigated them ages ago, but I killed some time looking at their services and pricing. Besides archiving services, they sold hacking protection and insurance against security break-ins—ha! First you freak out the client by showing how easy it is to crack their systems, and then you sell them just the thing to fix it.

The company's information wasn't, generally speaking, as unprofessional as of some of the other hawkers I had seen. Their information was well-presented, clean and professional, with logos and other marks of "serious" businesses that operated anywhere outside Barresh.

They spelled out what they did, what all the various plans entailed —they involved mainly buying data—and while reading through the various articles, I learned things I had never known about.

A business customer could, for example, track all of a buyer's purchases through Trader Guild records—this would mean that the company also had inroads to that system. They could then get back to the customer and offer goods that required repeat purchases for a cheaper price.

A political customer could buy tables of *gamra*'s likely future decisions sorted by subject and likelihood that the proposal would make it into law. There were prices on various levels of lobbying required to swing a decision one way or another. One could also buy agendas for future meetings of the *gamra* assembly. Those "products" just gave the date of the meeting with *agenda to be streamed later*.

I'd known that this was going on, and some of it was unavoidable, but the sheer blatancy of the activity of this company was as astonishing as it was fascinating.

As far as I could see, it was all white-collar rule-bending, and there was no conspiracy involved, no mafia or crime—although I agreed with Melissa that the Zhori mafia on Earth had been disturbingly quiet recently. This was a data-mining operation that appeared to be doing quite well for the company. They even included some quotes from people who had used the company.

"My sales doubled in the first month after I started using this program," one owner chirped.

Well, they had better, because the prices were a bit ridiculous, clearly targeted at more than just the small business owner.

Should I notify Federza that the Trader Guild systems had also been breached? Likely they would have been notified by *gamra* security already.

I yawned. Damn, why was dinnertime still so far away?

Back to the directories.

The door opened. It let in a snatch of sound from the hall: Eirani telling one of the domestic staff what to order from the grocery delivery people, and a squeal of Ayshada's laughter. At least someone was having fun.

Then the door rattled shut again.

Devlin had come in.

"I'm not quite ready for the next batch yet," I said. That's what you got from letting yourself get distracted.

"I'm not here because of that. There is a message for you, Muri, from the Exchange. It's important."

Just what I needed. *Gamra* security with an added disaster, no doubt. "Can I take it here?"

"No, it's off world, and there are visuals."

Even worse.

I got up from my desk and followed him into the hallway, wondering what the hell this could be about.

Eirani stood at the top of the stairs talking to one of the young girls from the kitchen. Her name was Yelida, and she had joined my household recently.

A loud squeal echoed through the apartment. A female voice said, in keihu, "Ayshada, be quiet. People are talking."

Which was followed by another squeal and a burst of child's laughter.

Devlin chuckled and I had to laugh, too. I was sure his being a member of the Azimi clan would cause problems, but for now Nicha's son was an utter delight and a true ray of sunlight in a household that had been far too serious of late.

The babysitter was just carrying the little boy across the foyer when we reached the door to the hub. Nicha was talking to someone in the living room, and his son had clearly decided to join him, testing the—excellent—acoustics in the hallway in the process.

There was no one else in the semi-darkness of the hub, with its control benches and blinking lights. Sheydu often sat in there, at the workstation at the back, but she must have gone somewhere else. I had to admit that the comings and goings of Sheydu were a mystery to me most of the time.

I sat on the central bench, normally Devlin's spot. I put on an earpiece. Devlin reached over my shoulder and hit a button.

A projection sprang into the air. First a brief flash of the *gamra* logo and then a man I knew well. It was Yetaris Damaru, the owner of the Barresh Exchange. He used live projection which showed the top half of his body as clearly as if he sat in the room with me. Showing off his new technology.

"Good afternoon, Delegate." It was eerie how it looked like his body and head grew out of the top of the bench that held the projector, as if he'd fallen into the thing up to his waist.

"Good afternoon. I understand you wanted to speak with me?"

"I received a communication from the Athens Exchange. Amarru wants to talk to you."

Normally these kinds of communications would go through messaging, but clearly she had judged this important enough to use voice and image. This was one expensive communication.

"I'm ready. I can talk."

"Good. I'll put her on."

He winked out and was followed by a number of clicks and crackles and flashes as the signal was relayed and relayed yet again as it spanned a good deal of the galaxy.

Another image sprang to life. Not three-dimensional and with a much poorer resolution. It showed a middle-aged, somewhat dumpy Coldi woman in a utilitarian unisex shirt with her hair pulled into a simple ponytail. Amarru was not known for her style.

"Cory." Her warm voice always made me feel at home.

"Amarru. How unusual to hear from you in this way." Everything about this screamed that it was not a social call. Amarru didn't make frivolous calls anyway, and she had probably the least-developed sense of humour of all the people I worked with.

A typical Coldi, she got straight to business. "I understand that you investigated two days ago about any people from Earth having travelled to Barresh recently."

"I did." Seriously, that woman knew everything. "Did you find anyone, because I didn't."

"Well, I don't know. Judge for yourself. I got a strange message from one of my local network publicity people. He was contacted by a woman who had clearly never dealt with anyone from off world before. She was very upset, very scared and my colleague took a long time to get out of her what the problem was and whether she was even in the right place to get help."

I nodded. If things were as they had been when I lived in Athens, it was not exactly easy to find Coldi people, or sources that put you into contact with them or their authorities, especially if you didn't know what you were looking for.

"My contact made a recording of the visit. I'm going to play a part for you, because I have no idea what to make of it."

Amarru's face disappeared and was replaced with a scene in an office, as seen through a camera that stood on a desk. It showed a good section of desk surface covered with a protective sheet and a few bits of electronics. A couple of armchairs stood around a low table on the other side of the room. A Coldi man sat there, as did a middle-aged woman with greying blond hair that hung loose to her shoulders. She wore a stylish pantsuit in pinstripe dark grey. She was in her fifties, I guessed.

I didn't know the Coldi man and had no idea where this was recorded. The view out the window showed another building which I presumed to be on the other side of a street. Maybe in the city of Athens somewhere. The blocky building style was about right for that.

The Coldi man said, in Isla, "Have you heard from him at all since he left?"

The woman shook her head, wiping her eyes. "I don't understand. I mean, he told me that he'd be somewhere extremely remote and I wouldn't be able to contact him. He'd let me know as soon as he was back in civilisation again, but that is more than four weeks ago now."

She had a strange, clipped accent that I'd heard before but couldn't remember where it was from.

"Does he often go to places like that?"

"He does. He loves adventure and he's been hiking everywhere and sailing and climbing mountains and kayaking down raging rivers. He's been away this long before, and no, he doesn't have a mistress if that's what you're thinking. I've been with him on some trips, but we have a disabled son, and someone needs to be home to look after him."

"So, when, after four weeks, you heard nothing, what did you do?"

"I went to the police, but they just nodded, took down all my information and I've heard nothing since. They seem to act like I'm crazy."

"Is that why you're here?"

"Well, they traced the location of the last message he sent me to Athens. Also, the police asked me to go through his desk and his computer and other things that belong to him. I found this."

She put a reader on the table. The Coldi man held it up slightly so that the camera could see what was on the screen and the image zoomed in.

It was an ad, laid out in a sparse, professional style. There was a picture of a couple of rocky islands with greenery on top protruding from a turquoise ocean.

Underneath it said, "A place of unrivalled rugged beauty, where you will be guaranteed to find privacy and walk on beaches where no human has walked before."

In smaller letters, it extolled the virtues of the company, called Exclusive Adventures, and they included, "exquisite food catering for all dietary requirements" and "guaranteed confidentiality". It said, "If you travel with us, we guarantee that no one else gets told about your adventure, so you can keep coming back to your favourite spots year after year, without the risk of your locations being spoiled by other tourists."

As activities they listed *survival camping* (No gun licence required!), *hiking, swimming, skindiving, sailing, surfing (with plesiosaurs!)*

I took in a sharp breath. Plesiosaurs. Beisili.

A message in a bottle.

"Stop the projection."

Amarru did, and her face returned to the projection, looking concerned. "Cory?"

"Yes. Yes."

"What, yes?"

"I think I know what this is about. This is my missing man, the sender of the message. Who is it? What's he doing in Barresh? How did he get here if he didn't show up in the Exchange records?"

"I don't know. What are you talking about?"

"You mean, you don't know? You always know everything."

"What am I supposed to know?" Why did I always forget that she had no sense of humour?

I quickly explained what had happened to us in the past few days and why I had been trying to find people from Earth through the Exchange.

She frowned deeply. "So you think this is the same person?"

"There is no doubt. It talks about surfing with plesiosaurs. I just did that, a few days ago. They're called beisili and they're not all that harmless."

"But why the note in the jar? I'm guessing this man would have been with a guide. Where is the guide?"

"Obviously something happened. We had a big storm a few days ago. Maybe their vehicle flipped or sank and he managed to get himself to an island but there are no other survivors."

"Ugh. What are the chances of him surviving for any length of time?"

"Depends on if he's injured and if he happened to have landed in a place that has fresh water. Some of those islands don't have any. Or if there are hostile tribes."

She blew out a heavy breath. "I don't like this at all, Cory."

"No, it could get messy."

"Really messy, for us, too. I checked and we have no records of him leaving Earth through the Exchange."

"How is that possible?"

"That is a very good question, but it's highly likely he travelled on someone else's ID, and that seems very odd for a legitimate tourist operation. In fact, the whole thing is odd. No one runs tourist trips off world. Not from Earth at least. Too much hassle, too expensive."

"This gig is only for very rich people. Have you seen what this company charges?"

"Yeah." But she didn't sound convinced. Amarru, who rarely left the Exchange complex, had very little idea of how little money some people had and how lucky she was not to have to worry about living expenses.

"Do you . . . want me to go and find this guy?"

"Yeah, probably. Be quick. It's not going to look good when the media gets a sniff of it before we've found him."

I could agree with that. "Could you send me all the information that you got from his wife?"

"Sending it now. There is a fair bit of stuff: the rest of the recording, communication details and other stuff that I personally haven't had the time look at. Good luck with it."

"Keep in contact."

"I will."

She logged off and I sat staring into the dark space where her image had been, while the transfer lights blinked.

"Muri?" Devlin said. "She is sending something for you."

"I know." I turned to him. "Go and call everyone in here. Tell them that it's important."

He nodded and left.

7

———————

W HILE I WAITED for everyone to turn up, I opened the first document Amarru had sent. It detailed the man's personal information. His name was Robert Davidson and his occupation was listed as Chief Executive of Execo Ltd., which turned out to be an engineering company that designed and adapted specialised mining equipment. He came from Cape Town. Ah, that accounted for his wife's strange accent. Did that mean she had travelled to Athens especially to see if she could find out why her husband had not contacted her? Likely, but that would be an expensive trip on the suborbital.

I also watched the rest of the recording at double speed, which made people's voices go funny, but it didn't provide me with that much more useful information. The Coldi man—some sort of legal representative like Nixie Chan in Rotterdam?—was cautious when talking to her. He said he'd investigate—and that investigation apparently consisted of contacting Amarru—and proceeded to ask her for some personal details that he cross-checked against the Exchange records to be sure that she or her husband were really not known. It didn't look like they were. Whatever possessed a man like that to come on this trip?

By the time I'd finished watching it, the first of my association were coming in. Thayu and Nicha, with Reida. Then Veyada and Sheydu and Deyu. Evi and Telaris were missing. I was beginning to have a feeling that sending them to visit their family might not have been as smart as I thought. For one, they had much more intricate knowledge about survival in the wilderness of Barresh than any of the others did.

"We've found the owner of the note in the jar," I began, and quickly brought them up to speed with what Amarru had said. I showed them a couple of still images from the recording, especially the parts that showed the ad.

Nicha's eyes widened. "He's paid *what?* to go on this trip?"

"Yeah, we're not talking about some down-and-out poor guy who got duped into coming here. He's paid for the privilege, and paid dearly."

"That's not Barresh," Veyada said, nodding at the image of the islands. "The sea is the wrong colour."

"You're right, but I think that whoever wrote this ad knew very well that the whole expedition was going to be illegal. Seeing as this guy is seriously rich, they might even have charged him for Exchange fees, and then used the permit of someone else whom they bumped off the flight." I was thinking on my feet. The possibilities for foul play were endless.

It might even be that marooning this guy on an island offshore, with no way for his wife to ever find out where he had gone, was the intended result. The unintended part about it might have been that he managed to send that message in a jar and that we happened to have found it.

Shit.

A lot of things suddenly made so much more sense.

Damn, how much more often had this happened? I hadn't heard anyone speak of a Bermuda Triangle for rich businessmen, but then again, what did I know about the most pressing news on Earth? Unless the Exchange was mentioned, news would never make it to Barresh.

"So," Nicha said. "What are we going to do?"

"Amarru has asked me to try and find him."

"Did she say where the budget for this activity was going to come from?" Count on Sheydu to be blunt. "Finding a single person out there would require aerial surveillance. We'd have to hire a solar plane and boats, and people to drive them, and possibly Pengali trackers.

Those can be a bugger, especially if they get a whiff of the urgency of the situation."

"We'll cross into Thousand Islands tribal territory," Veyada said. "By rights, we should first apply to them to mount an official search on their land."

I said, "I understand that the sand bar is in their territory. We didn't need a permit for that, did we?"

"No, because the sand bar falls under the more lenient *fishing grounds* provision, but if we are going to set foot on the islands, that is a different matter. We should probably also have a guide from that tribe."

"Good luck finding one of those," Sheydu muttered.

Thayu said, "It would help us a great deal if we knew how this man ended up where he did. What type of vehicle was used? We don't immediately need to resort to going out there and doing on-the-ground searches. We can search the Exchange records if we know what we're looking for."

There were nods all around. Thayu had taken a lot of training from local security people and it was starting to show.

That was the crux of the matter. Before we did anything, we needed to find out who was involved locally, because there would have been some local logistics for anyone to get out there. A boat at least, and someone to drive it. Possibly food and fuel.

Thayu said she would follow that up with the Exchange. Reida said that he knew people who hired out boats, and he would ask around if anyone had been seen gathering camping gear.

"We may have to use your Pengali contacts," I told him. "Anyone from the Thousand Islands tribe?"

He laughed. "When most of the local Pengali are from the Washing Stones tribe? Not likely."

Veyada said, "Yeah, that is going to be a problem. We can easily get permits to search in Washing Stones tribe territory. They're relaxed and many of them work in town or live in town. The Thousand Islands tribe is going to be a bit different."

Hmm, so going to the islands might require a visit to the Pengali Office but most likely the people there would be from the Washing Stones tribe, too. How did one even file a request to visit with the Thousand Islands tribe?

Sheydu was still unhappy about the matter of money.

I told her, "Look, at this point in time it's more important that this man gets found—"

"So that Nations of Earth and the Exchange can save themselves from embarrassment? They should send someone out there to do that job, because why should we risk our lives to do it? This man put himself in danger."

I spread my hands. "Look, I . . ."

Veyada shot his mother a sharp look. She pressed her lips together. Whatever went on there clearly had some history.

Nicha said there was money to cover any hire of equipment, if we needed it. We could worry about reimbursement later. The office staff would probably hit Nations of Earth for that. Those people were excellent in that way.

Thayu had taken her place at the second bench at the back, getting ready to dive into the Exchange records of vehicle movement out to sea.

I said I'd go into town to visit the Pengali Office to see if I could do something about visiting the Thousand Islands tribe territory.

But first, I went to get the jar with Robert Davidson's note from my office. I showed it to Devlin. "I would like you to see if you can match this drawing up with any geographical features offshore."

Devlin gave me a strange look. "What do you mean 'match up'?"

"He's drawn something here. Some natural feature of the location. See if you can find something that matches the shape. I will probably take you off the archiving. If we're going back out there, I want you to liaise with the Athens Exchange instead."

Devlin nodded, looking very serious.

I went to my office. I wanted to view all the things that Amarru had sent me, and perhaps write to Robert's wife with some more specific questions if necessary. If it had to go through all the channels, it might take a few days before I had an answer.

I had just sat at the desk when the door opened and Deyu came in. She crossed the floor and sat down on the very edge on the chair opposite the desk.

She was at that age where, when doing physical work, Coldi women would develop broad shoulders for the rest of their lives, and that classical triangle shape was already evident in her body. She looked quite pleasing now, but next year she would be formidable.

"Deyu? Is something wrong?"

"No, but there is something I want to say that I didn't want to say in there, because it might be embarrassing. It's about Sheydu."

"She did seem a bit out of sorts."

"Yes, and I'm not even supposed to know this at all, but do you know when we went on that nightly trip to the main island to destroy the relay?"

"The one where you showed off your train-driving skills?"

Her cheeks went red. "Well, yeah. I was a train driver, so that was easy for me. But Sheydu decided during that trip that she really doesn't like water. You know, most of us don't like water, but we can deal with our fear by training."

Like Thayu going surfing, which had been amusing, but I'd always had to be on the lookout for the possibility of a panic attack while either Nicha or Thayu were in the water.

"Sometimes, for some people, the fear of water is inbuilt and no amount of training can do anything about it. Sheydu is really embarrassed that she hasn't been able to shake her fear."

"Is that why she was so blunt? Because she is afraid to go out over the ocean?"

"Yes. But please don't tell anyone that I said this to you."

"It's all right. The secret is safe." No one made fun of Sheydu. No one, ever.

"She is extremely embarrassed."

"We are all afraid of something. I'll just put her on hub duties if we go out there."

Except after Deyu had left, I knew it wasn't as simple as that. Devlin was by far the best to be at the hub, and he didn't need a second person. And Sheydu was our explosives specialist. We might need her.

Gah, the complications.

I opened all of the documentation that Amarru had sent me. There was little more on the company Exclusive Adventures. On a whim, I translated the name into Coldi and searched in the information and news channels. I didn't find anything useful there.

There were some photos of Robert—balding, brown hair, bearded, a bit soft around the middle—at family gatherings, cooking a giant lobster, climbing a mountain in the snow, riding a kayak down a rapid. There were pictures where they had taken their disabled son on trips. I came across a wedding photo, dated 2108, over twenty years ago.

Just before he vanished, he had sent his wife a picture of a ring he had bought or was going to buy for her, with a stone in the shape of a bee. The wings consisted of closely-set tiny diamonds. The stone that made up the body was soft turquoise. I wasn't into this style of jewellery at all, but that stone was very pretty. And it looked expensive.

"I'll pick it up when I come back," he'd said. I presumed when he came back from his surfing trip. Cute.

Next I found some pictures to do with his work in the mining industry.

In one, he sat in an office with a group of other people. It looked like they might be well-known people, but I had no idea who they were. Another picture showed a piece of mining equipment where chunks of ore were crushed into smaller chunks. Two people in yellow overalls stood at the controls.

Then there was a picture of a view over an open-cut mine. Wow, I thought they'd shut down those eyesores ages ago.

I collected the pictures onto my reader. I'd take them into town to show people. I would be highly surprised if none of the Earth people I'd visited had any involvement with the organisation of this trip, even if only in passing. They might remember the man's face or might know who would be running tourist trips.

The fact that my visit to all the Earth people had brought up no information was strange. Either someone was lying or this venture was run entirely from Earth. But there would have to be a local connection. For now I wasn't seeing that connection, so I decided to make a start on the Pengali issue.

The train timetable didn't have any trains arriving in town before the close of business—or, I should say, before most administrative offices closed, because trying to pin Barresh to an opening and closing schedule was like trying to teach a fish to paint. The fact that Pengali were nocturnal, especially the tribal ones, might even mean that the office was open all night. Who knew?

I played it safe and ordered a water taxi.

Both Thayu and Nicha were busy. I would otherwise have taken Sheydu and Veyada, but now that I knew about her sensitivity I thought maybe not, so I went into the hub and asked Deyu and Reida to come.

Deyu jumped up immediately. "I need to put on my uniform."

"We're only going into town," I protested. I really didn't feel like the dress-up thing, but, *gamra* being *gamra*, it was unavoidable.

I tried to get ready as quickly as I could, but it still involved Eirani fussing over my hair and my clothing. When I came into the foyer, both Reida and Deyu stood next to the door in their black outfits, both of them carrying guns and looking very impressive.

It struck me that this was the first time they alone had accompanied me and, yes, both had developed from scruffy Outer Circle kids into fine young people. I must think of something to celebrate this special occasion for them.

We left the apartment. The area around the door felt empty without Evi and Telaris. I wondered if anyone had heard from them yet.

We walked at a brisk pace along the gallery, down the stairs and out the building past the uniform shop on the ground floor. The old fellow who ran the shop waved a greeting.

The boat was just coming in as we arrived at the jetty, and because it was coming up to high tide, we didn't have to climb down the ladder. It was funny how, since going out to the sand bar I'd started to take notice of things like tides, things that most people at the *gamra* island wouldn't give a second thought to.

As usual, the trip was quick and windy.

The driver dropped us at the jetty below the airport. We walked up the slope past the aircraft parking area with the sunlight at our back. No dark unmarked craft sat on the tarmac this time. The problems and mysteries were all mine and Asha would not come to interfere or help me. It was a little . . . disconcerting. I'd come to rely on the fact that someone was looking over my shoulder.

From the top of the path where it widened out into the square, it was only a short walk to the Pengali office, which was in the council complex. As expected, they had only just opened and the young woman in attendance was slightly flustered while we waited for her to flip all the wall levers to turn on the—Pengali-made—

pearl lights, so that the entire office became bathed in an eerie greenish light.

"Yes, can I help you?" she asked.

She wore an elfin-like dress of diaphanous material that showed off the leopard spots on her shoulders, upper arms and back. I saw myself reflected in her huge eyes.

I started, "We are looking for someone."

I told her our unlikely story. While I spoke, her frown deepened. I pulled out my reader and flicked through a couple of pictures of Robert. Robert smiling at the camera while climbing a rock face. Robert giving the thumbs up while skiing. There, the Pengali woman frowned deeply. She would know the concept of snow—for all that Barresh was tropical, Ceren was a cool world with extensive ice caps.

Then a picture of Robert on—

"What's that?"

—A camel.

She definitely did not understand the concept of camels. And she was getting distracted with too many details in the pictures.

"Please, have you seen this man at all?"

I flicked to another picture.

The Pengali woman gasped.

I looked at the screen. Dang, I'd accidentally copied across the picture of the ring. "I'm sorry. That doesn't belong in there."

She stared at the screen. "That is a sky stone." Her voice dropped to an angry whisper. "How dare they sell sky stones for the making of trinkets."

"It's a type of glass stone?" I very much doubted that the ring was a cheap trinket, but that aside—

"That type is only found in the territory of the Thousand Islands tribe. We call it that because it is the colour of the sky."

I looked from the picture to her and back again. "This stone has a special significance?"

She burst out, "It's a sky stone! He has put a sky stone in an ugly piece of metal. What is it for? Just so that he can adorn himself with frivolous glittery things?"

Whoa.

I involuntarily took a step back. Pengali often had a highly intense quality in their speech that could be very intimidating. Like everyone knew their customs. Like people were stupid for not knowing them. Maybe I was stupid, I don't know, but I didn't like being attacked. "Look, I have no idea where he got this stone—"

"It's a sky stone. It's from the Thousand Islands."

"He lives off world. People over there make glass stones in every single colour."

"You do not make glass stones. They grow in the rock for many ages. We search for the colours and make pretty panes and pretty windows. But you do not cut sky stone, ever."

I held up my hands. "All right, all right." I should probably have looked up the stone first, but then again how could I have known about this? Was this stone from Barresh? I guessed it could be. Would a mining executive buy his wife a fake stone? I didn't think so. Were these stones found anywhere else? No idea.

I flicked back to the last picture of Robert. "Please, have you seen this man?" I asked for the third time.

She squinted at the image with her large Pengali eyes that were dark brown, almost without whites, and bulging like deer eyes. "I don't know. I've seen plenty like him. They come here at times when it's unsuitable to go out fishing or whatever they come there to do and expect to be taken anyway."

"What sort of people are they?"

"They're usually rich, and they're from places like Damarq or Kedras or wherever that world is . . ." She gestured at the screen.

"They come for fishing?" Living at the *gamra* island, I was thoroughly unaware that this happened, but it probably shouldn't surprise me.

"Usually. I've heard that it all started when someone started telling stories about catching giant creatures with bait and a net. He must have been telling tall tales, because no one can catch beisili with a net. Or even catch them at all. They're too big and stroppy for that. But still these idiots come to risk their lives."

"Who takes them out there?"

"They try to hire anyone who has a boat. We told all our boat operators not to take them. They are poor customers. They want this, they want that or they threaten not to pay. They're more trouble than they're worth."

"Who takes them if none of your people don't?"

"Pah. I don't know. Other people. Or people who need money really badly."

"But who organises for them to come?"

"Organise? You misunderstand. They come by themselves. If anyone was organising it, they'd be smart and stay away in the wet season. Something like this was an accident waiting to happen. Probably he took a guide and the guide wanted to come back, but he didn't. They had a fight and the guide left him there."

"We need to help him."

"I don't know that you can. This man, he is in the territory of the Thousand Islands tribe."

"I understand that we need permission from the tribe to look for him on the islands."

"You don't get permission from them. You go, and hope they don't discover you or that you can talk your way out of it if they do. It's up to their generosity to provide for him. I'd say they are not keen to do so. They do not want anyone fouling their lands with their footsteps."

"I was hoping you could tell me where I could hire a guide."

She laughed, a snorting sound. "None of us would go there."

"Is there no one from the Thousand Islands tribe in town?"

"If there is, I am not speaking to them, and they are not speaking to us."

"*If there is?* Or do you know for sure that no one from the tribe is here?"

"I know for sure about my friends and people who come in here. But who knows what crawlers live in the dirty alleys of Far Atok? I would not recommend that you look for them. Your beautiful uniform will get dirty."

"So. If I offered a lot of money to find this man, would anyone help me?"

"Your money is not worth anything to us. We value peace. We stay away from uncivilised tribes. The Thousand Islands tribe are always looking for reasons to fight. They want our land, that's why. This man, why do you think he is worth the trouble of a war?"

8

"**WELL, I WOULDN'T** call that the epitome of useful," I said when we were outside. "I was under the impression that the function of the Pengali Office was to facilitate relations between the Pengali and other people in this city, but I must have been mistaken."

What was it about this case that thwarted all my attempts at finding out what was going on? There was probably something in my face that I wasn't seeing, but for now . . . I wasn't seeing it.

"I think she knows more than she's telling us," Reida said.

"She told us virtually nothing, so that wouldn't surprise me. But tell me why you think so." He had much more contact with the Pengali than I had.

We were walking down Fountain Street in the direction of the main square and the airport.

It was fast starting to get dark and groups of families, shoppers and social diners ambled up and down the street. Meili squawked in the trees above us. You could see them now, winged silhouettes flying from branch to branch against the dark blue sky, because at the end of the wet season and with the storm, these trees lost a good number of their leaves.

"That woman was just fobbing us off because she figured that we don't know anything and she could tell us bullshit. Not knowing where to find Thousand Islands people? Of course she knows where those people are. Not knowing who operates the other, non-Pengali boat services? Of course she knows. They are the Pengali's main competitors."

"Why didn't you say anything while we were inside? The Barresh Council pays her to provide a service, not to lie to people."

"Because . . ." He spread his hands and shrugged. He looked down.

Deyu touched his arm, a very subtle gesture. She looked down, too. We had almost come to a halt on the corner of Fountain Street and the main square.

People streamed past us on their way to the open-air markets and the many eateries, including Huang Le's, with its floodlit glasshouse at the back.

I knew why he had never said anything.

Because whenever something happened, someone in my association would blame Reida. Sometimes, it would even be me. Usually, it was a joke, and never meant in any other way. Or we would joke about things that he used to do, but that he hadn't done for a long time. And we would take him less seriously, and it led to the fact that he was usually the last person in my association to be offered training.

Of course.

Add that to the fact that he was one of the very few of the persecuted Ezmi clan left on Asto. Add that to the fact that he had zeyshi tattoos on his arms, and that he had probably narrowly escaped their stranglehold.

The world conspired to make him feel a lesser citizen.

And as usual, I was doing a pretty fucked-up job of managing this association, where everyone was supposed to feel useful and valued.

Look at the two of them, now standing hand in hand, like children being caught with their hand in the lolly jar. Two Coldi youngsters from the poorest of poor areas of Athyl, thrown well out of their familiar environment, and surviving, no, thriving on doing the things they had always known to do. For Reida, that was connect with as many people as possible. For Deyu, that was watching, learning and studying.

"I take your commitment very seriously," I said in a low voice, and then when they didn't reply, I continued, "I asked Nicha to find us some members who were not from the main ruling clans." The

Palayis, the Domiris, the Azimis, the Linguis, and, heaven forbid, the Vonayis. "Nicha did a good job."

I continued, "Thayu . . ." I was going to say, *I love her very much*, but the concept of partnership for life didn't appeal to most Coldi. "Thayu is from the Inner Circle. She chose Sheydu and Veyada as her seconds. They are much more like her than you two are like Nicha. That takes some adjusting. I'm doing my best."

Both of them kept looking down.

So I had to do that thing I hated: to push Reida's chin up with the tips of my fingers—apparently there was an intricate protocol involved with doing this properly, and I hadn't progressed much further than using the fingertips, but I had seen long descriptions of how you held your hand and what it meant. I hoped Reida didn't know about all those subtle signals either.

Reida's eyes met mine. His irises were very sparse in the gold flecking that characterised Coldi eyes. I still cringed at the meek expression in them. I knew this was a physiological reaction, but it still annoyed me that people thought they were worth less than me.

"Reida, I value your presence. Don't let anything tell you otherwise. Deyu, too."

I pushed up her chin as well. Her eyes were more typical.

Damn, I loved both of them, with all their angles and rough sides.

And then I did another very Coldi thing: I hugged both of them, and we stood in this threesome hug for a while. When we released each other, some of the tension seemed to have gone from Reida's face.

I resumed our conversation. "So, Reida, tell me: why do you think that this woman would hold back information? To keep from getting people in trouble?"

"That's one part." We started walking again now that some of the unease seemed to have been dispelled. "But more important is that boat ownership is a big thing for the Pengali. Most of them will never have a permanent house, because that's the way they are: they don't care about houses. But they will want to buy a boat, because having a boat means that they can earn money fishing or harvesting or transporting people or things. If they don't have a boat, they'll want to work and save up to buy one. They don't like the big boating companies, but they need them until they have saved enough to buy their own boat. The companies make their drivers work long, hard days, and will ask them to compete against each other. Pengali don't like competing. The drivers live in constant fear. They hate their employers and will never let an opportunity go by to make an underwater stab at these companies, if they can get away with it."

"What sort of things are we talking about? Stealing boats?"

"Not so much that, because a boat is easy to track, but little things like flipping the on switch on a competitor's boat so the charge drains overnight, or untying their boats when it rains so that they float away. For some of these people, it almost becomes a pastime."

"That's kind of petty."

"Yes, but boat ownership in Barresh is a harsh world. The Pengali consider it their territory. That's why some of the non-Pengali operators are real nervous about being singled out and to have it made publicly known what businesses are theirs. One fellow owns a whole slew of other businesses in the northwest. He gets hit a lot by his boating competitors. Another is a well-known councillor. This woman at the Pengali Office doesn't know that either of these owners have anything to do with this missing man, so she doesn't want to send you around to question them, because Pengali workers might well lose their jobs as a result and it will feed into this nasty boating war."

"So the reason she didn't name the non-Pengali boat owners had nothing to do with my question?"

"No. I dare say she couldn't care less about this missing man."

Deyu added. "You know, at the *gamra* island, people get carried away with the political consequences of something like this, but if every day is a struggle to survive, if you need to go out there and haul fish, and defend your fishing place against poachers and competitors and people from enemy tribes, then concerns about other worlds are . . ." She spread her hands. "Pffft, who cares?"

I nodded. Yes, I understood that sentiment well enough. What I hadn't expected was to uncover this cesspool of politics and backstabbing in addition to tribal rivalry and goodness knew what other foul practices surrounded the simple subject of boats. I mean—they were just a vehicle, right? A way to get from A to B.

But it sounded like the simple act of hiring a water taxi could be construed as a political endorsement. Those companies that ran the taxi services, and the ferries—

Wait. *Ferries!*

Shit.

I just realised: Clovis Keneally was the owner of a ferry company. We had briefly discussed it when I visited. No, it was Juanita who'd mentioned the ferries washing over the top of the lock into the marshlands. Because a competitor had untied the boats? Clovis had been a bit brusque about it. He had not wanted me to know that he owned that company?

Was it coincidence that Robert's help note was written on a ferry timetable?

Holy crap. There was the clue, right in my face. I turned to Reida. "I . . . have an idea that may or may not bear fruit. I'll have to check it out. Meanwhile, do you think you could try to find where these Thousand Islands tribe people are? We may need a guide later."

"I can try. That's all I can promise. Some of these people are a bit shady. I guess you want me to find one who's not going to lead us into a trap, either."

"That would be nice."

"I may need to go into Far Atok, but if you want, I can come back home with you first and then go back later."

"No. We're not going home either. You can go now and meet us later."

"Oh?" Deyu said, her eyes wide. "Where are we going?"

"We're going to check something out. Is that a problem?"

"No . . ." She hesitated.

"But what?"

"What about checking the directories that I was doing with Devlin and that needed to be done before the next assembly?"

Damn, that wouldn't be completed with all this going on. "We'll deal with that when we face the problem."

Which was not how I liked to do my job, not at all. I made a mental note to ask the office staff to look at it. They were not trained for this and wouldn't do as good a job as I could, but it was better for there to be some glitches than for us to still not be online by the time everyone came back for the assembly session.

Why did this bullshit always happen at times I could least afford it?

Reida went off and Deyu and I walked towards the station.

I began to see Sheydu's point. Of course I didn't mind helping find Robert—even if he was out there through his own stupidity—because that's what people did: they helped each other.

But at what point did I decide that these sidetracks were keeping me from doing the work for which Ezhya paid me, which had nothing to do with rescuing stupid humans out of difficult situations, in which, by the look of things, they had put themselves?

Why didn't Amarru ask Melissa to do it?

Because it wasn't Melissa's job either, and she had far fewer resources than I did. If I sent Melissa out there, she might well need to take her Kedrasi partner and they could both end up being killed.

"Where are we going?" Deyu asked when the train set off along the northeastern line.

"I'll explain to you when we get there."

She sat next to me, silently, while the train rumbled along the track. Reida's story had changed my mind about where I wanted to go. Initially, I had intended to visit Benton Leck after going to the Pengali Office, because he had returned from Miran, and maybe Clovis Keneally again because he'd seemed the most talkative of the Earth people, and show each of them the pictures of Robert. But certainly, if Clovis had seen Robert, he would have mentioned it before, because you didn't just "forget" that someone from your world visited in a place where there were only a handful of those people. Unless he didn't want me to know.

And I didn't want to tell Deyu where we were going because we were getting some curious looks from other passengers in the carriage. I guessed we were a fairly unusual sight: a *gamra* delegate in blues and an impressive-looking Coldi female guard, both armed more heavily than customary for the average citizen. If we talked about where we were going, they might remember if some kind of trouble blew up. Because both myself and Reida were fully qualified trouble-magnets.

Deyu and I stayed on the train until the second-to-last station. The line ended at the giant footbridge that connected the main island with Far Atok. It was one of the great idiosyncrasies of Barresh that there was no train line across it. You had to get off, walk across and catch another train on the other side. The footbridge had been deemed too culturally significant to deface it with rails.

Councillors kept promising to build a railway bridge, but none of the proposals had ever progressed any further than the council arguing over who was going to pay for it.

At the station where we got off, you could see the footbridge to the right, a giant structure built from stones the early inhabitants of the two islands carted, stone by stone, in punts from the escarpment and hoisted into place. Out there along the escarpment was an old quarry where you could see where the stones had been cut, made to measure and heaved onto boats by hand. It would have been a huge job.

To our left was another bridge over one of the city's drainage canals. This was a much lower and more modern construction of steel. On the other side of this bridge, a part of the canal split off into an inland harbour, with jetties and sheds: the ferry station.

A walkway led along the water to the main building, but the gate into the yard was closed.

A sign over the top of the entrance said, *Barresh Ferry Services*. I had seen it before, and it had always struck me as a bit odd. Barresh business people considered it crass to display one's business name too prominently, although the time that businesses had no names seemed to have passed with the coming of *gamra*. Maybe, too, owners of businesses to do with boats were reluctant to display too clearly who they were for the reasons mentioned by Reida: sabotage and vandalism by competitors.

If my assessment of all the facts was correct, Clovis Keneally owned this business.

"Is this the place we're going?" Deyu asked when we stopped at the gate. "It's closed."

"This is one of the boat companies owned by non-Pengali," I said. "What's more, the owner is from Earth. I don't know if there is a connection, but if you were a guide from another world, and you brought a guest from that world and you needed to hire a vehicle, wouldn't you choose an operator who was also from the same world?"

"I guess."

"The note in the jar was written on the back of a ferry timetable."

"There are two ferry companies in town."

"I know, but my money is on this one."

She grabbed the bars of the gate and pulled. "I can open this for you."

Coldi people would have no trouble with the flimsy structure. "No, I don't want to damage anything. We only do that if we're sure that we're going to find incriminating material. I just want to have a look." On the off chance that I found something interesting.

I walked to the side of the gate. The fence extended about a metre over the water of the channel, but the channel itself was open, because ferries operated at night. They would come in here for the change of shift or stuff like that, whatever it was that ferries did in here.

I knew that the water in the channels wasn't very deep, but I hated the thought of getting my shoes wet. Maybe I could . . .

I put my foot into the mesh of the fence that hung over the water, and then the other foot.

The fence was wobbly. Deyu held it in place while I shuffled to the end and then around and back to the shore on the other side. Then I did the same for her.

Well, that was easy. For a company afraid of sabotage from competitors, their security was unimpressive. Their loss, our gain.

Quickly and quietly, we walked along the edge of the water.

The canal went through a giant open-sided shed where at least ten boats lay moored. There was also a little office. I peeked in through the window by the glow of a few tiny pinpricks of light from the communication hub. The room contained two tidy desks, a workstation and a bay of shelves that contained wire baskets with various engine parts.

I tried the door—sturdy and possibly Coldi-proof—but predictably it was locked, and although I would love to poke around inside, we could not do that without going through the considerable effort of breaking the glass stone windows and we had no reason to do that.

We walked all over the yard and didn't find much of importance. It looked like the business was well run, the yard free of incriminating rubbish.

We climbed back along the fence without incident—and even without getting wet—and walked back to the station. A few other people waited on the platform, likely workers from the nearby industries or warehouses. I contacted Reida to see where he was and where to meet.

Then the train came in, the doors opened and . . . Clovis Keneally got out. He didn't see us, but made a beeline for the exit of the station in the direction of the boat yard. Well, that was interesting.

I held Deyu back when she was about to enter the train.

"What's going on?"

"Shhh. That man over there is the owner."

We let the train go, and followed Clovis at a distance. He stopped in front of the gate to the ferry yard to unlock it, and then went through, put the lock back on and relocked it.

"Do we climb around?" Deyu whispered when he had disappeared into one of the sheds.

"Better not do that, in case he only needs to pick up something quickly."

We waited.

The light went on inside the office. Not much later, it turned off again. There was the sound of footsteps, followed by a big splash.

Deyu gasped. "He's fallen in!" An involuntary dunking in ink black water was probably the stuff of Coldi nightmares.

"I don't think the splash was that big."

We waited, and indeed, Clovis came back from out of the shed. We retreated into the shadow of a neighbouring warehouse. He went out the gate, shut and locked it, and walked back in the direction of the station.

9

———

WELL, THAT WAS certainly interesting.

I contacted Reida. "Change of plan. Do you think you could meet us at the ferry yard soon?"

"I'm just crossing the bridge right now," he said. "If you're at the ferry yard, I could almost see you. I can see the roof of that big shed that's in the middle of the place."

"We're outside the gate. We'll wait until you get here," I told him.

He clicked off and we waited. There was no one in the street, and all the surrounding buildings were dark, being industrial warehouses where no one lived.

I asked Deyu about her studies, and then I asked her about her family. Her father had recently moved out of his furniture business in Eighth Circle, so that he could concentrate on his politics. Deyu had a half sister who lived with her father and had been, rich-people style, contracted by him by paying for a woman from Seventh Circle to have his child. One day not so long ago, Deyu had said at the table that the contract system tended to break down if no one had any money or owned anything worth inheriting.

That had earned her some strange looks from the others, but she was right, of course, even if Sheydu, Thayu, Veyada and Nicha had never been anywhere near poor enough to comprehend this.

I asked her about her father's politics. It was no more than a local wardenship, looked down on by people in the inner circles, but I understood one thing about Athyl's outer circles: they were vastly more populous than any of the inner circles, and to wield power over a single ward could mean having earned the respect and loyalty of close to half a million people. That was not nothing.

I had learned that if people in Eighth Circle were high enough in the hierarchy, they could find plenty of Seventh Circle partners happy to go into a contract with them. Which was how Deyu's father had worked himself up.

Being a child born to a low woman out of despair—she had forced Deyu's father to pay for the child—Deyu had missed out on such selection of genes, which was why she had been working behind the counter in a bar when Nicha found her. But she lacked neither determination nor her father's smarts.

Reida joined us.

I told him briefly what we had seen. "I'd like to retrieve whatever he threw in the water."

"What, now?" Reida said.

"Yes, there will be people here during the day."

"But it's dark."

"I've noticed. Come, let's go."

Neither of them said anything. It was probably their fear of dark, black water speaking. "Just help me get in there, and keep a look out. I'll go into the water and fish it out. The water in these channels isn't deep."

We climbed back around the fence and walked along the mooring spots and the quietly bobbing ferries to the dark overhang of the shed. I found a broom and tested the depth of the water: it was as high as my waist and smelled of rotting plants and silt.

How appetising.

"All right, I won't be long." I kicked one of my shoes off, then the other one, then took my blue *gamra* pants and shirt off. I folded them neatly and put them on a bench that seemed to have been put there for just this purpose. I sat on the edge of the canal and pushed myself in. The bottom felt disgustingly slimy under my feet. I shuddered and tried not to think about what might be down there.

I waded across the channel, pushing through the fetid, lukewarm water, feeling for something big with my feet, but I reached the other side without having found anything. Then I took a step to the side and waded back. I didn't find anything there either. Something nearby made a soft humming noise. I stopped to listen where it came from, but it sounded like a pump or some machine that came on automatically.

I waded back again. The water was waist-deep on the sides and a little deeper in the middle. Apart from being slimy, the bottom was surprisingly clean of debris. The bottoms of all the channels I had ever seen empty were concreted, although I'd been told that some were still made of packed earth.

Reida and Deyu stood on the side, silhouetted by the faint light from the office.

On my way back across the channel, my foot hit something. Ouch.

"Ah. I think I've got it." I pushed with my foot, but the thing was too heavy to move. I crouched as far as I could without submerging my head in the foul water. My fingertips touched the top of the thing. It felt like metal or wood, clean and not slimy. That was definitely the thing, a box of some kind. No, a crate, and it had a handle, which I could feel with my toes. The thing was very heavy, but if I could drag it as close as I could to the side, Reida and Deyu would be able to help me getting it out of the water.

I took in a deep breath and let myself sink under the water. I grabbed the handle and heaved, but I floated too much to have the strength to shift it.

I had a better idea. "Throw me a rope."

Reida went off looking for one. There were always plenty of ropes where there were boats, so he came back a bit later with a rope, one end of which he tossed to me. I waded back to the box.

I dipped underwater to pass the rope through the handle—

And something grabbed hold of my arm, a strong, snake-like thing, lashing around my wrist. I yelled underwater, letting out a burst of bubbles. Broke the surface.

"Reida! Deyu! Help me!"

I got water in my mouth. Coughed.

Someone jumped into the water.

Then I was pulled into the darkness again. I tried to grab the thing that was holding me. It felt like a snake of firm leather, wrapped around my wrist. I yanked. Slipped my hand out.

I broke the surface again, gasping. But now the thing had lashed around my foot and was pulling me into the middle of the channel. I kicked to get it off, threshing in the water.

Reida was next to me. He plunged his hand in the water, found the snake-like strap and pulled. My leg went up. He brought up a dark, black strap, and slashed at it with his knife. The material was tough, like rubber. But now I was being pulled closer to whatever was attached to that strap. It was big and it was bristly. It made a sucking noise and it moved. Sharp bristles grated across my shin. Ow, that hurt.

"Hurry up!"

Reida had finally sawed through the black strap, and pulled me along with him to the side, where he and Deyu heaved me out of the water. My left leg was bleeding with hundreds of little gashes that the horribly bristly thing had made. It was still down there, rumbling and sucking.

"Whatever the hell was that?" I called out. I was shivering all over.

"It's a bottom cleaner," Reida said. "They crawl over the bottom to clean the canals."

Shit. A machine? "With those black tentacles?"

"They are to gather rubbish to its mouth."

"And then what does it do?" This was the first time I'd heard of such a thing.

"It munches everything to shreds."

Great. I guess that was Clovis' purpose of dropping the box there. I felt ill and cold, and defeated. "Let's go home."

They helped me find my clothes and gun. I wrestled my arms into the shirt, left it hanging open, tied the gun bracket and jammed my feet into my trousers. My skin was still wet and the fabric stuck to it. My leg was bleeding and covered in leaves. Eirani would have something to say about having to clean my pretty uniform.

But as I was doing up the fastening on my shirt, Deyu let go of me and clicked her gun out of the bracket. The next moment, a beam shot across the shed, coming from outside, missing Reida by a hair's width.

He swore.

Deyu pulled me to the side near the office where we stood against the window.

Who was that? Reida asked through the feeder. Deyu held her gun raised. The feeder showed her to be more frightened than I was.

This had to be a guard employed by Clovis. And I did not want to get caught here. Clovis would expect me to support him, not snoop about in his business at night, interesting though my findings were.

"How about we try to get out the back way?" Reida said.

I looked over my shoulder to where pale moonlight from one of Ceren's tiny moons glittered on the water. Some larger boats lay moored out there, but nothing moved.

"There is a fence," I said.

"That has never stopped us before."

"True."

"Can you run?" he asked.

"I'll have to, won't I?"

"How well?"

"I won't know until I try. I think I'll be all right."

"Let's go then."

With one last look to the entrance of the yard, Reida set off across the shed's floor, sticking close to the walls.

Damn it, I had my fancy gun, but no armour. Thayu would kill me if she found out.

We left the shed, and zigzagged in between the boats in dry dock and stacks of transport crates and other things I didn't recognise in the dark.

Someone shouted behind us in keihu. Reida stopped and changed the setting on the gun to broad.

"No, don't shoot," Deyu said. "We want them to think we're unarmed vagrants so that we can take them by surprise when they're closer."

Good point.

"It means that you'll have to do something about the fence without a gun," I said.

"That's not a problem."

An amplified male voice shouted behind us, "Trespassers! Come out with your hands raised. Put down any weapons. Don't try to run or we'll shoot to kill." He spoke keihu, but with a strong accent that I couldn't place.

"Better hurry up," Deyu said.

She ran to the fence at full speed, jumped and kicked the top bar. It bent but didn't give. Deyu went sprawling.

She pushed herself up. "Damn it. That's stronger than it looks."

Reida said, "No, it isn't. You need to apply the right force at the right place."

He grabbed one of the metal fence posts and pulled it inward. It bent to about waist height. He climbed on top and jumped a few times. The post broke with a snap and the fence sagged further. "There."

Deyu scrambled on top of the wobbly mesh and pulled me up as well.

Reida had already jumped off on the other side. He was scanning the ferry yard through the infrared camera on the sight of his gun. "Quick, get out of here! They're just crossing the shed now."

We ran.

The land outside the yard was uneven, with surprisingly solid grassy tussocks that weren't always easy to see or avoid. Several times, my foot sank away into a hole dug by some sort of animal.

Someone fired over our heads.

I dropped face down into the grass. Deyu was close behind me and Reida was somewhere in front although it was too dark to see him.

There are four, Deyu said. She was looking through the sight of her gun, too, and on the screen over her shoulder, I could see them, too: four men now at the place where we had bent the fence.

Come over here! Reida said. He was closer to the water. I picked up from the feeder that he wanted to get away in a boat. I still couldn't see him, but started crawling through the grass. Those holes were really very annoying—

The ground gave way under one of my hands.

And something came out of the hole, growling and hissing. It closed a pair of horn-rimmed jaws on the sleeve of my shirt and a fold of my skin.

I couldn't help yelling out, "Hey!"

I pulled my arm up, dislodging the creature from the ground. It was one of those lizard-looking things that also lived closer to the ocean, about as long as my arm, not counting the tail.

I grabbed hold of its body and pulled. Its feet scratched my hand.

Ow, ow, stupid bloody thing.

I yanked. The animal lost its grip on my sleeve with a ripping sound. I threw the thing as far as I could throw it. It flew through the air and landed in the grass, letting out an undignified squeal.

Not a moment later, a white crackling beam—the narrow, deadly setting—flew from the gun of one of our pursuers to the place where the lizard had fallen.

Grass tussocks and dirt vaporised in a cloud of debris. The distinctive smell of ozone drifted on the air.

We kept our heads low in the grass, barely daring to breathe.

I strangely hoped that the lizard was all right.

They're Tamerians, Deyu said.

Artificial semi-human fighting machines, that some argued had been made to be better fighters than the Coldi. For one, they had excellent night vision, which was a known problem with Coldi people.

Shit, shit shit. I had toyed with the notion of identifying myself and talking my way out, even if it would lead to all sorts of trouble, but you couldn't argue with a Tamerian. They didn't speak much and listened even less.

Why the hell had Clovis hired Tamerians to guard his ships?

But I knew. Because someone untied his boats when there was a storm and they washed over the lock and he had to go and retrieve them at great expense. He was merely protecting his business. In the same situation, I might have done the same thing.

But they were Tamerians, and they were coming closer through the grass, where it was dark, and where they could see vastly better than any of us. Not long and they would discover us, and then we'd all be shot.

We should make a run for it, I said.

That would be stupid, Deyu said. *Sit still and grab your gun. Wait until they come closer.*

I clicked the gun from its bracket and set it to the most narrow-beam and deadly setting.

Behind me, I sensed Reida doing the same.

I acted while feeling as if this wasn't really happening and it wasn't really me.

The sight on the gun had a little infrared-light window. It clearly showed the four figures walking through the grass.

Closer, and closer, and closer. They *had* to know where we were.

Maybe they thought we were Pengali louts. Maybe they'd been given the order to try and catch intruders alive.

Now, Deyu said. *On the count of three, pick one, and shoot him. That leaves one Tamerian. We should be able to take care of him, too. One . . .*

I raised the gun.

Two . . .

I'll take the on one the left.

Deyu would take one of the two in the middle who visibly carried a gun, and Reida would take the one on the right.

Three.

I pressed the release. Three white beams crackled through the air. Two men went down. I couldn't see who missed. It was probably me.

The other two returned fire, hitting the ground so close to us that the debris hit me in the face.

I aimed—

Don't shoot, don't shoot! Deyu clamped a hand on my arm. *It's how they tell where we are.*

There were a hundred other ways to tell where we were.

The men were now running through the grass in our direction.

Reida commando-crawled a short distance away and fired again. Missed. One of the men stopped and fired at him. There was a sound like a cry.

Damn. Did that mean Reida was hit?

Look, there! Deyu said.

I looked. Three more Tamerians had come through the breach in the fence.

There was nothing for it. I had to try the only way I knew to get out of here: by talking.

I was about to get up when a big whooshing noise made the air vibrate. A vehicle rose over the roof of the boat yard shed. Deyu aimed at its pilot's window—

But I recognised that plane—one of the solar gliders that belonged at the *gamra* island.

"No! Don't shoot," I yelled. "It's our guys."

The plane landed in the grass between us and the Tamerians. Someone yelled from inside the darkness of the cargo hold, "Get the fuck inside!"

Sheydu.

Deyu jumped up. I jumped up. Oh, shit, my leg.

A spotlight went on, lighting the tussocks and uneven ground. Also, Reida running towards the plane. His side was covered in blood, but that didn't slow him down. He reached the door before either of us did. Sheydu hauled him inside.

Deyu reached the door as well, scrambled in and then held a hand out to me. I went sprawling over the dusty floor.

Someone in battle gear sat at the other door firing a heavy-duty gun on a mount. It was hard to see out that way. The engines were blasting dust and grass everywhere.

"All ready?" yelled the pilot.

It was Thayu, of course.

"Everyone's in," Sheydu replied. She heaved the door shut.

With a jolt, the plane took off again, while the marksman kept firing at the ground until we were out of range. Then he took his helmet and goggles off.

It was Veyada.

Phew.

For a moment, no one said anything. We were all too shocked.

Thayu gestured for me to come and sit next to her.

I scrambled to my feet. Whoa, the floor pitched under me much more than it should. My trouser leg was soaked with blood. I used the back of the seat to hold me upright.

When I had sat down, Thayu pushed her earpiece off. She gave me a blazing look. "What did you think you were doing?"

She only used that voice when she was extremely angry.

10

———————

I T WAS NEVER EASY to face Thayu when she was angry. Because I loved her, and also because she usually had a very good reason to be angry. And because I usually knew what the reason was.

I didn't dare look her in the eyes. "I'm sorry."

"Sorry doesn't even begin to cover it. Has anyone ever told you that despite your stupid acts, you are exceptionally lucky? We just happened to be making a reconnaissance flight based on the readouts from the Exchange."

"With weapons like that?" I cast a glance back into the cargo hold, where Veyada had taken the gun off its mount.

"*We* are prepared. *We* don't go into town barely armed, not wearing armour, and with only two junior staff."

Reida's voice came from behind. "That's not necessary! It's not that bad."

"Yes, it is, young man," Sheydu said.

"But that stuff stings—ow! Hey! Ow, ow."

I chuckled, but Thayu gave me a hard, serious look. "You brought them into danger unnecessarily. Tell me why you couldn't have let us know what you were doing and we would have helped you get in and out safely."

"You don't like this project."

"No, I don't. So I think it's even less worth getting killed for."

"But I can't just leave a fellow human marooned on an island or deserted beach in the territory of a hostile tribe."

"Let them rescue him. It's not your job, and if the *president* wants this man retrieved, why doesn't she employ people to do so, as well as pay for it?"

We were back to the same argument made by Sheydu. And yes, they were probably right in a hard-nosed Coldi way, but that was still not how people on Earth operated.

I said nothing for a while. We had been extremely lucky to only come out with minor injuries, although I would have to get someone to look at my leg. It itched and stung and to be honest I didn't feel too well.

"So, what were you actually doing here?" I asked. My mouth felt funny.

"I analysed the vehicle movement data from the Exchange and found a couple of interesting trails I wanted to look at."

"Interesting, how?"

"Businesses with boats that regularly go out to the ocean. We got coordinates and went out to take aerial scans."

"Find anything?"

"I'll show you when we get home. Oh. And we found the guy."

"Serious? You found him?"

"Yeah, he's got a camp on a little island just around the corner from the Thousand Islands tribe settlement. I'll show you that when we get home, too."

"For all that you don't want me to do this, you take a lot of interest in the project."

"You want this man recovered. So we do it, despite trying to change your mind."

I spread my hands, was going to say something, but I didn't. This was, ultimately, how associations worked. One person was at the top. What this person said went.

I blew out a breath. Anger rolled off her in waves, so I thought it wise to keep my mouth shut until she cooled down a bit and I found out what upset her so much.

To be honest I didn't really feel myself either. I was sore, hungry, shivery and smelly.

Eirani was going to have my hide for ruining my uniform.

But the fact that Thayu found Robert was a good thing, right? And the fact that he seemed to be alive. I should let his wife know.

Thayu landed the plane on the island's small airport, which was mainly used for service flights. There were no passenger services or comforts.

As soon as we'd touched down, Sheydu and Veyada got up and collected their gear. Veyada had packed the fearsome gun away into its case, which he slung over his shoulder. He carried the helmet and goggles in his other hand.

I rose from my seat—and the world turned black around me for a brief moment. I was holding the back of the seat, so I didn't fall, and I didn't think anyone noticed, but I should really get my leg looked at. It felt heavy and numb.

I managed to stumble to the door and down the steps, but it was a good walk across the tarmac and another good walk to my apartment. It had to be the sitting still during the flight. Maybe it would get better if I walked.

In contrast to almost everyone else, I had nothing to carry. The others were all talking, but I didn't hear anything of what anyone said. I just concentrated on putting one foot in front of the other—

—And my knee gave way. It felt like it turned to jelly. The next moment, I was on the ground and people were yelling around me.

———

When I next opened my eyes, I lay on my back in a bed in a strange, low-ceilinged cubicle. There was a wall to my right, painted creamy yellow, then a walkway through the middle of the cubicle and another bed to my left, empty.

The air was humid and laced with a strong scent of megon oil.

A window at my feet looked out over the roofs of the city. It was morning and sunlight streamed into the little cell. The door had to be behind my head. Above my bed was a shelf that contained blinking equipment, and a stand stood next to me with several "arms", each of which contained a bottle with some sort of fluid and a thin hose leading to two arm bands around my left arm.

What the hell? I was in the hospital. What sort of contraption was this? Why was I in this cell?

I tried to push myself up, but my muscles didn't have the strength. My leg ached. A vague memory came to me about blood running down my shin. Someone seemed to have wrapped it in a tight sock-like bandage.

Boy, I was really short of breath. I let myself fall back on the pillow.

"Oh, he's awake," someone in the room said.

I arched my neck on the pillow to look behind me, but as far as I could see, there was no one in the little cell with me.

I noticed the mirror at the foot end of the bed reflecting the door at the same time that the door opened with a hiss. It looked like there was some kind of air lock on the other side. Nicha came in. He wore a light purple gown of a thin, rubbery material that covered all of his arms and hung down to his knees, and a purple cap that covered his hair.

"Nich'?"

He walked to the bed and gave me a hug while trying to avoid all the tubes attached to my arm.

He sat on the edge of the other bed. Deyu came in after him, also wearing a purple gown and head covering. They looked like a pair of laboratory workers.

"You gave us a real fright," Nicha said.

"What happened? Why am I here? Why are you wearing that funny get-up?"

He pulled the gown. "This? Non-friction material. This is the high-oxygen chamber."

That explained the cubicle and the air lock, and the smell of megon oil, which was a strong fire retardant.

"But . . . how did I get here? The last I remember is getting out of the plane."

"You collapsed," Nicha said. "It was so scary. One moment you were walking home, and the next, you were on the ground with your eyes rolling back into your head."

"Ew."

"That's not the worst thing. Look at this." Deyu pulled out her reader and held it up so that I could see the screen. On it was a picture of some pale surface flecked with blood . . . I couldn't even begin to describe what that horrible thing was. Flesh-coloured and raw, encrusted with a multitude of black-brown bulges.

"Is that my leg?" What were all those brown, barnacle-like things attached to it?

I glanced down at my leg again and the sock that covered it.

I was beginning to get a horrible feeling about this. I'd sometimes heard people talking about the leech-like parasites that lived in the water.

"Yup, that's your leg," she said. "You fainted, and your trousers were wet with blood. When we looked at your leg, we saw this. We brought you straight here."

Holy crap and ew.

"These suckers really liked your blood. They told us there were more than a hundred of these critters on you."

Ew, ew.

"Dey', I don't think he likes hearing about this."

"Well, it's true." She put the reader back in her pocket.

"So . . ." My gaze followed the tube from my arm to the stand next to the bed with all the bottles, most of them with clear fluid.

"Temporary solution," Nicha said. "Fortunately, the medicos knew that your blood is incompatible with their universal serum so they didn't kill you, but you have to stay in here and you'll probably feel pretty lousy until you can hunt down a compatible donor, or wait until your body regrows its own. They put out a call for donors, but the only one who has responded so far—Melissa—is not compatible."

"I guess that's what you get when you piss everyone off. How long is this going to take?"

"They said at least seven weeks."

"Seven weeks!" A week in Barresh was five days, but still . . . "I don't have that much time."

"You have no choice. It takes as long as it takes."

Great. I was feeling mortally tired already. "Can I at least go home?"

"When the medico is satisfied with the condition of your leg. It's infected."

"Where is Thayu?"

"Asleep in the next room. She's been sitting with you all night."

Damn, now I felt even more terrible. Why did I keep doing these stupid things that upset the people I cared about most?

"I need to . . . there is so much to do."

"You have a good rest and look after getting back to health. We'll worry about the rest."

"But . . . the elections, and the security breach and . . ."

"Don't worry. We'll look after everything."

I made Nicha go through all the things he needed to look at. I was fading fast. I knew I was forgetting something, but couldn't remember what it was before he and Deyu left.

I slept a bit.

A nurse came with some breakfast, but eating made me so tired that I finished only half of it.

Thayu had woken up by this time, and did her best to feed me as much as possible. "You have to drink lots as well."

But just looking at that huge jug of water made me feel ill.

A medico came, and she undid the bandages. The smell that came from them almost made me throw up, and she confirmed my fear that I wasn't going home just yet. "The water in the channels is very nasty," she said. "There are many diseases. Your ability to fight them has been reduced because of blood loss. You really need a quick supply of clean blood. We've had a second person come in for testing. He was also incompatible."

"Who was it?"

"The academic, Benton Leck."

"I can go and ask the others," Thayu said. She'd been sitting on the spare bed, looking at this bandage-changing procedure with a slightly disgusted expression on her face.

"That would be your best bet," the medico said.

"What if we find no one?" My blood group was B negative and there was a real chance that no one who wanted to help was compatible, and the hospital wouldn't have the targeted immune suppressants that hospitals on Earth had.

"Then it will be a long recovery."

"Can we have a supply brought in?" Thayu said. "I'd be willing to go and get it."

"That's not necessary, Thay'—"

"Yes, it is. She says so. You could *die* if you don't get this."

"We can have it shipped. I can ask Melissa—"

The medico shook her head. "Unfortunately, the Exchange process doesn't allow for cooled products to be transferred without spoiling. It keeps everything at body temperature. By the time your blood is here, it will have spoilt."

"But what about artificial blood?"

"It still has a biological component."

I thought there was blood that could be stored out of the fridge but I couldn't remember the details. My brain was too foggy.

"My choices are to find a donor or face a long recovery with potential added illness?"

She nodded.

I attempted to push myself up, but couldn't even manage that. Then all of a sudden I remembered what I'd forgotten earlier. "What about Robert? We have to get him."

"Let someone else worry about that," Thayu said. "I'll ask Melissa."

Damn, no. "We can't ask Melissa. She has nowhere near our resources. I don't even think she's got a regular guard." She'd use guards from the *gamra* pool, if she needed guards, but could only do that if she was doing work for *gamra*.

"Please, Thayu, can you look after her? Make sure she doesn't get killed if she decides she wants to go out there?"

"I will try," she said. "But you know what Melissa thinks of me. I can only give her the information we have. Whatever she decides to do is her decision."

———

Thayu left after the medico was gone, and I stared at the ceiling, and slept and stared at the ceiling some more. I was so incredibly tired, and my leg hurt. That couldn't be good.

A nurse came to check me, and I asked her if she could put my reader on the bed. In the mirror, I could see it on the table next to the door, but there was no way I could reach it. I attempted to read some work stuff, but I could barely hold the thing up. Also, these annoying flashes kept going over the screen. I'd stared at them for a while before my foggy brain registered that this meant there was an urgent message for me.

Damn it.

I had to blink hard against the wish of my eyes to fall shut, but managed to open my inbox. Red flashing at the top was a message from Margarethe Ollund.

I opened it up and stared at the screen. The message was only two paragraphs, but it seemed like an insurmountable wall of text to me. Certain words penetrated the fog. *Consequences, press, assembly.*

It was important. I had to read it, but I just couldn't get past the first few words.

Then, to top it off, the reader beeped. I managed to find the right button and then almost dropped the thing.

"Yes?"

A male voice said, "It's Yetaris Damaru here. You just opened a message with an urgency alert. I have a communication waiting for you. Let me put you through."

"But . . ."

Oh man, I couldn't think straight, let alone discuss something of extreme urgency.

But he was already making the connection, and not much later a female voice came out of the loudspeaker.

"Cory?"

Damn it, that was Margarethe Ollund, and I was still trying to decipher her message.

"I'm sorry I haven't—"

"You've received my message," she said.

"I have, but . . ."

"We really have to act now, because—"

"Listen. I got the message. I haven't read it. I'm in the hospital and I'm not well." I was fucking struggling. "Just tell me what's going on, and I'll find someone else to deal with it."

There was a short silence.

"I'm sorry to hear that." Some of the urgency went out of her voice, and was replaced with something else that I couldn't place: a kind of cool annoyance. "What happened?"

"I did something stupid. Too long to explain." And entirely too revolting. "I'll be out of action for a few weeks. Tell me, what is this about? What do you want me to do?"

"Robert Davidson. I take it you've heard of him by now."

"Yes. We know where he is."

"Good. Get him out of there and bring him home. A lot of people here are very upset about his disappearance. It's all over the news. I don't know how this happened and why he was able to leave, but it's a big scandal here."

"As I said, we know where he is." Thayu hadn't specifically *said* that he was alive, but I assumed so. "I'll make sure he gets retrieved." I knew I was forgetting something.

"Good. Please do this as soon as possible. Preferably not in a body bag. Body bags are untidy and cause me all kinds of problems."

"I'll do my best."

She broke the connection and I was left puzzled. She hadn't even greeted me or asked how I was or wished me a speedy recovery. That seemed really out of character for her.

But I was simply too tired to think about it further.

I closed my eyes and when I next opened them, it was dark outside. There was a light on in the room, and someone was rummaging through my clothes which were on a chair next to the door.

"Excuse me."

The person turned around. It was Thayu. Wow, I was really out of it not to have recognised her.

She sat at the edge of the bed. "How are you feeling?"

"Tired. There is some problem on Earth. Margarethe asked me to return Robert as soon as possible. She didn't say why there was such urgency." She also hadn't said anything about a budget.

Damn it, that's what I should have asked, if I hadn't been so tired. I could barely recall what the president had said.

"I went to see those people," Thayu said.

"Which people?" What the hell was she even talking about?

"All the ones from your world who live in Barresh."

Oh, I saw. This was about the blood transfusion. "And?"

"They're . . . funny."

"Not in a good way, I gather."

"Yes, well . . ." She folded her hands. "That fellow in the main square with his eating house almost chased me out of his shop. The tall old fellow who works at the History Centre has been in, but his blood is not compatible. He also said, and it really makes a lot of sense, that he stores a supply of his own. Why haven't you done this?"

"I . . . I don't know." I guess I should have, and at some point someone might even have mentioned it to me, but I'd never done anything about it, and in hindsight that was fairly stupid.

"As usual, you think you're invincible."

"I'm sorry."

"From now on, I will see to it that you do it. He also said that if you find no one else, you can use some of his supply, if you can find a way to make it useful to you . . . I'm sorry, that's not what he said, but I am not familiar with the things he did say. He said it was hard." She spread her hands. "I don't know. I'm not a medico."

"What about the others?"

"The old guy and his wife didn't open the door. They were at home, but I guess they don't want to help."

"He is the one who owns the ferries whose yard we blew up last night." Was it last night? I had no idea.

"Right. I guess I can see why he's not interested in offering help." She thought for a while. Then she said, "The most interesting reaction came from that guy who owns the warehouse."

"Jasper Carlson. You mean, he actually spoke to you?"

"He did. His Coldi is almost as good as yours."

"Not quite?"

"I said: almost. He and his partner run a courier business exclusive to the Trader Guild. They're preferred suppliers." That was a much-coveted label amongst merchants. Preferred suppliers to the Trader Guild usually made a lot of money. Again, I cursed myself for being so preoccupied with *gamra* things that I never checked out the people from Earth in Barresh.

Thayu continued, "He told me some very interesting things. I'm still hunting some of them up, but he will probably come to see you as soon as you return home."

"Well," I said, wiping my face. "That is quite a big change in behaviour for someone who couldn't be bothered to come to the door when I went to see him."

"It's all about the pretty girl with the pretty smile." Thayu grinned.

She could joke, but I knew the signs. One: he kept quiet and never volunteered information. Two: he spoke to Thayu, not to me. Three: he offered help only when Margarethe had gotten upset.

I would hazard a guess that he worked in intelligence, possibly for Nations of Earth. Possibly, too, he was reporting back on me and the other people from Earth on the orders of men in grey suits at the top of the various departments, men like the despicable Simon Dekker who I'd dealt with briefly and who had fortunately been sacked. Men who collated huge files on people of interest that were still stored on paper, and digital versions destroyed unless they were safe and verified. I knew this data-gathering on top employees was common practice, but the thought made me uncomfortable. I didn't work for Nations of Earth anymore but, obviously, that hadn't stopped me being a person of interest.

I wasn't sure what to feel about that, although in my current state, "nothing" would be correct. I felt confused, alarmed that he wanted to see me. "If Jasper Carlson wants to visit me, tell him I won't be going home for a while yet."

"I have some different news about that, too," she said. "I ran into Lilona in the foyer, and she asked why we hadn't been back."

Oh, crap, did I have to deal with all of this at once? "Did you tell her that we'd come after the election?"

"I did. We need to make an appointment." Her eyes were intense. Yes, I would do it, but I still didn't know what to think about having my entire genes changed, and I was in no state to discuss that, either.

Thayu continued, "Anyway, we got talking about why you're in here. She said there is a kind of plasma she can give you that is a—what did she call it again?—primer, that's it, for the gene treatment. It doesn't actually change anything inside you, but makes you more receptive to all types of medicine, including hers. She had names for all this but seriously, don't ask me about them. I don't know how any of it works. But she said she'd contact the medico to see if she can give you this stuff."

"That would help me?"

"She thought it might, but she needs to investigate first."

"When would we know this?"

"As soon as possible."

I nodded. I was bored. I wanted to go home. I didn't want to stay in this claustrophobic cubicle for seven weeks. Hell, the election would be on by then.

"Anyway, about what Margarethe told me: We need to get Robert."

"I spoke to Melissa about that. She agreed to go out. Apparently she also got a message from Margarethe. She's leaving this afternoon."

Shit. "I hope she taking a good team, because otherwise, we'll have to go and rescue her as well."

"That won't be necessary, and you're going nowhere for quite a while. Melissa took a few people with her, including a Pengali guide. They will be fine."

"I hope the guide was from the right tribe."

"I have no idea."

Oh, damn it. I was guessing probably not. Probably Melissa had taken one of those Pengali people who advertised themselves as guides, but who only took visitors to historical sites near the escarpment, an area they were familiar with in the hands of their own tribe. I felt cold inside.

The door hissed open and Veyada came in, carrying a basket. He set this on the table and unpacked a variety of containers. Lunch. "What would you like? Nut bread, fruit?"

It was customary in the hospital, I had learned, that the family provided food, unless the patient required a special diet.

Eirani's bread smelled wonderful, and I asked for a piece.

Veyada smiled. "You must be getting a bit better. You're very chatty."

"I just had my ear bitten off by Margarethe." I told him about the brief conversation I'd had with her, and he was equally puzzled about the urgency.

Thayu spread her hands. "I understand they'd want him back, but since the fact that he got lost out there was his own fault, and he's in a dangerous place, I don't understand why they don't accept that getting him back is not so easy."

"The longer we wait, the less likely he will be to survive, especially since he's on an island that has no fresh water."

"Yes, but she doesn't know that."

No. She only spoke of the fallout and Robert's wife. I wondered if this wife was perhaps an employee of Nations of Earth, but even if that was the case, Margarethe wouldn't have told me through the Exchange link, where everyone could listen in.

11

———————

L ILONA SHRAKAR came to my room not long after Veyada and Thayu had left. I hadn't seen her for a while.

She looked a lot healthier than she had when I had first seen her. Her hair, then, had been dull and grey; and her skin, lifeless and pale. Now her skin had acquired a healthy glow and her hair was darker. She still had some grey hair, but it possessed a lustre it previously lacked. I could see that even from the wisps that protruded from underneath the purple cap.

Wow. That showed how stressed the crew of the Aghyrian ship were, and how much they needed to find a place to settle and replenish their resources.

She carried a clear container with medical equipment, syringes, boxes, tweezers and other metal implements, which she set on the bed. Then she took the reader that held my medical data from the shelf. She read, nodding.

"Interesting medical file," she said. "The list of diseases found in your system is quite impressive. How did you collect all these?"

"I went for a swim in the channel and got set upon by a bottom-munching machine. And then I got besieged by blood suckers."

She pulled a face. I remembered the time we walked through the drainage pipes and she got upset about getting dirty, after having lived in the clean ship all her life. We hadn't even encountered nasty creatures back then.

"They tell me it's going to take a long time to recover unless I get a blood donation from someone. We can't find a suitable donor. I don't *have* a long time."

She nodded. "That's what the files tell me. They tell me that you're impatient as well. It says 'At risk of abandoning treatment without authorisation.' "

"It doesn't!"

"It does say so." She showed me the screen. She was right.

Well . . . I spread my hands. The assessment was not wrong, but who the hell had time to be sick anyway? "Thayu tells me you might have a solution."

"I don't know. Seeing this long list of infections on your file, I'm not sure. My potential solution comes with disadvantages."

"Doesn't it always?"

Her face remained very serious. These were clearly not disadvantages to be taken lightly.

"All right, what's the option?"

"I was wondering if it would be possible to give you the primer that lets your immune system cope with the extra genetic material I would be adding when you receive the Coldi genes, should it be your wish to go ahead with that."

Her eyes were intense.

I was in no state to make that decision now, but I also knew that given the choice, I would make it anyway.

Lilona went on, "But I would have to give you drugs to suppress your immune system to begin with, and you've got almost every infection known in Barresh, so I can't, or you'll die. The primer would take about two weeks to work, during which time you'd be kept in a coma —but first, the infections need to be cleared up."

"That doesn't sound like it saves a lot of time either." That was the understatement of the century. Changing my genes was not about time.

"I agree. This is not something you'd do to get out of here quickly. It would be something you might do to save your life. I also didn't get the feeling that you were totally committed to it yet. If I give you the primer, it would set changes in motion that are . . . not entirely irreversible, but hard to undo."

I nodded and sighed.

Seven weeks in this tin can, it was.

———

I fell asleep before dinner and slept for a long time, until Nicha came with breakfast, and Veyada brought some stuff from the office. Then I had to tell Thayu that Lilona's option would be too risky in my state. I couldn't tell if she was disappointed or not.

"I want to get out of here," I told her. "This place drives me nuts."

"The medico tells me that first you'll need to be well enough to spend time on a normal ward, outside this room."

I sighed. "Has anyone else come forward?"

"No one compatible."

"Didn't they tell you that some stored their own blood? Is there a way we could check? They might have a universal blood product. Even if it is illegal to import it."

"I can go and see what I can find out."

I sighed again, and she sighed, too, and put her warm-skinned hand on mine. "It was really very stupid of you to go into that channel."

"Yes, but he threw something in the water. He came back from his house in the dark especially to do that. Wouldn't you have tried to fish it out?"

"Oh, I would, but only after I'd established a safe perimeter. It was stupid of you not to check. It was stupid not to wear armour."

And so the conversation went around and around in circles.

Then I asked her, "Has anyone heard from Melissa?"

"No. But she's out of range of just about every piece of communication equipment, so that doesn't surprise me."

She didn't sound worried, but I was. I shouldn't have let her go.

"By the way, Evi and Telaris are on their way home."

"Already?"

"They heard what happened and decided to come straight back."

"That's not necessary."

"Yes, it is," Thayu said. "Their main job is here, especially when there's trouble."

"But they're allowed some time off, and I'm not going anywhere."

"If they didn't have this job, they would have no time off, they wouldn't even be alive."

There seemed no arguing it, and to be honest, I was glad. Any extra hands were welcome.

Thayu stayed with me for the morning, wearing the funny purple anti-friction gown. She made sure I ate my breakfast and drank enough water. She helped me turn around and helped me with various bodily functions. She even stayed in the room when the nurse came to rebandage my leg, and didn't pull a face when the bandage came off.

I asked, "Does it look a bit better?"

The nurse went, "Hmmm."

I guessed at least it meant it didn't look worse.

I hoped.

After she was gone, I slept some more.

Thayu was sitting on the other bed, doing some work, when the power went off. The lights went off and the machines started beeping. A moment later even that stopped.

Without the humming and clicking and hissing air, it was very quiet in the cabin.

"What's going on?"

Thayu got up and opened the door.

Someone came in, wearing a purple gown.

He was a thin man with a narrow face and intense dark eyes. He wore his black hair in a ponytail at the back of his head. His chin had a distinct five-o'clock shadow.

Jasper Carlson.

He sat down on the other bed, silhouetted by the light that came in from the window. Thayu had gone outside, presumably to deal with hospital people coming to investigate the source of the power outage and the lack of alarms. I really hoped Thayu hadn't turned off anything that kept me alive along with the equipment that recorded voice and visuals in the little cabin.

Jasper folded his hands. "I would have preferred to come to a place where the walls don't have ears, but I'm told you need to spend some time in here." His voice was quite dark.

"Seven weeks." I was beginning to feel tired again. This was not a social visit, and I really didn't feel like discussing any kind of sensitive information or politics.

"Unless you find a donor."

I sighed and nodded.

"You're not going to find one in the places you're looking. You're B negative and you can accept donations from people with the same blood group or O negative. There are none of those in Barresh."

I wanted to ask, *How do you know that?* but didn't have the energy.

"Some of us store our own, but those who are smart have a supply of artificial blood."

"But you can't—"

"You can't take that through the Exchange? I know, that's the bullshit they sell you when you ask about it. The problem is not with the processes of the Exchange. It's with their bureaucracy. Artificial blood falls under medicines, and as such, it needs to be dealt with by the Trader Guild, who need a Quarantine Approval number to be able to complete the formalities. Of course it doesn't have that number, and no one is interested in completing all the formalities, so it can't be imported legally. But there are lots of things that make their way in and out of Barresh illegally."

That seemed a remark designed to make me curious. I was supposed to ask something but couldn't remember what. I wished he'd get on with it. I was fading fast, and why was it so cold in here all of a sudden?

"I'm going to tell you a secret." He inserted his hand in his pocket and held it out to me. On the palm of his hand lay a glittering stone about as wide as my thumb, clear but with a bright turquoise hue.

"This is what it's all about," he said.

I frowned. I had seen this before, but where? My head was swimming.

"It's a blue diamond," he said, probably expecting a reaction that I wasn't giving him. I don't know that he appreciated just how unwell I was. "They have become quite the thing to have on Earth. Someone waged a very clever advertising campaign. Blue diamond rings are *the* thing to have when you're getting married. A lot of people are paying a lot of money for these babies."

"Don't they . . . make artificial diamonds in all kinds of colours?"

"Yes, but if you really love a girl, you can't give her a fake stone, right?"

True.

"All the stones are sold by one single company, Fleming Diamonds. They've spent a fortune in advertising. It was very smartly done. They're the sole suppliers of these diamonds, so they can ask whatever they want. And they're getting the stones here, where they are quite common. Illegally, of course."

Ow. This made my head hurt. "Who are 'they'? Do we know who is involved?"

"Pretty much everyone, but especially Clovis."

". . . Everyone?"

"Clovis Keneally, Juanita, Huang Le and his wife. I'm not too sure about Benton Leck, but he certainly never tried to *stop* them, either."

"Wait. These people are smuggling diamonds?"

"Taking them in their luggage and bringing them to Earth."

"But they don't travel. I've checked."

"Oh, no, they pay people to deliver the stock on their behalf. And they are cleverly disguised as travellers. Not that a little handful of stones would be easy to detect, especially since they have no value here and no one cares."

"Does Robert Davidson have anything to do with this?" My teeth chattered. I was getting really cold. I was tempted to ask him a *get to the point or get out* question.

"Clovis has run a few of these adventure surfing tours for rich men. He uses them to carry packages."

"Wait, there could be more people involved than just Robert?"

"I don't know about this trip. It might have been just him. Clovis has done it a number of times before, and those tours were with small groups. On one, I remember, he had three people, another time he had four."

Damn. I felt sick. "But wait, Clovis is here. Why is Robert out there?"

"I don't know what happened, but I can make some guesses. At some point Clovis might have found out what industry Robert works in and put the two together: that Robert wanted to start his own diamond-importing business. Robert is well-positioned to do this. Execo owns most southern African diamond mines. He would be in an excellent position to do so, in fact."

"But *is* he actually thinking of doing this?"

Jasper spread his hands. "He may, he may not. Probably not,

because the money involved would be small fry for him. But men like Clovis have small minds. They probably had a fight and Clovis might have thought it safe to abandon him out there, knowing that he would be unlikely to survive. He would not be terribly keen on knowing that Robert is still alive."

Oh shit. And I'd gone around advertising the fact that I'd found the note in the bottle. And . . . "I sent Melissa out there to get him."

"Melissa Heyworth," Jasper said, his voice flat.

"I don't know of any other Melissas."

"Shit." He stared at me.

My heart jumped. It probably wasn't a good idea to get agitated in my state, and I paid for it by feeling terrible. "Any trouble in particular?"

"Well," he said, fingering his upper lip. "She's a woman, alone."

"She hasn't gone alone."

"Then I hope she's taken enough people. If Clovis has really left Robert out there to die, he's not going to want anyone finding out what he did. It won't be pretty if something happens to her, being the *gamra* delegate."

"No. Please can you make sure she comes back safely?"

"If they're in Thousand Islands tribe territory, it's out of my hands. I don't know anything about his business, or about boats. Clovis is the only one who has any contact with those people. All the Pengali he employs are from the Thousand Islands tribe."

Something clicked in my mind. "The ones with the giraffe patterns."

"Yes. That type of patterning is much more common with the Thousand Islands tribe. The skin spots get bigger the further from the equator you go."

"Is that why the other Pengali are sabotaging his boats?"

"Are they? As I said, I'm thoroughly unfamiliar with that business. He's a bit of an unsavoury character, as I've already told you. I know that when he goes out there, he buys the tribe's stones that young guys go out to collect for him. It's a bit dicey, because some Thousand Islands elders believe that they shouldn't be sold, because it's not a hugely common colour, but yeah, otherwise he's friendly enough with most of the tribe."

"Why is Margarethe Ollund so keen to have Robert back?"

"Is she?" He gave me a sharp look.

"She contacted me about this. She wants him brought back as soon as possible." I was gasping for air.

"She probably fears for his safety," Jasper said. "The debate about whether Nations of Earth should join *gamra* is flaring up again. She may be under pressure from people who don't want Earth to join and are using Robert's case as a reason. Barresh never ceases to supply the *gamra* opposition on Earth with material to make their case."

I was probably supposed to chuckle here, but I couldn't muster the strength.

"As for the president being keen to have him returned: Robert Davidson is a high-profile mining magnate. People make a lot of noise when he disappears. That's inevitable."

"Well, I've sent out a team. So all we need to do is wait until we hear from them."

"Understood."

He said nothing for a while.

"What is your function in Barresh, Mr Carlson? Are you a spy?"

He laughed. "No. I'm just a businessman."

"Do you know Robert Davidson in that capacity?"

"No, that would be too handy. I have never met Mr Davidson and I have no idea why he would be more important than for the reasons I just said. Because he's a rich man with powerful friends. When governments make decisions, those decisions are not always made for the reason the public thinks they are."

"I'm . . . well aware of that."

"Good." Another silence. "Because there may be some things that I could tell you that could be of interest to you."

"Does it have anything to do with this case?"

He laughed. "Always practical, aren't you?"

No, but I'm fucking dying in this airless tin can. "Please, if you've said all the things that you've come to tell me . . . turn everything back on. I can't do anything about any of this, and I need a clear head to think about it . . . I am really not very well."

"All right." He rose. "I'll go now, so your woman can turn everything back on, so you stay alive." He walked to the door. "Oh, before I forget. As a gesture of possible future collaboration, an assistant of mine is waiting outside. There is no need to beg these crooks for donations of their smuggled artificial blood. They won't give it to you anyway. My assistant is a perfect donor."

He opened the door and went out.

A moment later, the light came back on and the vent blew out a hiss of oxygen-laden air. For a while, I lay on my back just concentrating on breathing.

A businessman indeed. He sounded more like a skilled lobbyist. Given his status with the Trader Guild, that was probably a fair assessment of his capabilities.

The door opened again.

"Thay'?"

"He's gone. I turned everything back on. Sheydu would have something to say about the warning system in this place. No one even came to check the outage."

"That shows us . . . really how much they care . . . about us." I was still gasping.

"They care about things that get them into trouble."

"What about this assistant of his? Is he there?"

"He is." The expression on her face showed that she felt very ambivalent about it. "He's Tamerian."

I met her eyes and her expression was one of shock, but in a way it made perfect sense. One philosophy about creating an artificial race would be that they were as compatible with everyone else as possible to enhance their chance of survival.

Did that mean . . . I felt cold. Did that mean they could cross-breed with all other races, too, and that they would spread their silent, obedient, non-communicative stain across humanity?

Thayu said, "He's gone to the lab for testing. They expect to have the results later today."

She sighed. She didn't like it. I didn't like it much either, but there might not be another option. Even if none of the medicos had explicitly told me, I understood very well that my low blood count hampered my ability to fight the rampant infections, and that letting my body fight them on its own might well lead to a much longer recovery than normal, or worse.

Thayu sat on the edge of the bed.

I told her what Jasper had told me, and she nodded. It appeared to be a repeat of what he had said to her.

"Do you know who he works for?" I was starting to feel a little better. "Nations of Earth?"

"He reports to a small intelligence company in Athens. They probably work for Nations of Earth in some way, but I don't know that they work for any person in particular."

It was amazing all the things Thayu knew. Although to be honest, she probably had help from Amarru on this one. "Do you trust him?"

"You should never trust anyone who is not in your associations." And if I was Coldi, that would be all I needed to know.

No, I didn't trust him, either. He was too forthcoming with information, trying to impress me with his stealth ways, commanding that equipment be turned off as if his words were top secret.

But what was his game? No idea, besides trying to butter me up.

Later, when Thayu had left and I lay alone staring at the extremely boring ceiling in this extremely boring cubicle, I thought of some of the questions I should have asked him. About Margarethe Ollund, for example.

I wondered how much she was using Robert's case as a political vehicle from her own platform. I didn't see a need for her to become involved in this case, unless she wanted to use it to prove that yes, Earth should get on with *gamra* membership or this sort of thing was going to happen over and over. And that the current situation did not prevent criminals from doing what they wanted. It just made it harder to persecute them.

I had heard it all before. I'd been a political football once, and wasn't keen to repeat the experience, especially since I no longer had a horse in this race.

12

———————

NOT MUCH LATER, the door opened again and the medico came in. She shut it carefully and set a tray on the table next to the bed. On it stood a bottle with syrupy, dark red fluid.

"I have really good news. You won't believe this, but they've found a donor."

"I heard something about that. Who is he?"

"I don't know his name. He's Tamerian. We'd never tested one before at the lab, and they're perfect donors for just about anyone."

Perfect so as to be completely interchangeable with any other individual. One could keep a bunch of Tamerians purely for backup organs. The thought made me ill.

She took one of my drips off, undid a connector and clipped on another.

"He hasn't left yet, has he?"

"Excuse me?"

"The Tamerian. Has he left the hospital?"

"No, he's having some food in the observation room. We took as much as we could." She hung the bottle up on the stand, attached another lead—I had no idea what that was for—and attached that to one of the machines.

"Can I see him?"

She switched the machine on, frowning at me. "If you want. They're not exactly very talkative."

"He's saving my life. I can at least say thank you."

"I guess."

She checked the machine, seemed satisfied, and gathered all her things into her box and went to the door. "I'll ask if he would like to come in here. I'll send a nurse to check your leg. The nurse will also take off the drip when it's finished, and will give you your antibiotics."

More poking and prodding with needles. Whoop-de-doo.

She left and I lay back on the bed, staring at the dark fluid in the bottle on the stand. The machine was making little puffing noises. It probably did something to increase the pressure in the bottle so that the blood would flow into my arm more quickly.

I knew it was impossible, but I felt better already.

After a while, there was a soft noise at the door, followed by someone coming in. The Tamerian. He wore a protective gown and came in looking like a purple ghost.

"Sit down," I said.

He did. Like most Tamerians, he had dark hair and olive skin. His deep-set eyes were grey.

"What's your name?" I asked.

"Puck." Or maybe he said *Buck*.

"Thank you, Puck."

He looked at me and then at the stand that contained his blood, only his eyes moving.

"Do you work for Jasper Carlson?"

"He is my boss."

"What sort of work do you do for him?"

"I do what he tell me to. Move boxes, unpack, clean."

"How long have you been here?"

"A year and fifty-two days." The way he said it sounded like a jail sentence.

"Do you want to go back to Tamer?"

He gave me a blank look.

"Do you like being in Barresh?"

Again, no reaction. The expression on his face remained neutral.

"I don't know much about Tamer. Tell me about the world."

"Tamer is a medium-sized world, the second planet in the system on a class 5 star. The orbital period is ninety-six days and a day is two point zero five times the *gamra* standard day. Gravity is one point one seven times the gravity of Ceren. The planet has a cool temperature and the surface is fifty percent covered in permanent ice. The dominant life form is a symbiont migrating plant. The top life form in the ecosystem is a warm-blooded predator. The human population of Tamer measures five thousand."

"Well . . . thank you. You must like snow a lot."

Another blank look. I cringed. This was more awkward than speaking to a teenage boy.

"Can you ski?"

"Yes. We ski."

Another thought. "Can you surf?"

"Surf?" He frowned, the first sign of emotion on his face.

"It's a bit like skiing, but on water."

His frown deepened. "How? You sink in water."

"No, you stand on a board that floats, and you slide along the side of a wave. Like this." I had a picture of Thayu attempting to catch a wave and I brought it up on my reader.

He frowned at the screen, his expression deeply intrigued. "Surf." And then again, "Surf."

"I like it better than skiing. It's not cold."

"But if you fall, you get wet."

"Yes, you do. But that's all right, because it's warm. I could teach you if you want."

He shook his head, still looking at the screen. "Surf."

And then he said nothing for a while. The screen switched itself off. Some people were talking outside the cabin. I thought I heard Thayu's voice.

"Anyway, thank you for saving my life."

No reaction. He still stared at the dark screen.

"You can go now."

"All right." He almost jumped up and went to the door.

"Puck?"

"Yes?"

"Thank you."

"Yes . . . Surf." He opened the door and he was gone.

The door shut again, but didn't remain shut for very long. Thayu came in gasping with laughter.

"You're priceless. You want to teach a Tamerian to surf?"

"I don't know what that conversation was about. But he seems to respond only to descriptive language. He doesn't understand or know how to use abstract concepts at all."

"Those Tamerians are not really the superpeople they are supposed to be."

"I think the Aghyrians didn't like the fact that their creation, the Coldi, had a mind of their own, so they overdosed on the toning down of personality and social intelligence."

"The two go hand in hand."

"Yes, but the Aghyrians themselves aren't particularly socially adept."

"Lilona is doing a lot better."

"True. I wonder how much is learned." Maybe I should try to teach Puck to surf. It would be an interesting experiment.

At some point someone was going to have to investigate the situation on Tamer, what the mysterious anti-establishment group of people was still doing there despite the fact that the Aghyrian ship was gone, who those people were and what the point of Tamerians was, other than that they made excellent bodyguards or soldiers who didn't have opinions of their own.

Maybe the Aghyrians were unhappy with Coldi because they hadn't followed their blueprints of what society should look like. At least the Coldi had been able to grow into a well-rounded people. If these Tamerians never had opinions and never argued, then they would never be any good for anything except menial work.

I *hoped* none of these characteristics carried in the blood.

Although I *was* feeling better. It wasn't my imagination.

By the time Nicha came with lunch, I was sitting up in the chair in front of the little window, dragged there by Thayu and the nurse, who needed to change my bed. The sheets were disgusting from fluids leaked from both my legs. Apparently the barnacle-like leeches injected an anti-coagulant in the blood that kept the bites weeping. But they had finally scabbed over.

"Wow," Nicha said, setting down the basket on the clean bed. "How does it feel to have a bit of Tamerian in you?"

"I'm in no danger of blindly agreeing with everyone, if that's what you want to know."

He laughed. "You sound better. You certainly look much better."

"I feel much better, too." For one, the awful throbbing in my leg had almost gone, and I'd been able to put some weight on it while hobbling from the bed to the chair. I was even hungry.

Nicha had brought a selection of Eirani's breads, noodles, chunky mushroom sauce with bits of fish and a crispy salad.

"So, have you heard from Melissa?" I asked while we were eating.

"Not yet. We've been extremely busy, Reida and Deyu especially."

"Did the security breach give you that much grief?"

"No, they finished doing all that. It's probably going to be a bit of a hack job, but it will do for now. One of Reida's Pengali friends brought in a huge soggy, stinking pile of notebooks and documents."

"Whatever is that for?"

"For whatever reason someone decided to dive in a drainage channel and get attacked by a bottom muncher."

"Wait—are you saying that they found the stuff that Clovis tried to dump? Wouldn't it be all munched up?"

"People dump all sorts of stuff in those channels, and the cleaner is there for a reason: to pick it up and remove it. That's its function: to keep the channel clean of large items of rubbish. It can't be too fussy about how to remove the rubbish. It just gobbles the whole thing up and dumps it at the outlet in the marshlands."

"But what about . . ." I looked at my leg.

"Those were just the metal bristles that it uses to pick up things."

"There is nothing 'just' about them."

"Sorry."

He chuckled, and I laughed, too. It was ridiculous, really. I was here because I'd been run over by a fucking pool cleaner.

"So, Reida got that box he dumped?"

"Yes, and the two youngsters have spent most of yesterday drying out the pages and piecing them back together on the floor of the hall, 'helped' by Ayshada."

I laughed. I could just imagine that, and his frustration if he wasn't allowed to 'help'. "And? Did they find anything interesting?"

"Very much so. It looks like our friend has been paying bribes to just about everyone. Look." He pulled out his reader and showed me a picture on the screen: on the achingly familiar tiles in the hall—and oh, how I wanted to see them again—lay a collection of scraps of paper. Painstakingly pieced together, they formed a page out of a notebook such as merchants in Barresh would use at the markets, or at least those who still wrote everything down on paper.

There was a tally of a number of widely known councillors, with in the left column the amount of money given, by Clovis, I assumed, and in the right hand column the type of favour bought.

Of the well-known councillor Remiru, it said, *Waive application process for new shed*, and of the head of the Barresh guards, it said, *Careful.*

It was good to know that at least someone had some integrity left in this cesspool of a town.

I said, "Very interesting indeed. Did you find anything to do with Robert?"

"A printed copy of the advertisement that Amarru showed you."

"So that mystery contact address that Amarru couldn't reach would bring interested parties to Clovis?"

"Eventually. But there is more, because Huang Le is involved as well."

Exactly as Jasper had said. Which meant that Clovis and the others would indeed not be too keen on being unmasked, by Robert, Robert's wife or one of us.

"Nich', I want to warn Melissa to get out of there quickly. If Clovis used Tamerian guards to protect his property and to kill any trespassers, I don't like to think what he would order Tamerians to do to people who would try to uncover his tracks." I did have trouble imagining the old man ordering people to be killed. Corruption, yes, that I could believe, especially in Barresh, where corruption was often the only way of getting ahead. But he didn't seem the killing type.

"Melissa is out of reach."

"Shouldn't we have heard from her by now? I mean—how long does it take to get out there and back? No more than two days."

"That's only if he's sitting on the beach waiting for her. If she has to do any looking around because he's scared witless, it will be longer."

True. Yet it seemed to me that she had been away forever, and I wouldn't feel happy until she came back safely.

"I'm worried. I know it's early days, but I'm worried that I sent her out there. If these people have this level of organisation, they won't think twice about knocking Robert off, as well as anyone who comes to look for him."

I hoped Melissa had been smart enough to bring guards.

But I also knew that, being someone from Earth with still a very Earth mentality, she wouldn't have.

"Nicha, is there a way we can send her help? Are Evi and Telaris back yet?"

"They'll be back tonight, but they also should be staying with us. Now that we know these things, we may be at risk right here. Criminals do strange things when their anonymity is threatened. Melissa out there may well be safer than we are here."

That was always a possibility, but I still didn't like it. *I* had sent Melissa out there. If something happened to her, it was my fault.

———

It still took another two days before the medico would allow me to go home. On my first day out of the high-oxygen chamber, I developed a rash and they had to check that it wasn't some sort of allergic reaction to the blood I'd received. My leg was on the mend but she wouldn't let me go until it had fully scabbed over. She also insisted that I allow house visits by her and came back for checkups. It almost sounded more tiring than staying in the hospital.

But I was glad to go home. Thayu hired a water taxi that took us right to the jetty just outside our building. It was midday. The sun on my face and the wind in my hair were heavenly.

I came out of the lift to Eirani running out onto the gallery and giving me a hug, and Evi and Telaris in their familiar spots at the door. All the domestic staff were in the hall, as were Veyada and Sheydu, and Devlin, and the nanny with Ayshada who was singing at the top of his voice.

Everyone was smiling. I had missed them.

I hugged all the members of my extended household, who had become like a virtual family to me, but when I came to Devlin, he said, quietly, "There have been a couple of messages for you. I haven't sent them through because I knew you were coming home, but some of them look like they might be urgent."

"I'll have a look at them later."

First, there was lunch: a wonderful selection of breads, and fruit, and fish and fresh salad and tea and juices.

Eirani had put a comfortable armchair in the living room, which was fine for today, but I told her it would need to be shifted to the hub.

Eirani exclaimed, "You're not going to work, are you?"

Well, actually, I was. I hadn't liked the look on Devlin's face when he mentioned those messages.

I asked, "Has anyone heard from Melissa yet?"

There were shakes of heads all around the room.

"She doesn't report to us," Sheydu said.

Maybe not, but this was getting ridiculous. "Can someone check out where she is?"

Later, I shuffled into the hub, where Eirani had set up another chair. She even came to bring me *manazhu* while I sat down. "I feel like an old man now."

"I will be an old woman long before you're an old man, Muri," she said, putting the steaming cup on the sideboard of the control panel and fluffing one of my pillows.

Devlin gave me the earpiece so I could finally look at these urgent messages.

I opened up the list, and there they were, in orange: Margarethe Ollund, Margarethe Ollund and Margarethe Ollund. Damn.

I checked the time. She would be asleep in Rotterdam.

I opened the first one.

Cory,

I have heard nothing and I presume this means you haven't yet found Mr Davidson. Please reply by return message with the status of your search. I have the press breathing down my neck and members in the assembly baying for blood.

Then the next one,

Mr Davidson's wife has been giving damaging reports to the media. She claims that her husband was abducted by offworld people with ulterior motives. She claims that Nations of Earth has acted in support of these people. Nothing could be further from the truth. We need to put a stop to this now and return him home so that we can get to the bottom of this.

The last message was the longest.

It said,

You may not be aware that we are in a time of election campaigns for the Nations of Earth assembly. I personally think, and I am sure you would agree with me, that we need to keep the dialogue between Earth and *gamra* going. I don't think it can be rushed. I don't think we need to get impatient. Balance is important. We cannot allow the situation to get out of hand when people start acting from the point of view of panic. These events of the past few weeks are a serious threat to the stability of our relationship with *gamra*.

What was she on about?

Some people were talking in the hallway. I called, "Nich'? Can you come in here for a moment?"

He did, carrying his son, who watched with wide eyes.

"Can you read this for me and see if it makes any sense to you."

He read, his dark eyes moving from side to side. "Why is this so urgent?"

"That's what I'm trying to establish. She seems to be trying to tell me something without actually saying it."

"Why?"

I spread my hands. "I don't know. I'm not getting the message. All I can gather, although she hasn't said it, is that he's not a simple tourist and not just some rich guy with more money than sense. He's here for a reason. She probably knows what it is, but most likely she doesn't want to say more through the Exchange." Because communication through the Exchange wasn't secure and couldn't be secured and everybody who wanted could listen in, or ask for the transcripts. "Jasper told me that he seems to think that Clovis smuggles diamonds and that Robert might be trying to pull his business out from under him."

"Pah. Diamonds. I don't understand why people get so excited about them. I'd say it's probably something political."

It could be that, too. A cold shiver went over me. "All I can do is tell her that we're working on it."

I wrote a brief message to Margarethe, saying that we were working on it, but that it was not easy, and dangerous. I wished I could say more, but likewise I had to keep it annoyingly vague. I wished I could ask for her to send me a secure message—the old fashioned way, on a piece of paper in a sealed container—but even that would raise eyebrows. And even if she sent that information, it might not get to me before I needed it.

Something was going to blow up soon, and I wished I knew what it was.

13

I N THE EVENING, we all gathered in the living room for dinner.

Everyone cheered as I came in, walking independently across the hall from the hub to the table. I was improving in leaps and bounds. My leg was still a bit itchy, but no longer painful. I would almost be back to normal after a good meal and a good sleep.

Eirani clasped her hands together. "Look at you, Muri, getting so much better already."

I sat down at my usual spot: in the middle of the long end of the table, facing the window. It was dark outside, and beyond the balcony —where the evidence of the storm had been cleaned up—loomed the black darkness of the marshlands, where Robert and Melissa were in some sort of trouble.

"He'll be back to annoying everyone very soon," Nicha said, still talking about me.

"Well, let's hope he's learned a lesson." Thayu met my eyes across the table. "This is why we spend so much time preparing every job. What looks simple rarely is."

"You're channelling my grandfather."

She gave me a blank look, and I remembered too late that anything to do with belief and spiritual language usually went over Coldi heads, and that I'd probably bent the use of the word channelling to mean something it normally didn't.

She continued, "I'm right. You almost got yourself killed. Next time you're determined to get yourself killed, let me know and I'll come with you. I might even bring some other people to greatly reduce the chance that you're successful."

"Oh, come on, Thay', back off," Nicha said. "He's learned his lesson."

"I hope so, but I suspect he doesn't really understand."

"You have to accept it," Veyada said. "When we worked for Ezhya, he would sometimes do things that we would have advised against. Sometimes they worked to his advantage; sometimes they did not. You can warn a person, but ultimately, they have to lead their own life."

"But did you ever think your life would end if something happened to Ezhya?" Thayu's voice sounded close to breaking.

An uncomfortable silence followed her words. I met Thayu's eyes, glittering with moisture.

I cringed. I hated embarrassing her, even if embarrassment didn't appear to be an emotion Coldi felt in great doses. I felt it on her behalf, and I hated it. "I learned my lesson, really."

She nodded. I had no doubt there would be more words said about this later when we were alone.

The rest of dinner was a chaotic, noisy and jovial affair. Eirani hovered behind my chair, jumping every time my cup was empty or I had eaten a slice of bread. She wasn't happy with the amount I ate—although it was a lot more than I'd been eating in the hospital—and kept commenting on how thin I was.

I had to tell her several times that I could not possibly eat any more.

I called everyone to an informal meeting afterwards, just to keep tabs on what everyone was doing. We moved to the hub for this, where I sat next to Devlin on the central bench and everyone else either occupied seats at the other workstations or leaned against the walls.

Devlin and Deyu reported on the security situation, and that appeared to be a little more worrisome than I had expected. They had run checks on the entire system, found some bugs, and found some additional bugs that no one had known were there. Those had to be fairly recent, and I suspected that the loading of advertising messages with buggy code was not a one-off restricted to this one company. I had often wondered why the person who set up the apartment had made such a clear separation between the office and hub systems, and this was clearly why. Because of sneaky Barresh merchants inserting sneaky code.

Thayu and Deyu had investigated the bugs that we did know about, and that had come through the advertisement sent to the office that had sparked the alert. When activated, the code opened a direct link to outside that could be accessed by a small piece of corresponding code that could be automatically sent out by a reader, even by people just walking past who had no idea that their equipment was being used in this way.

I asked, "And then what does it do with those snatches of information?"

Deyu said, "They can be sorted based on key words that indicate what a particular office is talking about and would be interested in paying for. It's not a high-tech spying operation, but it would lead to people sending you lots of business solicitations."

"Is this why we've been getting so much advertising?" And here was I thinking that I was becoming popular.

"Likely."

"Whoever they are, they're much more interested in business matters than in *gamra* politics."

Thayu said, "Yes, but we would need to look at who uses the information, because these businesses are not the end users. They merely gather the data. Who are their customers? Suppliers of office equipment, yeah, I'd have not that much trouble with, although we don't exactly *want* anyone listening in, but it worries me when they start selling information to lobbyists and other people who have political motives."

I agreed that was a worry. The idea that people would pay for this, too. "Is this even legal?"

Veyada said, "Not within *gamra*, it isn't, but because these are local businesses, they don't fall under *gamra* law, and local laws relating to business concerns are much less strict, and in general, data-gathering is considered *fair game* as long as it concerns publicly available data—"

"I would hardly call this publicly available."

"No, but to comply with the *legal* part of the business, they will filter out the publicly available data, never mind that the method of collection was illegal, because they have ways to obscure that, too. This will be where your solicitations from businesses selling office equipment come from. There will also be a much more interesting shadow market in illegal data. It will still only concern insignificant-looking, very low-level security data that no one cares much about, but when you collate it, you can form a complete picture of a person or business' behaviour and know where to target them for lobbying."

Or, I realised, for damaging a rival company. If you knew such things as where they bought their supplies and when they did their accounting, who did it, and how much they were paid, then you could target a business with cheaper prices or someone who had more skills for the same price. Then you could also plant spies in your rival's company.

The possibilities were endless.

Devlin was right: not only did we need to stamp this out, we needed to make sure it never happened again. How this could be achieved was another matter altogether. Not only that, if it was happening to us, it would be happening across *gamra* and probably even the council.

"Who are the people buying this illegal stuff?"

"Shadow men and shadow companies. People we've never heard of and companies we've never heard of in places we've never heard of."

Sheydu said, her voice dark, "Like Tamer. They'd been doing their thing for ages before someone took notice."

There were nods all around. Like Tamer, and likely just as disturbing. Someone had turned data collection into a form of art.

Devlin said, "So, I guess you want me to disable the directories and destroy the document and all the links related to it?"

"No. Leave it."

He frowned at me.

"Make it so that to the outside world it looks like everything is still working, but disconnect that part of the system from everything else. Reinstate some of the old operating data from Renkati. I don't care what, just dump something in the partition that looks like real data, so they don't know that we're onto them."

"Certainly they already know that?"

"Maybe. These sorts of scam merchants don't always think everything through."

Sheydu nodded her approval. "You can usually catch them when they do something stupid, either because they *are* stupid, or because they don't have enough people to cover every part of their butts."

There were nods all around. Waiting for the opponent to do something stupid was always a good tactic.

The medico had said nothing about getting my leg wet, so after the meeting, Thayu, Nicha and I retreated to the bathroom where we had a drink, and where, when Nicha had gone to look after his son, Thayu washed me all over, and I proved to her that I was getting back to normal.

I asked if she wanted to talk about what had happened, but she said she did not. Everything had already been said, and perhaps it was best that we move on.

I promised her to try not to get myself in other similarly dangerous situations, but also said that I couldn't absolutely guarantee it would never happen again.

"Just promise me that if you ever get yourself in danger again, you are with me."

"I think I could live with that promise."

We slept in each other's arms.

———

Being at home did wonders to my health, because when I woke up the next morning, I felt almost completely normal. It was quite early and the light filtering in through the window was still misty and grey. Ugh —it was raining, a steady, grey drizzle from an equally grey sky.

I slipped from the bed, letting Thayu sleep. She must have gone through a hard time trying to keep the household together, but would rather die than admit she was exhausted.

There was no one in the hub, so I sat down at the central bench to check the overnight news. We'd set a flag on the location of Melissa's boat—and the satellite had travelled directly overhead very early in the morning—but the boat hadn't moved.

I stared at the little dot in the 2D projected image that I had pulled from the satellite data. The boat lay at the western end of the beach on a little island. You could see a little boat-shaped dot on the image. It also showed the remains of a fire on the beach—no megon trees there—and a square patch of something grey that could be a tarpaulin or a tent, it was impossible to see what because of the dense tree cover.

What worried me most was that the island's scan which Devlin had completed late last night did not show any significant sources of fresh water. Surely, she would have had to move to collect water? Had she at least brought a solar distiller? But even so, why hadn't that boat moved for the last two days?

I was certain: we had to do something because she had run into trouble. We had run out of excuses to wait any longer. We had to go after her.

I went into the service directory and tried to find someone who owned a boat—someone who was not connected to Clovis, or the Barresh Ferry Company, or the company that officially owned the Barresh Ferry Company—which was Clovis' of course. Tracking down that company showed up that Clovis also owned a good number of shops, the water taxi company that we used to get to the island quickly if needed, two accountancy firms, a health practice and several building companies, most notably the one that held the contract for the constant and ongoing repairs and maintenance on the ancient council buildings.

This guy literally had his nose everywhere, and yet his name never appeared on any of the contact information of those companies. I wondered if by chance he was involved with this data-gathering company, but I couldn't find a connection. That company had its address at a locker number at the Courier's Guild headquarters, which usually meant that it was either off world or, more likely, it didn't have a formal office in town, and for a business that dealt with virtual goods, that was not unusual either.

"What are you doing?" Thayu asked at the door.

I looked up, realising that a chunk of time had disappeared and I'd been so busy that I'd missed Eirani coming up with the breakfast things. The plates were already on the table and the members of my association were coming in.

"Melissa," I said.

"Heard anything from her?"

"No. The boat is still on the beach in the same spot."

She stared at the image.

"Something has happened. We're going to have to help her."

She stared a bit more, her eyes blinking.

"Thay'?" I knew she didn't like this. I knew she didn't want us to be involved, but she knew Melissa. It was hard to guess what she was thinking.

She breathed out. "Why don't we discuss it at breakfast?"

We went across the hall into the living room, where Sheydu and Veyada and Reida and Deyu already sat at the table. Nicha was at the door to his room, talking to the nanny, who, by the look of things, had just arrived. Her hair was wet from the rain.

We sat down at the table.

"Call Evi and Telaris in here," I said.

Reida got up and went into the hall. A moment later, he returned with both men. Eirani bustled around pouring tea and bringing extra plates and cups.

"We have a problem," I said, when everyone was eating. I went on to explain the situation with Melissa. I ended with, "So she is out there, and some of you may disagree with me, but I think we have a moral duty to help her, because she is out there because of us."

"No," Sheydu said. "She is out there because your *president* makes both of you nervous. Why don't you ask your *president* why, if this man is so important to her, she isn't offering any assistance."

"She can't, officially. She has no people out here except Melissa, and no authority to command any kind of skilled, military-type assistance for the logistics of this operation."

Sheydu snorted. "There are ways. I hear Tamerians are for hire for anyone who requires them."

"Maybe, but she is not familiar with this situation, because that's what Melissa is for. Her influence stops at pleading the Chief Delegate for assistance, and I don't know that she could make a strong case that he should give her that assistance."

"Excuses," Sheydu said. "All it would need would be for her to contact Federza with an official request, with an explanation. If she really wants you to retrieve this man, why doesn't she provide you with the proper documents and a budget?"

Sheydu was right, much as I hated to admit it. *Get him back here* was an order Danziger would have given, and he had suffered badly in the election, because people thought he was aloof and distant and didn't appear to know what he was talking about. I desperately wanted to believe that Margarethe was not like that, but I had to admit there were aspects of this mystery that I didn't like at all.

I sighed. Spread my hands and let them sink again. "Look, I don't know. All I know is that a man is out there, lost. I have no idea why he came, but clearly when he wrote with sulphuric ochre on the back of a ferry timetable, he had been abandoned, left for dead, and he was afraid of dying. And we have Melissa out there, and the *president* urging us to do something."

A heavy silence followed my words. At least no one protested. That was progress, wasn't it?

I continued with that hopeful sign. "We can hire an aircraft and be there and back within a day."

"You're not going anywhere," Thayu said.

"I've had two days to recover. I'm fine. I'm bored with all this doing nothing."

"It's out of range for the solar planes to fly in one go," Veyada said. "Especially if we're heavy, and we will be."

That was a bigger problem. "I was wondering about that. Is there anything else we could use?"

"Boats are a much better option. Planes are vulnerable to weather —" He looked out the window where it was still raining. "—and suitable landing spots. Most of the islands have sheer cliffs and tiny beaches that may even consist of only rocks. If the sea is too choppy and there is no nearby shelter, we can't even reach the location."

The beach where Melissa's boat was looked safe enough, but I got his point. If we needed to go *somewhere else*, we wanted to have a versatile vehicle.

"We could take a boat and a plane."

Veyada and Sheydu gave each other a meaningful look.

Sheydu said, "You would need two boats, one especially to carry the plane."

"I suggest we take *three* boats: two for us, and one for the folded-up plane."

Another meaningful look.

"You have thought a lot about this, haven't you?" Thayu said.

"Tell me what else I was supposed to have done, lying in bed staring at the ceiling in the hospital?"

"All right," Thayu said.

Sheydu looked like she wanted to protest, but Thayu waved her hand. "Let him have his expedition, or he'll never shut up about it."

She didn't *like* admitting that she cared about Melissa's fate, but I thought she did, even if only because I did.

"Are we all going?" Reida's eyes were shining. "I've always wanted to see beisili. I hear you can ride them."

"I hear that you will attempt nothing of the sort, young man," Sheydu said.

"Goodness, no," Eirani said. "It's their breeding season and the big females get very territorial."

"Don't worry," Sheydu said. "I will personally see to it that he keeps out of the water."

Reida grinned.

All of a sudden, the narrative had changed. Someone had decided that we were going. Was it because of my proposal to take three boats and a plane?

After the kitchen staff had cleared the table, we all went into the hub. Devlin pulled up all the maps of the area, and none of them were terribly detailed. The reason was given as *Thousand Islands tribe territory*.

"What are we going to do about getting a permit and a guide to visit?" I asked.

Thayu grinned. "Do you want to ask any of Clovis' Pengali helpers?"

"No way."

"There is our answer," Thayu said. "We go in, we get them out and leave quickly. If they turn up, there are enough of us to get out of trouble if necessary."

I couldn't help having a dig at the members of my association who had berated me for doing ill-prepared things. "That sounds like an excellent plan. What can possibly go wrong?"

14

───────

WHILE WE WERE discussing the details of travel, Devlin asked the office downstairs for safe places to hire boats. This whole episode had been highly educational to me. Previously I would have thought you "just" hired a boat, and that boat hire was a service you paid for and someone delivered in the same way you ordered groceries or laundry services, and that the quality and timeliness of the product or service was the main consideration in choosing a service.

But that was not the way with boats in Barresh.

We couldn't hire from any of the companies associated with Clovis. I still wasn't one hundred percent sure that Clovis personally had anything to do with Robert's marooning on the island—he just didn't seem the type of person who would do this—but I sure as hell didn't trust him. I didn't really trust Jasper's version of events, either. He had been too forthcoming with his accusations.

But we needed boats and this boat war meant that hiring someone was a political statement.

This made me wonder about the *other* boating companies and what affiliations they had and what data about us *they* had passed on to their owners every time we had hired a water taxi. And it made me think that maybe we should just buy the damn boats and be done with relying on others. That was an educational thought, too, because all of a sudden I saw why those extended keihu families living in their obscenely large mansions with obscene numbers of staff had come to operate in the way they did: they kept everything in-house. Because having to deal with sabotage as a result of this type of rivalry got old, fast.

Not just that. I realised I had a big, gaping hole in my household: I desperately needed Pengali workers. I had always shied away from hiring them, because the silly Earth human in me felt uncomfortable with the "colonial" aspect of hiring "noble savages" as domestic staff. Seeing Pengali work and live with those rich keihu families, toiling away at the menial tasks, always made me feel a bit ill. But of course that was a silly notion that came from my cultural background, that I pretended I didn't have, but that, at times, proved stubbornly resilient.

Pengali were neither noble nor savage. They were very *different*. That was the most important reason that I needed one or two in my office or other staff.

Unfortunately, this was not going to help me now.

Devlin found a company happy to let us have three boats without drivers, and then Reida found three drivers for us, none of them boat owners themselves. It seemed a decent solution to the problem.

"They're still from the Washing Stones tribe," he warned, "But they say all this tribal stuff is highly overblown. It may be important for the older folk, but the younger ones just want to get jobs, and they don't see any problems in working alongside other tribes."

I hoped he was right.

Those Pengali came to the apartment in the afternoon. There were two young women and a slightly older man, all three dressed in neat, clean clothes, minus all the tribal gear—the belt with the skulls and teeth and glass-stone knives I always found a little intimidating. They were polite and quietly-spoken. Their names were Maray, Della and Langga. I made up some excuse for them to sleep in the guest quarters, mainly so that they could not pull any last-minute tricks on us. They chose one of the rooms downstairs, one of those Melissa had used at times, and rolled out their mats on the floor. No matter how much Eirani urged them, they would not use the beds.

I was unsure of their diet, but they went out and came back with fish and lizard eggs which they cooked themselves in the kitchen, while being extremely quiet and polite to the kitchen staff.

"They're the strangest people to have in the house," Eirani said. "It's like I can't do anything for them."

Coming from her, a lifelong Barresh resident, this was a telltale remark. I truly needed to employ some Pengali.

I went into the hub to check with Devlin if any messages had come in. I had written to Margarethe that we were about to go and retrieve Robert.

She had not replied, but two solicitations had come in to the link that we had left open. Both were for boating companies.

Devlin stared at me. "How did you know that was going to happen?"

"I didn't, but I suspected. This data-gathering process looks automated, and clearly someone neglected to go through to delete us from their list after *gamra* made it public that we'd been breached. Or maybe someone else had already taken possession of the list with our data on it. Keep an eye on it while we're gone. Track what comes in, or who or what tries to access the link. Try to find out who they are."

He said that he would.

Evi and Telaris had collected a veritable pile of survival equipment in the hall. With satisfaction, I noticed a large first-aid kit, since this was their secondary capability.

We had dinner—without the Pengali—where Devlin reported that the weather was expected to be partially overcast but otherwise fine for the next few days, and we decided to leave early the next morning.

During dinner, a message from Margarethe came in.

It was as short as it was uninformative.

Robert Davidson is a respected member of the South African community. His wife has taken a strong anti-*gamra* stance and is gathering a lot of support. Until the time that we can investigate how he ended up in Barresh, public opinion will focus on the side of "evil aliens". The longer this case lingers on, the more damage it will do.

She added a news article that showed Fiona Davidson agitating and claiming that she and her husband were innocent victims of people who had ulterior motives, wanting to get their hands on their money. The holiday brochure, she said, was a scam. The aliens had abducted her husband, who was innocent.

It was almost believable.

But no one said anything about Robert's position with a mining company, or about diamond smuggling.

And yes, Margarethe could be right. I could fully imagine how public opinion would savage her and the assembly over the disappearance of an "innocent" man, but it didn't address a couple of key questions. The most important one: why would anyone in Barresh be interested in abducting this man? He had nothing that was of use to them.

The media were selling it as a sob story, and it was clear to me, this *wasn't* a sob story. When her husband went missing, Fiona Davidson had gone straight to an Exchange agent in Athens, and she couldn't have done that unless she knew where to find such a person. Fiona Davidson clearly knew a lot more than an average partner in the same situation, had her husband's disappearance been as accidental as she suggested.

But Margarethe clearly wasn't able to tell me what I needed to know.

Melissa might have been able to, but this stupid delegate had jumped the gun and sent her away to solve this mess much too early. Yet I desperately needed some independent information.

When I first came to Barresh, I had been able to see the news as reported on Earth. But since I no longer worked for Nations of Earth, I had lost access to this network. Nations of Earth paid for the transmission of this information, and it was accessible to their employees. It was stupid, but it was their policy, and I hadn't been able to change their mind on how stupid it was.

All I could get was a poorer version compiled by the Exchange, in which news items from Earth had to compete for space with thousands of other news items from all over the inhabited worlds—all of which were freely accessible to me if I was interested and could read the language—and it should come as no surprise that other events were judged more important than one single missing man.

Melissa had access to the Nations of Earth network. How could I get into her apartment?

I asked *gamra* security, but they wouldn't open the door for me unless I had written permission from a higher authority. When I grumbled about this, Sheydu remarked that *gamra* security only existed to make our lives harder: they botched operations where they should stop people accessing certain data or locations, and they stopped people having access to data or locations who *should* have access. This pretty much reflected my recent interactions with them.

I didn't press the point with them, because we had a secret weapon: Reida.

When I told him I wanted him to break into Melissa's apartment, he grinned at me. "How come every time someone berates me for doing stuff, the next thing someone comes around and wants me for that very skill?"

"*I* appreciate your skill. Just don't expect me to approve of it publicly."

I went with him and Deyu to the apartment after dark, and he had the door open in no time.

"Quick, go in and do your thing," he said. "I don't know how long it will be before someone comes to check out the break-in."

"I won't be long," I said, and went inside.

Reida and Deyu would keep a look out on the balcony and warn me in case someone came.

It was dark in the apartment and the air smelled stale and musty. I stumbled through the hallway in the pitch dark, until I came to the living room, where the very faint glow of the city lights from the other island produced just enough light for me to see the outlines of major items of furniture.

I remembered the pearl lights with the little lampshades, and ran my hands over the wall until I found a lever and pushed it up.

Light flipped on.

The room was tidy, clearly left like this by someone going on a trip. The apartment didn't have a luxurious hub like mine, but it did have a small, windowless study that Melissa had set up as such. There was only room for one chair, in the middle, and the wall space was taken up by desks and shelves with equipment. A couple of lights blinked in the darkness.

Wow, this was really ancient equipment.

I switched on the receiver. I had feared that I might need a passcode, but the Exchange recognised Melissa's apartment and I was able to get through into the Nations of Earth portal without any trouble.

Sheydu would be impressed with the lack of security.

The portal had changed a fair bit since Danziger had banned me from it. I suspected I could probably organise being reconnected, but I hadn't wanted to test my good relationship with Margarethe, because she would probably get in trouble if that came under scrutiny.

But damn, seeing all those news services lined up filled me with irrational nostalgia, laced with a good number of stressful memories. When Danziger had cut me off from communication, this was the only way I could access the news.

There was World Newspoint, which usually delivered dry and boring stuff. Flash Newspoint, Melissa's former employer, which was entirely the opposite. There were two news services I hadn't heard of and there was also a general feed, which consisted of an amalgam of all of them. That opened up a huge long list with articles about disasters, politics and various flotsam from all over the world. I stared at it for a while before realising that I barely recognised any of the names and even fewer of the issues. Whatever the hell did the headline *Strange In Many Pots* even mean?

Oh. *Strange* was the name of a man suspected of being involved in bribery.

Sheesh, this was like looking at an entirely different planet.

Since when, for example, did travellers need to submit to full profiling before being able to leave a country?

Amarru had said nothing about that. I was guessing that she had ways around it that she used when I came to visit my father. It also brought home the point that I hadn't even been to Nations of Earth, my former employer, since my contract ended, and that I had no desire to do so.

I went to Flash Newspoint, and searched *Robert Davidson*.

A list of about twenty articles came up.

Apparently, there was also a Robert Davidson who was a tennis player. Awesome.

In between reports of his latest tournament win, I found an article with the title,

Davidson's Wife Claims: No Help From Nations of Earth.

Hmmm. Interesting interpretation.

I opened that one.

Fiona Davidson, wife of missing mining executive Robert Davidson, claims that she was forced to seek help directly from the Athens Exchange when Nations of Earth was stonewalling her requests for assistance in finding her husband. Mr Davidson went on an adventure trip with a travel company called Exclusive Adventures, which specialises in adventures for the very rich.

"When I asked Nations of Earth to help me locate my husband when he failed to return, they said it was outside their influence and that was the end of their help," Ms Davidson said.

The article went on to complain about how unfair it was and how Nations of Earth had a moral obligation to look after its citizens everywhere. The journalist had concluded with a parting remark, *This process would become much easier if Nations of Earth could get over its indecision and finally decided to join* gamra.

It said *gamra*, not *Union*. That was a step in the right direction.

At the bottom, there were lists for keywords and a few related articles. One of them said, *Execo to shut diamond mining operations in southern Africa*.

That article explained how the company, and its predecessors, had a long history of exploitation of the local workers it employed, in many cases, to hand-dig for jewellery-grade diamonds. Over the past two hundred years, the soil in the area had been turned over so many times that good finds had become increasingly rare.

My attention skipped to a snatch of dialogue.

"We understand that a good percentage of the local economy is dependent on the mine," Davidson said, "But we have continued this operation for as long as it was feasible."

Davidson?

He was introduced earlier in the article as Mr Davidson, head of mining operations, Execo Africa.

That had to be the same one, right?

So, could I conclude that, having closed mining operations in Africa, the company wanted to sell premium diamonds from Barresh? And that it was pushing for Nations of Earth to do so legally? That was a valid cause, wasn't it? Maybe when he found out, Clovis was unimpressed with that. Unimpressed enough to maroon Davidson on an island?

On a whim, I searched for Fiona Davidson's name, since she seemed to be more forthcoming with information. After a few false positives, I found her: *Dr Fiona Rachelle Davidson, General Practitioner*.

Besides pictures of her at work, there were pictures of her brandishing a gun and standing with one foot on—I wasn't sure what that animal was, some sort of antelope.

There was also a picture of her and her husband at a gun show.

Educational.

I went back to the main list of articles, but it wasn't very informative.

Oh well, at least I had tried.

I was about to go, when I had another idea. I searched, *missing rich people*. Because if this was an adventure tour, there would have been others. The Pengali woman at the Pengali Office had said as much.

The search brought up a lot of socialite shenanigan rubbish that— well, I had no idea how the hell the search thought it was relevant. But in the middle of articles about misbehaving princesses, actors, animators or film producers, I found a small article.

Gusamo Sahardjo still missing.

I opened that one.

There has still been no sign of Gusamo Sahardjo, the Jakarta-based owner of CreativeMinds.

Damn it, I had used CreativeMinds in the past. It was a great place to pretty up your correspondence with designs and interactive graphics and logos for a small fee.

Mr Sahardjo travelled to Europe four weeks ago to join a tour that indulges in one of his passions: extreme surfing.

Shit.

It looked like I might have found another of the participants in the tour.

Gusamo was a short, thin man with an open smile. He called himself an artist first, despite spending most of his time on his business. According to him,

Indonesians are blessed with a developed sense of art that is both practical and adaptable for business purposes and attractive to all cultures. The use of colour, the use of modern imagery and the latest digital techniques are not unique to us, but the combination of all three plays a large role in our success. In short: we produce design that the entire world can relate to.

He was talking up his business, of course, but from what I remembered, if you wanted to have something designed—for a hefty price tag—the hip digital art community in Jakarta was your go-to place.

Gusamo also had a love for anthropology and the ocean. He had contributed extensively to a sea turtle conservation project, and—

My reader sent a warning beep.

Security on the ground floor, Reida said through the feeder.

All right. I could read this sort of stuff all day, following links from links to other links, but at this point, I couldn't do much more, and sadly I was still little wiser about Robert Davidson or about what it could be that Margarethe was hinting at.

Well, at least I had tried.

I shut down the hub and I joined Reida and Deyu on the balcony not much later. Reida relocked the door and he assured me that no one would ever know we'd been there. I hoped so.

On the way home, we passed the jetty outside the front of our building. The three boats lay there, ready to go, guarded by Evi and Telaris.

"All quiet?" I asked.

"Nothing interesting happening whatsoever," Evi said. In security speak, that was a good thing.

I glanced at the boats. They were sturdy vehicles, bigger than the one we had taken out before, with more powerful engines. The solar plane lay folded up on one of them, hidden under a thick waterproof cloth.

At home, Veyada and Nicha were in the hall with a big stack of camping gear and some basic food supplies for twelve people. Sheydu came to drop off a tightly shut crate. Explosives, I assumed.

She grinned. I wondered what had happened to her being terrified of water. She had not protested or thrown up any excuses for not going and had, in fact, said very little.

I hoped the issue was not going to surface at an inopportune moment.

I told them that there might be a second person in need of rescue.

"Not a problem," Sheydu said. "We've got enough for an expedition double the size."

We were packed. We were ready. I had done the right thing and involved all of my association. No lives would be risked.

15

STILL, I SLEPT BADLY that night.

My mind kept churning over things that might possibly go wrong; and in the dark, at night, those things had a habit of multiplying. It might rain, we might not get enough sunlight to charge the engine, the sea might be so rough that one of the boats would flip, and few in my association could swim. Or we might find that the boat we'd seen on the satellite image was there, but no people, and the island was guarded by a bunch of vicious Pengali from the Thousand Islands tribe who would only communicate through the use of weapons.

When I did doze off, my active mind provided me with a plethora of absurd, far-fetched and just plain horrible dreams.

A herd of beisili chased us from the island, overturning the boat that contained all the people in my association who couldn't swim.

They all fell in the water and were bobbing around screaming in their life jackets, when a beisili decided that it liked to test its teeth on the jackets. When we tried to chase them off, they came and overturned the boat with the plane, which was our only means of getting back home, because somehow the other boat had disappeared. Everyone was in the water, and everyone was screaming. Nicha grabbed onto me, and then Veyada and Sheydu as well. I started sinking and Thayu couldn't even reach me.

I yelled, "Thayu!" but water came into my mouth.

I woke up, sweating. I sat up in the dark, panting. Stupid dream. Stupid overactive brain. Beisili were scared of people. Only the young ones ever came close. They were certainly not strong enough to overturn boats and I very much doubted they'd be interested in life jackets.

Thayu lay next to me, out cold, on her stomach with her face pushed into the pillow.

I wiped my face and lay back down, staring at the ceiling, feeling numb. This expedition worried me. I was missing something, and I wished to hell I knew what it was.

I mentally ticked off all the preparations we needed to have made. Tents, food, water, guns, first aid, emergency beacon, solar chargers, fishing gear, ropes . . .

I dozed off briefly and then woke up with a shock to Thayu getting out of bed.

"Time to go," she said.

I stumbled out of bed and looked out the window. The suns had not yet cleared the escarpment, and a soft layer of mist lay over the water. At least the weather was cooperative.

Damn it, I felt woolly-headed and ill. Eating a quick breakfast only marginally improved things. Eirani was bustling about, making sure we ate enough, asking Veyada whether we had packed this or that or the other, because Veyada was the only one not to snap at her questions.

Nicha was at the door to his room, giving instructions to the nanny. Little Ayshada had not yet woken up. I could see him in his cot, sleeping on his belly.

Telaris opened the door, and one of the kitchen staff brought in a trolley—because we used the building's lift for moving large items between the ground floor and upstairs in the apartment.

We loaded everything on the trolley, or I should say that the others did, because Thayu wouldn't allow me to help.

I protested. "I'm not an invalid."

"The medico would have a fit if she knew that you were going on this expedition."

"But she doesn't. They always think that you have all the time in the world to spend lazing about recovering."

"Sometimes, there is a point to these warnings, Muri," Eirani said.

"You should take it easy, because you were very sick." She stood at the point where the hallway opened into the foyer, her arms crossed under her considerable bosom. I suspected that she spoke to me because she had given up trying to appeal to any in my association.

And yes, she was right, but there was no way I'd let everyone go without me. It was my project, my idea, my people and you just didn't let members of your association go off to an important task by themselves. That was not the way associations worked

Everything was on the trolley, and Evi and Deyu wheeled it out onto the gallery observed from the foyer by Veyada. The big tottering pile of things just fitted through the door.

"Well, there we go," I said to Eirani and Devlin and the others of my staff who stood watching in the hall.

"Good luck, Muri, and please take care."

Devlin merely waved. We'd be talking to each other as soon as we were on the water, and until we were out of reach of the Exchange, which was usually just before the sand bar. After that, we would have no connection until Thayu set up the satellite transmitter.

The trolley took up all the space in the lift so we went down the stairs and then helped Deyu and Evi wheel it out of the lift. It was a slow and cumbersome procession through the atrium, out the building's entrance and down the sloping walkway to the jetty, but finally we arrived, everything was loaded in the boats, covered with oiled cloths and tied down.

It had been decided that one of the Pengali women, Della, would take the boat with the plane, and that Nicha would go with her.

We divided the rest of the group between the other two boats. I went with Langga, Thayu, Telaris and Reida. Veyada, Sheydu, Deyu and Evi went with Maray in the last boat.

By the time the boats finally pulled away from the jetty, sunlight streamed over the roof of the building onto the quay and jetty. A couple of *gamra* guards watched our departure. I wouldn't be surprised if they knew exactly what we were doing and where we were going. Little as she thought of them, Sheydu would not keep them in the dark about these kinds of operations.

For a long time, the boats moved in convoy at a steady pace. The weight of people and gear made our pace much slower than on our previous trip.

We stopped for lunch at the island with the ruins. Pengali would rarely drive a boat without trailing a few lines with hooks and bait, and we had caught a couple of medium-sized fish.

Langga took them to a tree trunk that lay at the high tide line on the beach. The top of the trunk's curve formed a flat surface that he used to clean and gut the fish and cut the pink meat into wafer-thin slices. The blade of the knife was glass-stone, diamond, polished only around the cutting edge. The rest was dark, covered with a gummy substance, into which a row of signs was engraved.

He noticed me looking at it.

"In our traditional ways, we use the land, but don't change it. When a tree washes up, we make the top flat so it's a table. We don't move the tree, we don't cut it into planks. We just use the tree."

"I was looking at your knife."

"I made it myself." He gave it to me, enveloped in a fishy smell. "When I was a boy, the elders would make me sit there and grind it by hand for many, many days. It teaches angry young men patience. I would have to recite old stories while I did it, and they would berate me if I got it wrong. I was a very angry young man back then." He laughed, which sounded like a kind of piggy snort in Pengali.

I turned the knife over in my hands. It was an instrument made with incredible patience and skill with a meticulously sharp edge. It looked very old and well used.

Meanwhile he pulled apart some kind of fruit, and squeezed juice from the individual parts out over the fish slices. Then he took a little pouch from his belt and sprinkled some red powder over the fish. He massaged it into the flesh with his fingers.

I recognised the dish. I'd had it before.

I returned the knife to him. I felt like it needed to be handled with reverence. This was not just a carving knife; it was the evidence of a young man's journey from impatient youth to an adult.

He stuck it in his belt, pushed all the fish together onto a large leaf which he presented to the group.

The fish was delicious. The juice was sour, which complimented the salty taste of the fish.

Veyada, Evi and Telaris also enjoyed it, but the others preferred Eirani's bread. That was their loss, but at times I got a little annoyed at the Coldi unwillingness to try different foods. Being able to eat red-coded food, few foodstuffs would be harmful to them.

Seeing us enjoy it, Reida got curious, so he tried some, too. We all laughed at the face he pulled at the uncooked, soft texture. But then he wanted more, and the pile of fish slices was soon gone.

It was time to move on. We clambered into the boats, pushed off and soon came to the channel. By now it was well past noon and the tide was rushing in. The boats slowed to a crawl, engines going full blast against the mass of churning water making its way into the delta. Being the heaviest, the boat carrying the plane had the most trouble getting through, but we all made it out to the ocean. The water was clear, the waves small, despite a bank of clouds sitting over the islands in the distance. It looked like there might be small storms out there, too. Langga steered the boat in a lazy circle while studying the sky before setting off in a southerly direction, apparently satisfied.

To our left was the sand spit with the patch of rainforest where we had camped. The wind, rain and waves had long since erased all evidence of our presence.

Once we'd left this part of the coast behind, we were in utter wilderness where very few people from the city ever came.

The boats maintained a steady pace. Thayu checked our location on the map on her reader. We no longer had connection to the Exchange, so our location wasn't being logged other than through the engine's beacon, but that was all automated and a one-way communication.

"There," she said, pointing. "It's that island, in between those two bigger ones."

I squinted against the sunlight. Like all offshore islands, it rose out of the water with steep sides. "Why would anyone go out there to surf? The best surf is at the spit."

"That piece of land to the left is not an island. It's a *peninsula*." She used the Isla word. The oceans on Asto were not nice: too salty and with poisonous upwellings. Few people went there and, therefore, Coldi had little terminology that dealt with water and boats and shores.

The lay of the land became clearer when we had come closer. In this section of the coast, the escarpment, the tall cliff on the eastern side of the Barresh delta that marked the edge of the huge Mirani plateau, lay much closer to the ocean, and it formed an outcrop that sloped into a long finger pointing west into the ocean.

I looked in amazement at the vast display of untouched wilderness. Ceren was an agricultural world, and yes, it was sparsely populated. This was also because, the tropical climate of Barresh aside, it was a cool world with extensive ice caps and a lot of rugged, mountainous terrain that was either too high or too cold for farming.

A sight like this was what old explorers would have seen when they first came to the coasts of Africa or South America: vast swathes of untouched jungle, sluggish, silty rivers, pristine beaches.

Oh, I understood why people from Earth wanted to come here.

"What's that?" Reida said.

I followed the direction he was pointing. We had just rounded the tip of the peninsula and had a view down a silvery beach on the southern side. At the far end, something white stuck out from the tree canopy.

Thayu used the magnifying lens on her reader to have a closer look. "Some sort of tower." I looked at the screen over her shoulder. It was a structure made of wood, a raised platform over the canopy.

Reida leaned over for a look. "We're being watched."

Thayu nodded. "Probably."

Langga was looking at the screen as well.

"Do you know what is there?" I asked him.

"Thousand Islands tribe," he said, in his clipped accent. "They live there."

"The traditional settlements are like big hives made from dead wood," Reida said.

I knew. I'd seen pictures of the main settlement of the Washing Stones tribe, at the mouth of a creek where a waterfall cascaded from the escarpment onto large boulders called the Washing Stones. The story had it that the people would stand under the water to clean themselves.

The other two boats veered away from the coast, and Langga followed their example. No good seeking unnecessary trouble with the tribe. Yes, we were probably being watched, because besides these platforms—and the Pengali had excellent eyes—they were not shy in using modern technology. I'd seen many a traditional-looking Pengali fisherman with a satellite transmitter in a pouch.

Once we were in the shelter of the offshore islands, the sea got a lot less choppy. The island where Robert and Melissa were was the furthest from the shore out of a group of three. The islands stuck out of the water like giant boulders, with steep sides and forested tops. The island in question was no more than a rocky knoll. The beach was visible as a fine white line at the point where the cliffs met the sea. The water was very calm here, almost mirror-like. You couldn't see the bottom, but on occasion, we crossed underwater ridges covered in sea growths.

Thayu was studying the island through the lens on her reader, her brow furrowed.

"There!" Reida called out. He pointed in the water ahead.

I saw them, too, a group of beisili frolicking on the surface.

"There's at least five of them."

One of the animals stuck its head up, looking at us. Another pounced in the water close to the first one, and the first one grabbed the second one by the scruff of the neck. The two rolled in the water with a lot of splashing of flippers and tails.

"Oh, they're having a fight," Reida said.

"Mating season," Langga said, his voice dark. His huge eyes scanned the water.

Then another animal surfaced really close to us. The light grey colour made it a female, and it was huge. Its back was heavily ridged, as was the top of its head. A carpet of marine growths grew on its back and neck and the top of its head. Its eye was about the size of my hand, and deep cobalt blue. There were two smaller animals with it, last year's young probably.

Langga let out a loud whistle and cut the engine. The boat floated forward, and he had to steer it to the side to avoid coming too close to the group. The other two boats did the same.

The large female looked at us, then pulled its head under the water and flapped away languidly, not fast enough to let us through, and not deep enough so that we could go over the top.

We followed the animals in the direction of the island.

Reida was mesmerised. He sat in the bow and Sheydu in the other boat kept yelling at him to keep his hands out of the water. He seemed determined to touch one of the animals.

Meanwhile, the skirmishes in the other group continued. There were now three animals threshing and rolling in the water and the mother and two young we were following appeared to be going in that direction. The group was tossing something around. A dead fish, Thayu said.

When we came closer, we saw that it wasn't. It was a body, half-eaten, with bits of dark-coloured clothing still adhering.

Thayu yelled, "Whoa, stop!"

Langga reversed the engine and the boat stopped. The other boats stopped, too. We drifted together again.

"Did you see that?" Thayu asked, her eyes wide. "They're tossing a dead body around."

"They're scavengers," Langga said, as if he witnessed this every day.

I remembered that traditional burials in Barresh involved putting the dead person on a raft made from reeds and pushing it out into the channel. The current would take the raft out to sea, until it sank and nature could reclaim the body. I didn't think too many people still used that type of burial. Maybe the Pengali did. On second thoughts, I was sure it was a keihu custom, not a Pengali one. And the rafts I had seen would never have made it this far out.

I felt sick.

This had to be someone from either Roberts or Melissa's party.

"We should go and look," I said.

Langga gave me an uncertain glance. "They're fighting. They're mating. You don't go near beisili when they're mating."

"We need to know who that is." And we needed to do it quickly, before there was nothing left.

Langga eyed the fighting and jostling group. He called something in Pengali to the other boats. Della replied, and accompanied it with a snap of her tail. Maray waved her tail from side to side, almost hitting Veyada in the face.

"We can go a bit closer," Langga said. "Not much. Maybe you can see. Maybe not." He reversed the engine flow again. The boat moved slowly forward.

The big female we had been trailing stuck its head out of the water, snorting. The two younger ones had gone ahead and were now joining the other group's fighting and jostling. We followed carefully. Langga scanned the water, his big eyes roving. Every muscle in his arms and legs was tense, ready to spring, ready to flip the rudder around, to reverse the boat away.

The group moved away a fraction. We moved closer. They moved away again.

Then the female let out a loud hooting honk, punctuated with clicking sounds. All of a sudden, the other animals stuck their heads out of the water, and then, as one, took off in the direction of the open sea.

The boat with Maray led our convoy to where the group had been. We searched, but found no sign of the body. We brought our three boats together.

I breathed out heavily. "It looks like they took it." I had half expected to find Melissa or Robert, or Gusamo.

A heavy silence followed my words. People nodded, most still searching the glassy surface.

"We need to go ashore," Thayu said. "We can't risk getting stuck out here at night."

"If there is anyone on the island, they should have seen us by now," Nicha said.

Nods all around. We were not that far from the shore. From here, we could just make out an upturned boat and something that looked like a shelter under the trees. The solar panels that we'd seen on the satellite image were gone.

If someone had been alive, and able, they would have run onto the beach, waving their arms.

"Maybe that body was the last survivor," Evi said, his voice dark.

I sighed. "Maybe. But either way, we need to know. We need to bring back evidence, because if nothing else, Nations of Earth is going to ask for it."

We kept going, a lot more subdued, afraid of what we would find.

Thayu stood on the bow, studying the island through her reader. The beach was on the southeastern end, facing the mainland, and the light from the low suns hampered her vision. The island showed up as a black silhouette and, to get any kind of resolution in the shade, she needed to dial the contrast so far down that all lines acquired an aura.

"It's hard to see," she complained. "I think there is something on the top of that rock, and there is also something in the forest. The infrared is useless because all that rock is still radiating heat."

We were already in the shade of the island, gliding into the bay. A second boat became visible on the beach behind the first.

Not a sign of life appeared on the beach.

We came closer and closer. Telaris took his gun from the arm bracket, constantly scanning the forest and the cliffs behind it. The bay was like a mirror and when Langga cut the engine, the boat glided over the shallow water to the beach. The other boat was slightly ahead of us. Veyada jumped into the thigh-deep water, holding the rope to pull the boat up onto the sand.

Then Thayu yelled out, "Action!"

16

———————

VEYADA DROPPED himself in the water. Sheydu, Deyu and Evi dropped as one to the bottom of the boat. A shot flew over the top and hit the water just in front of the bow of our boat.

Splash. A bullet.

Thayu pulled me down. Reida and Telaris also fell between the benches.

I lay, panting, on the hard and disgusting bottom, half in a puddle that stank of rotting fish.

I said, "What the fuck do they think they're doing?"

"They don't want us around," Reida said.

Telaris muttered, "Someone recommend that kid for a prize in logic."

Damn it, I hadn't yet spoken to my association about easing off on teasing Reida.

I carefully rolled onto my back.

Langga sat behind the engine housing, holding the rudder with his tail. If ever I was going to die and come back in a different body, it would have to be one with a tail.

Thayu was using her reader to spy over the boat's side.

"What's happening?"

"I can see Veyada. He's on our side of the boat."

"He's all right?"

"As far as I can see. He's got his gun." That had to be a measure of being all right.

"What about Nicha?"

"I can't see their boat."

"They're behind us," Telaris said. "I think they've already backed away. I can hear an engine."

I heard nothing except the roaring of blood in my ears. What the hell, just what the hell was going on?

"We need to get out of here," Thayu said. "We can go around the point to another beach or something, but it's fast getting dark, but I don't want to fight any Pengali in the dark."

These were likely to be Thousand Islands tribe fighters. Pengali were nocturnal. Of course I had come here with a group of highly trained people, who were also known to have rotten night vision.

"All right." I turned my head to Langga. "Can you reverse the boat from where you're sitting?"

"Not a problem." He opened a little door in the engine casing, where there was a second control panel. He turned a knob which reversed the engine's airflow. Air roared over my head. The boat moved, backwards, I hoped.

After a while, Thayu pushed herself up and I followed her lead.

We had moved a good distance away from the beach.

Veyada had climbed back into the other boat, and he and Sheydu had their guns trained on the shore, probably peering through the sights to spot signs of movement in the infrared scan.

I was glad to see the third boat, with the plane, Della and Nicha, safely with us. Telaris had been right, they had backed away earlier, and Nicha was using his reader to study the beach.

The drivers steered the boats close together.

"See anything?" I asked Nicha.

"There is a little hut to the side. I could see some movement in there for a bit, but it's gone now."

"I'm guessing they're from the Thousand Islands tribe?"

"No," Langga, Della and Maray said at the same time.

"Well," Langga added. "At least not from the settlement. There would have been more of them, and they would have chased us much further."

"How many people do you reckon there are?"

When Pengali shrugged, they flicked their tails. "Hard to tell. There could be one, there could be more." That was a typical Pengali answer.

"But less than there would have been if they were from the settlement?"

"Yah."

But it was getting dark, and whoever was there had the advantage of being hidden and knowing the place, and we did not.

"Change of plan," I said. "We'll go around the point to another beach and we'll camp there. Then we'll figure out what to do tomorrow morn—"

Someone behind us yelled, "Oy!"

I looked over my shoulder. The beisili had returned. There were at least twelve of them, a varied group with dark-coloured males and several large females. They circled our three boats. One stuck a head out of the water, floating closer. Its eyes were deep blue, and the top of its head was so heavily encrusted with growths that it looked like a carpet of thorns. It was a huge, mature animal—female, judging by the light grey colour of the parts of the skin that were visible.

"Get the fuck away from us!" Sheydu yelled.

She had drawn her gun. The animal observed her coolly, blowing out a snorting breath. Then it languidly sank under the water with a couple of lazy flaps of her flippers. Another one swam right behind it. This one was also a female, but much younger. The skin on its back was smooth, with only a few encrustations, and the ridges were only starting to develop. This animal, too, stuck its head out of the water to gawk at us. Its eyes were bright blue.

A third animal rushed up from below. Darker, its back full of growths, male. It tried to push itself in between the two females, who pushed close together. They swam in circles, the females keeping together, the male jostling, coming really close to our boats.

Langga shouted something in Pengali to the others. Della had already started the engine.

And all of a sudden, the male jumped half out of the water, on top of the younger female. The big female seized him by his neck and pulled him over the top of her, into a roll. Tails and flippers cast a wide spray of water. They went under, came back up in a tangle of tails and bodies and necks. They rolled around, coming perilously close to the boat with Sheydu and Veyada. Maray was frantically trying to start the engine on their boat.

The female honked. She had him in a death grip, holding him so tightly with her flippers that they almost vanished in the soft rolls of flesh on his underside. He threshed in the water, letting out a squeal. A cloud of red bloomed.

The other animals joined, threshing tails and flippers. The water became a boiling pool of froth.

And then the fight stopped as suddenly as it had begun, and the beisili all bobbed up, skimming the froth off the water, slurping and licking, and smacking their mouths.

"What the hell?"

Langga stood staring at the animals. The engine was running, and we were slowly drifting back from the group.

"Beisili mating," he said. "Few people ever see this."

Holy crap.

I went back through the events. The two females, mother and daughter, the male showing an interest in the daughter, but the mother got jealous and claimed him for herself. Was that how it went? And the red stuff was not blood but sperm, which they also considered a delicacy?

Ew, seriously.

The boats started making their way around the point at the end of the beach where sheer cliffs met the ocean. Both suns were now under the horizon and the sky above turned purple and dark green.

"These beisili, they will be a problem for us," Langga continued. "This is their territory. The male wants the young female, but the older female won't let him have her. The longer the fight goes on, the more beisili will come, and the more they will mate. The seed attracts others, and it attracts fish and can even bring eels out here."

For now, the sea was deceptively quiet.

The beach around the corner wasn't a beach as much as a collection of boulders at the bottom of a cliff. It was utterly unsuitable for going ashore. We threw out anchors and tied the boats together into a large platform.

The shore was close enough, but not even the Pengali were keen to get into the water to check it out. Beyond the boulders was a narrow section of dense shrubbery and behind that the solid, inhospitable cliff face, with not as much as a tiny ledge to climb it.

The stone looked like a type of granite, and rainwater and algae had painted dark and lighter stripes across the vertical face. The only vegetation that grew on it was at the very top.

By the last of the dying daylight, we unpacked some of our supplies and ate bread and fruit. We filled up the space between the benches with bags and rolled out our mats over the top. There wasn't nearly enough space, especially for Evi and Telaris.

We tied the oiled cloth over the top, held up by the engine housing, in case it rained, and it looked like it might.

We gathered in Maray's boat by the eerie green glow of a pearl light that Thayu had brought.

It was a group of miserable-looking faces.

"Well," I said. "That changes things a bit. Anyone got a clue about what's going on and what we should do tomorrow?"

"We should try to approach the beach from another side," Sheydu said.

"*Is* there an approach from any other side?" Nicha asked. "I mean . . . look at these cliffs."

Thayu was studying a generated 3D image of the island on her reader. The bluish light lit her face from below. "The western side of the island looks a bit more accessible. There is another beach on that side, and the cliffs are lower and less solid."

"Is it a real beach in the way this here is not a beach?" Reida said, gesturing at the boulders.

"The map isn't that detailed, so yes, maybe, or maybe not."

"That side of the island is exposed to the ocean," Langga said. "It will be a lot harder to stay close."

"We can use the plane," Veyada said.

"Yes, we can," Sheydu said. "But first of all, we need to figure out what we're doing. Simply said: we need to know how many people with guns there are and whether we care if we kill them."

Trust Sheydu to make a blunt remark.

"What we really need to know: this Robert guy of yours," —she looked at me— "was he the one at the end of that gun, or was it someone else?"

I would have loved to be able to say that it would be someone else, but I remembered those pictures of Robert and his wife at the gun show. That splash in the water had been created by a projectile, not a discharge. Pengali sometimes used darts, but our drivers would have known if Pengali were involved.

It *did* look like it was Robert. But why send us a help note and then pick off any help that came?

Margarethe said that she wanted him returned to Earth, but was the reason that he was a wanted criminal? But if so, she could have told me that, couldn't she?

I didn't know. I wish I had a better idea.

Thayu said, "Whoever it is, I am reasonably sure that there are not many people involved. The problem is, as we've already established, accessibility. The easiest, dare I say the only, route of access to the camp is via the bay, where this person can see us coming from a long way off."

"And which is infested with violently amorous creatures," Sheydu added, her voice dark. She was looking at the water lapping at the sides of the boat as if it were poison.

"That, too. If we use the plane, we can make a very quick approach, but I still suspect the beach is the only point of entry. We can use it only once, because once he knows we have a plane, we've lost the element of surprise. He—or whoever it is—has dug into an exceptionally defendable spot. We are likely a majority, but we're not sure, and we don't know what weapons he has."

I said, "What about Melissa?"

"No idea. Her boat is here, that's all I can say."

I shivered at the thought of the macabre sight of the beisili tossing a body around. "What I mean is that if anyone is being kept prisoner in that hut, then the sight of us might well propel the captives into doing something."

"Yes. But we don't know. And 'doing something' could hinder us as well as help us."

True.

The fact remained that we knew nothing.

It was decided that we would try to see what the other beach was like. The island was tiny and as soon as daylight came, we would pull up the anchors and go around the other way. If the beach there was more promising, we would set up camp there.

Maray suggested waiting a few days so that they might think we'd gone, but that would never work. Whoever had shot at us would know who we were and would know that we were there for Melissa and wouldn't leave until we had her.

The light was starting to attract various winged creatures that flapped and fluttered around, annoying Sheydu in particular. When a big ringgit-like creature fluttered around with a *frrrrrrrtt* and landed on the light, we decided enough was enough. Della grabbed the thing by the wings and whacked it against the side of the boat. Its body was almost longer than her hand. Thayu switched the light off.

We stumbled around in the dark to find our mats. I took off my pants because it was too hot and airless under the low canopy of the oiled cloth, but either imagined or real insects kept crawling over my skin, so I had to put my pants back on, disgusting as they were.

The water was calm, but not entirely still. With each ripple, I imagined beisili lurking underneath us, ready to resurface for another display of mating rituals.

But I was tired, having slept poorly the previous night, so I dozed off for a good proportion of the night.

I woke up when the palest of pale glimmers of daylight coloured the eastern sky. Something splashed in the water nearby.

It was Langga pulling in his fishing line and throwing the catch—jumping and flopping—onto the bottom of the boat.

Maray said something in Pengali in the other boat. She came over, silhouetted against the lightening sky, holding something large and spiky. Langga laughed his snorting Pengali laugh. This was followed by a snap-snap-snap sound of something breaking.

By the time everyone was awake, and the sky in the east had turned pink, the three Pengali were cooking breakfast on the solar heater, using seawater and something from a small bottle. I had a look in the pot, and it was filled with froth. The raw fish yesterday had been good, but I wasn't sure about this.

Neither, by the look of things, was Sheydu.

Reida wanted to know what was in the pot, and Langga fished out a—well, whatever it was. A big, brown thing with a lumpy surface and a couple of stumps where I figured he must have snapped off the creature's legs. He took his knife out of his belt. He cut the lumpy, rubbery shell, peeled it open and scooped the white greasy-looking contents into the pot, and tossed the skin overboard.

Ew. It looked like I'd be sticking to a vegetarian diet today.

He declared breakfast ready.

Maray and Della had been hovering around and attacked straight away. Langga offered some to us—a white soup in a bowl, with bits of froth still floating on top.

The look of revulsion on Deyu's face made everyone laugh, but only Reida was game to try some. He pulled an 'eh' face, but finished all of it. Langga clapped him on the shoulder. It struck me that Reida was the only one of us who had any kind of relationship with these people. They even seemed to find it hard to tell the difference between the Coldi, saying "him" when they meant Thayu or "her" when talking about Veyada.

The Pengali polished off the rest of the soup while we ate the by-now slightly stale nut bread.

Then it was time to go. We untied the boats, pulled up the anchors and set off in a northerly direction. The sheer cliffs continued on the other side of the "beach" that wasn't. We drifted past the granite walls with their patterns of algae. The island was utterly hostile, uninhabited and inaccessible.

Langga had been right about the ocean side being more exposed. The wind picked up and the waves got choppy, casting sprays of salt into our faces.

We rounded a rocky point to the bay in question, and there was a white beach—and big pounding waves breaking on the sand. Our boats were far too low and cumbersome to handle surf. We'd be smashed against the rocks if we came too close.

Crap.

But it was better than the other side.

We threw out anchors and Thayu, Reida and I used the tops of the benches—that we had removed to make room to sleep last night—as surfboards, and paddled ashore. Thayu trailed a waterproof box with all our weapons.

The water wasn't deep, the bottom was firm and I suspected that once the tide went out, we'd be able to pull the boats in from the shore.

We dragged our makeshift surfboards onto the beach, where Thayu handed out the weapons and equipment.

The beach was fairly wide and ended abruptly at a thick wall of forest.

At the boundary between the beach and the forest, we found the remains of a camp. A pile of ash from a camp fire—because you could make fires away from the areas where megon trees grew—a couple of fish skeletons, and a jar.

Just like the one we had found on the beach at the sand bar.

Shit.

I looked at the sea where the boats lay anchored.

"What is it?" Thayu asked.

"Look at this." I showed her the jar.

"The same as we found."

"Yes. Someone camped here. Is there a current here that would take floating things to the mainland?"

"Maybe. We can ask. The wind would carry anything that floats to the spit."

I nodded, still looking at the makeshift camp as we continued into the forest.

The vegetation grew incredibly dense. Reida used his knife to cut a path for us, going uphill.

In the claustrophobic greenery, it was humid and hot. I was helping Reida pull aside vines and other vegetation, and the sweat was soon rolling off me.

Then we got to the bottom of a giant rounded boulder. Reida climbed up like a goat, but I couldn't manage it until Thayu leaned a tree trunk against the rock to use as a stepping stone.

Whoa, the sun beat down here.

We climbed the rough granite surface. Behind us was the bay and the ocean, with our boats bobbing at the point. I could even see someone moving. Of course, the Pengali were fishing again.

At the top, the rounded surface fell away suddenly, as if the giant boulder had split when falling from the sky. One half had sunk into the depths and the other made up most of this island. It was exposed and windy here.

We dropped to our bellies and crawled the last bit until we could see over the other side, down a sheer cliff, over the bay, the beach and the forest.

A man walked on the beach directly below us, carrying a net with several of the brown lumpy, bristly things that Langga had caught for breakfast this morning. He carried a gun slung over his shoulder. He wore shorts and a shirt. His skin was pale, his hair brown. He had a beard.

Robert Davidson.

He turned around and yelled at someone in the shade of the trees out of our vision. It was impossible to hear what he said. I was also pretty sure that he hadn't seen us, and he wasn't looking in our direction. He disappeared underneath the trees at the bottom of the cliff.

So we could see the beach from up here, but there didn't seem to be an easy way down. Bugger. That meant we would have to use the plane. Maybe the plane and the boats, coming from different directions at the same time. He had at least one accomplice.

I let myself slide back down the rock. Thayu and Reida followed.

"So it was him," Thayu said. "What is his game? If he wants to be rescued, then why shoot at us?"

"I wish I knew."

But we had to do something quickly, because I really didn't want to have to spend another night here.

We walked down the giant boulder, the last bit of it sliding on our backsides, used the tree trunk to climb back to the forest and followed the path we had made. Thayu went first, Reida next and I came last.

And all of a sudden, Reida gave a surprised squeak and disappeared into the moss-covered ground. A dark hole had opened up in the path where the soil had given way.

I yelled into the hole, "Reida! Are you down there?"

There was no reply.

17

———————

SHIT.

I fell to my knees and clawed at the ground, pulling rocks out of the opening.

It was deep and dark and sounded hollow.

Did I hear splashing? Had he fallen in the water and was he now unconscious and drowning in an underground pool?

"Reida!"

My voice echoed in there, and I realised immediately that I'd made a mistake and might have given away our position.

Crap. But I had to go after him.

"Give me the rope."

I yanked it off Thayu's shoulder, tied it to a tree, then around my waist and let myself sink into the hole. The entrance was narrow and little avalanches of dirt trickled into my face and down my neck.

The ground crumbled away under my feet.

In a moment of panic, I fell a short distance until the rope yanked taut—ouch—and dangled in nothingness.

Shit. How far down was it?

I pulled the gun from the arm bracket and used the infrared sight. There was a lighter patch to my right—if only I stopped spinning around—but no sign of a person. The patch bubbled and swirled. Possibly a warm spring. How deep was it? It was hard to tell.

"You're OK?" Thayu called above me.

"Yeah. There's a big cave down here. I think there's water at the bottom. I can't see a sign of him. I can't go any further. The rope is too short."

"I'll pull you up."

"Wait."

My eyes were starting to become used to the ink darkness. There was a glimmer of light in the bottom right corner: an exit to the beach? Which beach?

"All right?" Thayu called.

"Yeah."

The rope shuddered and I went up. Then someone down in the depth of the cave yelled, "Hey, keep your hands off me. I'll go and do what you say, just point that thing somewhere else, all right?" That was Reida.

A man replied. Robert, perhaps. It was definitely not a Coldi voice.

I entered the narrow hole in the ceiling of the cave, and Thayu helped me clamber out.

"There is an exit to the beach on the other side," I said. "Reida fell down there and Robert has him. There is water in the cave. He must have been dazed and his gun wet."

What a bugger of a thing to have happen to him, and us. Now Robert knew we were here, and he'd be expecting us. Well, to be honest, he probably expected us already.

"We need to talk to the others," I said. "See what we can do."

"Better hurry up. We don't have much time left in the day."

We started walking down the path that we had made on the way up. The beach was already bathed in rich afternoon sunlight. Beniz and Yaza had long passed their midday zenith, but were still bright enough to appear as one spot of light. They were close at this time of the month, and the double edges on the shadows almost invisible.

We dragged the makeshift surfboards into the water. I stacked Reida's onto mine, and we paddled back out to the boats, where Veyada and Telaris helped us board. Deyu looked on with wide eyes.

"Where is Reida?" she exclaimed.

We told them about what happened.

Deyu's eyes widened even further. "We have to get him!"

"Yes, but we couldn't do that with just the two of us. We came back to get you. It's time to move. We don't have a lot of supplies to stay out here. There is fresh water in the cave, but we don't have any here. We'll move this afternoon."

"We can attack from two sides," Veyada said. "We should use the plane to fly into the bay, the boats can follow us and the main party can go through the cave."

Langga pulled a face.

"What?" I asked him.

"Beisili. A big group of them went around the point while you were out there."

"They didn't harm us yesterday," Veyada said.

"That was only the beginning of their mating time. It was a little game."

Sheydu said, "A game? They nearly flipped us over."

Maray nodded, her face grave. "That area around the corner is a mating bay. They will all come together there and have a big mating orgy and the beach will turn foul with foam. I don't like taking the boats in there today. I'll refuse to go in tomorrow."

"Can we land the plane on the beach?" Veyada asked.

Thayu thought for a bit. "It's a bit short, and there is not much of an approach, but yeah, probably. It would be rough."

"Let's do that, then."

We agreed that the Pengali would take the boats further out to the point, throw out the anchor and wait in case of an emergency. Thayu said she would set up the satellite communication for them.

The people who were good at hand-to-hand fighting would go through the cave. This included Evi and Telaris, Sheydu and Deyu. We took all of the heavy weaponry out of the boat for them, as well as armour, ropes and temperature suits, since their task might involve waiting in a damp and cold cave.

This was the heavy-duty group. Robert would expect an attack from that direction.

Thayu, Veyada, Nicha and I would take the plane to land on the beach and provide a surprise.

I said, "You're sure you don't want me to go with the other group? I'm not a sharpshooter like you." Although I would probably get in the way of the others. Maybe they were sparing me because of my recent stay in hospital.

"Normally, you're not a sharpshooter," Veyada said. "Except when someone holds a gun to your head. In that case, you develop into the best sharpshooter ever. That's a valuable ability, to deliver under extreme pressure. You can teach that, but it's much easier when it's inborn."

"Well . . ." I wasn't sure what to say to that. That was a very high expectation to have resting on your shoulders: this guy is our secret weapon in an emergency. I think I was happier with the "too weak" and "gets in the way of good fights" tags, because you know, that thing where I'd accidentally hit my target in an emergency, I wasn't sure how replicable that was.

We went to work to put the plane together. The tide was going out and the waves had become small enough for us to drag the boats onto the beach.

Thayu set up a whole bunch of solar chargers and transmitters on the sand. While she bustled around, contacting people and sending reports, we pulled the cover off the plane, and lifted the frame out of the boat. We inserted the struts for the wings, pulled the cloth over the top, attached the solar sails. Then we put the seats in. Thayu wanted the ski-like undercarriage. We put that together, set it on the sand and lifted the plane on and tightened all the bolts.

Then we pulled it to the high tide line, facing the slope of the beach. The skis were wide and slid easily over the sand. Thayu seemed happy.

"Just leave it at the top there, and we'll be able to slide right into the water."

Then we helped the other group get their combat gear out of the boats. It made a compact but very heavy pile on the sand.

We distributed the heavy items over the number of packs that were small enough for cave-crawling. Sheydu had to leave the solar charger. She was not happy about that.

She stated, "There are two things that you can never have enough of in a fight: energy and weapons."

I agreed, but we were also faced with a distinct lack of space and a limit on what everyone could carry and still have enough freedom of movement for a fight.

Finally Sheydu was satisfied. She had put on her temperature-retaining suit, which others had done, too, except Evi and Telaris.

Armour went over the top. Not the civilian grade which I wore, and still found much too hot, but military grade. She shouldered the pack and others did, too. The gun brackets went on both arms. Her belt with pouches containing explosives went around her waist. Deyu shouldered the ropes while Telaris carried two mounted guns and their mounts and a camouflage net, which was a very nifty thing that, when turned on, produced a light-bending field the same way the surface of most Asto-produced aircraft did.

Sheydu then clasped Veyada's arm and clapped his back, one of the few times that I'd seen them display any sign that they were mother and son.

Then they set off into the forest. The last thing I saw was the bobbing coils of rope on Deyu's back.

Next, we took our weapons from the boat: the mounted gun for Veyada, Thayu's arsenal of secret weapons. She gave me a knife with a belt to wear under my shirt, and a handful of her marvellous emergency blasters to go in my pockets. "Keep these ones handy. They will work when they're wet."

I put them in the pockets of my jacket.

Then it was time for us to go. First we pushed the boats back through the surf, so that the Pengali could take them to the point. The wind had strengthened and the waves had come up alarmingly. From where we were on the western side of the island, our view of the eastern sky and the escarpment where thunderclouds formed was blocked by cliffs. But it was the time of day for thunderstorms, and we were coming into the part of the year that they rolled in from the east almost every day.

I trusted that Thayu had checked the weather when consulting with her people in the city through the satellite.

She climbed behind the controls. Veyada and I each grabbed one of the plane's side struts and Nicha the tail. We pushed the plane over the sand towards the water. A wave broke just in front of us and washed us back up the beach. We all got very wet.

"Whoa, are you sure this is a good idea?" I asked her. "The sand would be easier."

"Yeah, but I want to conserve the charge." To take off from the sand, the engine would be blowing sharp jets of air out of a mesh of little holes at the bottom of the landing gear.

"Try again," Veyada said.

We pushed. A wave broke over our feet and dragged the plane down the beach into the water. It tilted sideways a bit.

"Jump on," Veyada said.

I did. Nicha swung himself up, dangling from the tail. Another wave broke. A churning mass of foam and sand washed over my feet and bottom half of my pants. Thayu gunned the engine.

Veyada yelled, "Hang on!"

We hit a third breaking wave.

The plane's nose went into the air. Oh fuck, we were going to flip. We were— The engine roared right next to my ears. I held on, oh, holy crap, I hung on. The plane became airborne. It flew low over the breakers and landed gently on the choppy surface on the other side.

We clambered in. I was shivering.

"Holy shit, Thayu. Were you trying to drown us?"

She was fiddling with the instruments. "Nah. I knew those *surfing* lessons would come in handy one day. Sit down, put the seat belts on. It could get rough."

"No kidding." Crap, why did I always get myself into these situations?

Veyada, Nicha and I strapped in. I was half-sweaty, half-wet, but it was hot and airless in the plane, and the air smelled strongly of resin. Veyada insisted on sitting next to the open door.

While Thayu steered the plane to the relative shelter of the shallow reef on the southern end of the beach, watched by the Pengali in the boats motoring out to the point, Veyada proceeded to open his gun case and took out the stand. He bolted the legs onto the back of the pilot's seat and then the main barrel onto the pivoting stand.

All this while the plane gathered speed, bumped over the water and finally took off.

We quickly cleared the lump of rock that had been at our backs and had a wide view of the coast. The eastern sky was black with a giant thundercloud.

"Thay', look at the weather."

"I know," she said, her tone laconic. "Once this is done, no one is going to go anywhere for a while, so we might as well do it now."

We circled the point, without coming into view of the beach.

There were the three boats making their way across the choppy water to the point. We couldn't see the other group in the thick forest.

"Look," Veyada said and pointed.

I looked.

While we couldn't see the beach where Robert was from here, we could see part of the bay. It was full of large, light and dark grey shapes. Beisili. Hundreds of them.

"Holy shit!" Nicha said. "How many of those fucking creatures are there?"

"They probably feel bad weather," Veyada said. "They come to shelter."

I needed to ask him one day where he had lived, because Veyada always gave the impression of having a far wider knowledge of wildlife than a Coldi on Asto would have.

At a couple of spots, fights had broken out between the animals. Flecks of pink-white foam dotted the water. All right, I saw what Langga meant.

From above, I spotted a couple of familiar shapes: the very large female with the younger female swimming very close and the dark grey male pushing the large female aside. Wasn't he just like a leery old man chasing after that young virgin?

We followed the rocky contour of the island to the highest point, a weather-blown, treeless crop of granite without a sign of human habitation. I had no doubt that Pengali would have been there at some point, but they had a habit of not leaving evidence of their presence. On the other side of the top, the ground fell away quickly to the cliffs we had sailed around this morning. The island was really tiny, with only two beaches.

Thayu appeared to be waiting for something, so when we were on the northern side of the island, she banked the plane in a sharp turn, and I had a dizzying view of the emerald waters and sheer cliffs.

But I didn't like those dark clouds.

A flash of lightning bloomed inside the billowing masses. Already, it was raining at the escarpment, veils of grey reaching down from the clouds.

Thayu said something into the microphone. And then, "All right. They're all in the cave. We're going in."

We had to approach the beach from over the southwestern point of the island where the Pengali waited with our boats. I could see them bobbing on the surface. They had taken down the cloth shelters, probably because they caught too much wind.

Then we passed really low over the headland at a crazy speed.

"Whoa. Too much tail wind," Thayu said.

She pulled the plane up, just missing the rocks at the northern end of the beach—or at least that was what it felt like to me—and made another sharp turn. I grabbed the edges of my seat with sweaty hands.

The plane barely straightened out before the gliders hit the sand. A vicious hissing noise indicated that the air jets blasted at full tilt.

The plane slid to a halt. Veyada took the gun off its mount and jumped into the sand.

"Look at that," Nicha said. "We have half a beach left to spare."

Thayu wiped her face. She picked up her weapons and arm brackets from the empty pilot's seat next to her and put them on.

Oh no, that had not been the way she had planned to land. For one, the nose was facing the wrong direction and we would need to turn the plane around first before we could make a quick exit if that proved necessary.

In the bay we were out of the influence of the squalls of wind that made the sea at the point choppy. The movement of the water also helped whip up the frothing foam from the beisili's mating, which washed up onto the beach in big rafts, as if someone had dropped a bottle of detergent in the water.

The animals themselves were still at it, carrying on and squealing and honking. Most of the action was a fair distance from the shore and the squally wind carried snatches of noise to the beach.

Nicha was watching the makeshift shelter under the trees, an oiled cloth strung between a couple of tree trunks. I could see a variety of containers and something that looked like a table. The boats were also there, but one had been moved much closer to the water. The drag marks in the sand were fresh.

"Where is everyone?" Nicha asked. He peeked around the side of the plane, his gun at the ready.

"They're likely to be wherever that cave comes out," Thayu said. She glanced up at the cliff face behind the camp, but it was impossible to see where we had looked down this morning. It might even be further up. I didn't think we could see this part of the beach from up there.

"Come on!" Thayu took off across the beach.

Nicha and Veyada followed her and I trailed along.

Thayu arrived at the edge of the forest, and urged us to join her.

We ploughed our way through the sand over the exposed beach to the forest's edge.

"We're being watched," Thayu said, showing me her screen. It clearly displayed two human forms in the shelter.

"They're behind those containers," Thayu said.

"I can give them a warning blast." Veyada motioned with the gun. "We might be out of their range, but they're not out of ours."

"I don't think we're out of theirs either," Thayu said. "I don't want to take any chances. We don't know who they are."

We kept walking along the forest's edge, guns in hand. The shelter was primitive, consisting of just an oiled cloth, flapping in the wind. Something moved inside.

"Stop," Veyada said.

We did. A person ran out of the shelter in our direction. It was a woman, yelling, "Cory! Cory! Don't shoot!" It was Melissa.

The next moment, a gunshot echoed over the beach from inside the shelter.

For a brief, terrible moment, Melissa froze in mid-air. Then she fell face first in the sand.

18

N O. SHIT.

Melissa lay in the sand with her head facing down the beach. A red stain bloomed on her back below her right shoulder.

Shit. Melissa. I stared at her motionless form, my heart beating like crazy, blood roaring in my ears. Was she breathing? I thought so. Or maybe not. I couldn't tell.

The shooter used an Earth-style hunting rifle with bullets. That had to be Robert. What the hell was wrong with him? "We have to help her."

I made to get up, but Thayu held me back. "Stay here. He'll shoot you as well."

"But . . . Melissa!"

"Let's flush him out." Veyada extracted a device from his pocket.

I asked, "Does the cave come out in the shelter or somewhere else? Where are the others?"

"Inside," Thayu said. "They descended into the cave, met with some trouble and are still inside."

"Trouble? None that Sheydu can't solve?"

"She's waiting for the right moment. The guy shut a metal door on them and they're locked inside the cave. She's got the gear to blow it up, but we need to time our actions well. We get one shot at this. She says the ceiling of the cave may collapse, causing further problems.

Besides, the guy is extremely dangerous, armed to the teeth with equipment that we're unfamiliar with and highly trained to use it."

I could kick myself. The signs had been there in all the information I had about Robert. Yet I had so desperately wanted to believe that he'd been an innocent victim of some sort of scheme designed by Clovis and company to divest rich men of their money. But I should have known that rich people are rarely rich because they are dumb.

"All right, then, can we at least get to Melissa?" I couldn't stand the sight of her lying on the beach like a discarded doll. It had started to rain, big fat drops that made little plop-plop noises when they fell.

Thayu shook her head. "Not yet. Too dangerous."

"Do something, then."

She could be slowly dying of her wounds down there. Something we could do might save her, if we got the opportunity to do it.

"We're working on it," Thayu said.

It took far too long for my liking. The rain became heavier. Big drops of water fell from the trees above us. Thayu was talking to the others, then she complained about the reception. Then she said that the receiver was no longer charging. There was no sunlight on the other beach where the transmitter stood, and the equipment might even have blown over.

I'm losing reception. It is now or never, she sent to Sheydu.

"I don't like it," Nicha said. "Too much stuff doesn't work in this weather."

"We don't have any other time. Let's go."

Veyada took a little device from his pocket.

He clicked it on and his voice was amplified over the beach. "Anyone in the shelter, come out immediately. We will shoot."

A man yelled inside the shelter, I couldn't hear what was said. The next thing, a couple of people ran out and a giant explosion rocked the ground. A spray of rocks, wood and other things burst out from underneath the shelter.

A strange hissing noise approached from behind us.

I looked over my shoulder, but saw only trees. "Veyada, what's tha—"

The heavens opened. Big fat drops fell from the sky as if someone had turned on a shower at full blast. A clap of thunder made the ground shake. The air turned misty, obscuring our view of the shelter.

Veyada had dropped to his belly and was firing at that end of the beach, wiping rain out of his face. Raindrops hissed where they fell on the barrel of the gun. The discharge beams flew, sizzling, through the rain, producing flashes where they met raindrops. I looked over his shoulder at the infrared screen, but could not make out anything shaped like a person.

After a while, he stopped firing. "I think they're all out." He carefully got to his feet.

A few people had taken cover behind some trees closer to the shelter. From our position, we could see their backs. I only recognised Deyu because she was still carrying the rope over her shoulder.

In the pissing rain, one person ran to Melissa and dropped to his knees next to her. He set a box down on the sand and moved her shirt up.

That looked like Telaris with the emergency kit, thank the heavens. If anyone could help her, he could.

"Look, there," Thayu yelled.

Two people were moving across the beach, one holding a gun to the other person's head.

Veyada turned his gun on them.

"Who is it?" I asked.

"Robert."

"Who has he got?" Thayu said, wiping water out of her eyes.

Lightning cracked and struck somewhere really close. I winced and ducked my head. The ground shook with the clap of thunder that echoed through the bay. Holy shit.

The rain intensified. I didn't think that was possible.

"I think it's Reida," Veyada said. He was wiping water out of his face.

"What's he doing?"

"He's making for that boat. Damn it, I'm out of charge." He wriggled his recharge pouch from his belt, opened the pearl chamber in the gun and shook the spent pearls onto the sand. They hissed when drops hit them.

"Look at the bay," Thayu said.

The part of it I could see before it disappeared in the pelting rain was covered in pink foam. There were at least three beisili fights in that area, globs of foam flying through the air. The sound of the honking females carried even over the roar of the weather.

Veyada swore.

He had reloaded the large gun, but now Robert and Reida had arrived at the boat and Veyada couldn't blow up the boat without hitting them. I presumed that had been his intention. He was out of reliable range for Nicha and Thayu's guns, even mine, and the others couldn't see him, and we couldn't warn them.

Thayu jumped up and started running towards the pair.

Robert forced Reida into the boat. Then he went to the controls and started the engine with a roar that rose over the noise of the rain. Another clap of thunder broke nearby.

Thayu ran past Telaris and Melissa. She yelled something. Some others also started running. Deyu, Nicha, Veyada.

The engine roared again. He was nuts to go out in these conditions. The water was hardly visible, let alone all the beisili in it. But the boat moved off the sand onto the water, where it quickly gathered speed.

Thayu reached the spot where the boat had been, followed by a couple of others. None of them could do anything about the retreating boat. It ploughed through thick layers of foam, until the boat was pushing so much of it ahead of the bow that the buildup started to spill over the sides. Robert slowed down, yelling at Reida, who bailed foam out of the boat with his hands. But there was far too much of it. Foam spilled over the sides and over the engine housing. The engine stalled. Robert took off his shirt to wipe the air inlets clean.

A beisili raised its head nearly. It was wearing a little cap of foam like snow on its head. Then another one came up. One, a big female bent her neck and nudged the boat. Robert raised his gun.

Bang

A couple of other animals bobbed up.

Robert fired again.

Bang, bang.

But that only brought more animals to the boat. They jostled through the mass of foam, tails and flippers threshing. The boat rocked. Robert lost his balance and stumbled. Reida seized the opportunity and flew up from the bench. He hit Robert on the side of the head.

Robert went down. I'd heard Coldi crack skulls that way.

The beisili were carrying on and fighting, occasionally upsetting the boat.

Reida had to hang onto the side. It was rocking violently, embroiled in a boiling patch of beisili activity. Huge rafts of foam heaped up against the sides, and spilled over into the boat. The wind whipped some of it into Reida's face.

Robert raised himself. He aimed his gun . . .

"Reida, watch out!" My voice drowned in the sound of pelting rain and thunder.

Veyada raised the big gun.

Deyu yelled, "No, don't!"

And Reida leapt onto the edge of the boat and . . . jumped out. He plunged into the foam. Robert was firing indiscriminately into the water. Then he ran out of ammunition.

Could Reida swim? I had no idea.

"Reida!"

Shit, we had to get the other boat on the water.

Deyu and Nicha had already turned it over and were running down the beach with it.

Reida rose back up out of the foam. His head and shoulders stuck out of it as if he was standing in shallow water. He . . . moved. Holy crap, he had jumped onto the back of a beisili. The animal rolled on its side, waving its flippers around to try and get this thing off its back. Reida slid forward until he could grab the animal's neck. It rolled and threshed in the water, but Reida held on to the neck as hard as he could.

Meanwhile, Robert had reloaded his gun. He raised it—

Thayu shot at him.

The white sizzling beam missed by a hair's width.

Robert stumbled back and fell in the boat. He scrambled to the engine and, like Langga had done, opened the panel at the back to control it that way.

The engine roared.

Veyada aimed his gun, but didn't fire.

A moment later, Robert's boat had disappeared in the mist and pouring rain.

What the hell? I burst out, "What's wrong with you? Why didn't you shoot him? You had a hundred opportunities to do it."

Both Veyada and Thayu looked at me. Thayu said, "Because the *president* told you to bring him alive."

And it would never do for them to get me into trouble with the president.

Shit. That was how loyal Coldi were, and I still managed to forget it. And yes, Margarethe had said that, and I had assumed that this was for a very different reason: because if Robert died on this illegal holiday, there would be trouble for her, because Fiona Davidson was an innocent victim. As it turned out, the trouble was way more complicated than she had been able to divulge over the open link of the Exchange. She wanted Robert Davidson alive, so that he could be questioned and convicted.

And I assumed that, given the choice, even she had rather that he died than that he escaped our clutches. I had simply forgotten to update my orders last night.

Shit, shit, shit.

"He won't get far," Veyada said. "His boat will be full of water long before he reaches the city."

But this man was smart and dangerous, and had already been responsible for the deaths of a number of people. Where, for example, were all of Melissa's crew?

I left the shelter of the trees since there was no point staying either for safety or against the rain. I was soaked. Deyu and Nicha were just coming back with Reida, who was completely covered in foam.

I ran to check Telaris who was still with Melissa. He had rolled her onto her side and had bandaged up her right shoulder and upper body.

"Fortunately, it doesn't seem to have hit anything too damaging," he said. "The projectile is still inside. I'm not game to touch it, but I've given her a sedative to keep her quiet. She should be taken to the hospital as soon as possible."

"Yeah," I said. I was shivering. Water was running through my underwear. The sky was deep grey. I couldn't even see the plane at the other side of the beach, let alone imagine that someone would fly it.

Thayu said, "The transmitter charge is completely flat. We need sunlight to charge it. We probably need to go back to the other beach to put the charger back in the right position."

"Do we have enough charge in the plane to do that?"

"Yeah. But I'm not going to fly in this weather."

Fair enough.

"Where are our boats? We should warn them that Robert has escaped."

"They're not going to want to come into the bay in this weather."

True, too.

"At least let's get Melissa out of the rain."

Telaris had already shoved the camouflage netting under her. He and Thayu picked up both ends, forming it into a hammock, and carried Melissa up the beach.

In the shelter, it wasn't much drier than on the beach, so Thayu and Telaris continued into the cave. The back half of the oiled cloth had blown loose. In the mess of pots and jars and cooking and other survival debris, I found a travel bag with a luggage tag.

I turned the tag over. In neat letters was written an address in Jakarta.

Shit. That would have belonged to the missing Indonesian businessman Gusamo Sahardjo. I thought of the body we'd seen the beisili throw around.

Had Robert shot his co-traveller, too?

What was going on inside this guy's sick head?

I scratched my head, staring at the bag.

"What's that?" Thayu asked.

I showed her and told her about the other person on the surfing trip. "Have you seen any other survivors?"

She shook her head. "I don't get what his game is and why someone would do this. This is up to you to explain. I'm out of my depth."

"I don't understand it either. He's flipped, or something. How is Melissa?"

"Sleeping."

"Where is Robert going to go?"

"In this weather, most likely the Thousand Islands tribe," Telaris said, coming up behind Thayu. "Or that is where I would go."

Well, damn it, this Robert Davidson was one slippery character.

"Was he the only one here? No accomplices?"

"He had two helpers, but we dealt with them in the cave."

Nicha came into the shelter with Reida, who was pale, covered in disgusting foam and soaked to the bone. But his eyes shone.

"He got away, but did you see me ride a beisili?"

Thayu said, "I saw a beisili trying very hard to throw someone off its back."

He grinned.

"You know what Pengali do, right?" Veyada said. "To stop the beisili diving, they stick seeds in its nostrils so it can't close them and it can't dive. The problem is steering them because the beisili just heads to the nearest beach to rub the seeds out of its face."

"I didn't happen to have any seeds on me," Reida said.

"I'm bitterly disappointed," Veyada said.

Reida grinned. Veyada gave him a bone-shattering clap on the shoulder.

"What are we going to do now?" Sheydu said.

I asked, "Is there anything we can do besides wait for this weather to stop?"

No one made any suggestions.

So we investigated everything in the shelter, in the burned-out remains of what looked like a well-appointed field station at the mouth of the cave. Someone had evened the floor and made tables out of driftwood, on which stood flat trays, some filled with dirt. The next cavern contained drums with water, a solar power generator—off—a supply of light pearls—all flat—and a portable charger. There were a couple of guns, including some Asto-made ones. A pile of empty cans and jars stood against the wall, some still with bits of food in the bottom.

"It looks like he's been holding out here for a while."

Telaris and Thayu put Melissa down on a clean sheet on one of the mattresses against the back wall.

She was breathing, although shallowly.

"Any medicines?" I asked.

"I haven't found any yet," Telaris said.

"Is there a lot more to this cave system?"

"There is another room next door," Sheydu said.

"The main cave is quite amazing," Evi said.

"If you discount the bodies on the floor," Deyu said.

We left Melissa in peace and went further into the cave. At the end of the passage shards of metal had peeled back from what had been the metal door.

I looked inside.

Evi was right; the cave was nice. Being formed out of granite, there were no stalactites or other rock formations, but salt had leaked through cracks in the rock and had formed great encrustations of coloured crystals on the walls.

Three bodies lay on the ground, one half in the pool. Two were Pengali, both well dressed in leather and resin armour. I'd never seen that type before. The gear hadn't been sufficient to save their lives. Both were female. The third person was a keihu youth, dressed in the traditional khaki tunic made from seagrass felt. Damn, there would be trouble over this. He looked like a youth from one of the major families.

A shaft of pale light pierced the roof of the cave. That was where we had come through. Water trickled into the pond somewhere out of view of the glow of our light.

Deyu told me how they had let themselves drop through the hole, and had found these three people waiting for them at the bottom. Being Pengali, they had much better vision in the dark.

"We didn't want to shoot them, but there was no choice. They would have killed us." That was Veyada's training coming through. He was always about never using weapons unless there was no other option.

"It's all right," I said. "I understand."

"Then we found that the guy had just slammed the door on us, shutting us in with his assistants." She sounded horrified. A Coldi association leader would never do that. Coldi found displays of selfishness like this profoundly disturbing, especially by people who were leaders of small teams.

"I wonder what happened to any of the people who came with Melissa? Was there anyone here except her?"

"I don't know."

"She was not in a condition to tell me," Telaris said.

On the other hand, I wasn't sure if I wanted to know.

"I've seen no one else," Deyu said. "Reida might know."

But Reida was standing outside, under the run-off from the rock, trying to wash the foaming beisili sperm off him.

Opposite the room with the tables where Melissa lay was another room. It was dark, but Deyu flipped up the switch. When my eyes had become used to the greenish light, I saw tubes and metal parts of a machine inside a glass case.

Thayu went over to it. The case was taller than her. A single piece of apparatus took up most of the space inside, together with some control screens and panels.

"What is it for?" I asked.

The central part of machine had a clamp to hold something, which sat at the end of a hydraulic arm. The case had a door that I presume you needed to open to put something in the clamp.

"It's a . . . well . . . I don't know." She frowned. "It looks like you put something in this part, and then it . . . probably grinds something with those disks."

I hadn't noticed the disks yet. They sat neatly tucked away in a recess along the side.

I wondered . . . I looked around the room. There was a table against the wall. On it stood a couple of velvet-covered trays in which lay a handful of glittering, faceted jewels. Some stones were the size of the nail on my pinky, but a couple were wider than my thumb. Blue diamonds. Sky stones.

This place was where they produced the stones like the one I had seen that Robert was taking home for his wife.

Either the stones were found on the island or brought here by Pengali. This was Clovis' business. But what had happened? Had he tried to recruit Robert as an accomplice, because of Robert's work experience? Or Robert had tried to steal diamonds, knowing how much they were worth? Or . . .

I didn't really know. It was very strange.

19

GREAT PEAL of thunder rumbled outside.

We went back to the cave entrance where we found the rest of the team taking shelter. The beach and the bay had vanished in a curtain of rain. Water tumbled off the rock above us, over the cave entrance in between the rock wall and the soggy remains of the canvas shelter.

We had nothing to eat, but Evi found some dried fish and a couple of cans. Thayu and Nicha weren't sure of the coding of the contents—which turned out to be Mirani beans. Those were really bland, but better than nothing. We found a water heater that still had a bit of charge and made something that resembled soup from the dried fish and beans. It tasted terrible, but it was warm and filling.

Deyu and Veyada walked out to the point in an attempt to get the Pengali to come in with our boats, but it was raining too much and the boats were too far out for them to be visible from the shore. Deyu and Veyada came back by the time it was getting dark, soaked to the bone, cranky and arguing about whether the Pengali would or would not have been able to see their lights from the boats. If even Veyada started arguing, you knew things were very bad.

It got dark. We took it in turns to sit with Melissa. Telaris clicked a new ampule of sedatives in the band around her arm because he was afraid she would move too much and damage the wound.

It was still extremely humid and, when the storm had passed, still and airless.

I finally slept some after going out to the shelter, where the sand made for a softer bed than the rock in the cave, even if it wasn't entirely out of the rain.

I was wakened, when it started to get light, by a honking sound.

The rain had stopped, the sky had lifted and it was again possible to see all of the beach and the bay, and what a sight it was.

Thick rafts of pink foam covered the entire beach and adjacent water. Big globs of it also floated on the waves, turning the water oily.

I couldn't see any beisili, but I could hear them honking. Here and there, the water rippled with their presence.

Thayu was out on the beach, inspecting the plane. I strolled across. If I hadn't been hungry and feeling filthy, it would have been a perfect morning. Well, except for the foam, which was beginning to smell bad.

"Any damage?" I asked her.

"What from? It's seen a lot worse weather than this."

True, although mostly the planes would be brought inside during storms.

"Do you think you could take Melissa to the city?"

"I think so. Charge is fine, structure is fine."

"But?" I sensed hesitation in her voice.

"I very much doubt Robert has gone. He'll be back, and he might bring supporters from the tribe. I want to be out of here as soon as possible."

She might be right about that. If the Thousand Islands people had some sort of trade going with Clovis or Robert, they might not be impressed if we came to disrupt it.

There was a noise behind us.

Thayu turned around and gasped.

A beisili was really close to the shore. It was a young female, judging by the colour and size. She hobbled into the surf, using her flippers in the same way a seal did, and lay down, flat on the sand, surrounded by foam. She didn't move, didn't even lick at the foam, but regarded us with a baleful eye.

"I had no idea that they came out of the water," I said.

"Wow, she looks exhausted," Thayu said.

"It's probably from that male chasing her all day for the past two days."

"Do you think it's the same female?"

"I don't know, but—"

Another head broke the surface and a second animal came out of the surf—definitely the very dark male that I had seen before. He hobbled up to her like a sea lion. It was a strange sight to see such a large animal move so clumsily. How much did these adult beisili weigh?

He nudged the female with his head. She didn't react.

He pushed his nose into the side of her neck and attempted to lift it.

She did nothing.

He bent over and grabbed her gently by the skin of the neck.

"Do you think he's . . . going to force himself on her? Rape her?" Thayu sounded revolted.

"If she doesn't move, probably."

"I can shoot him." Thayu clicked her gun out of its bracket.

"You can, but I don't think that's going to kill him, only make him angry."

She let the gun sink.

The male shuffled half on top of the female. His weight pushed her into the sand.

"He's going to suffocate her," Thayu said. She raised her gun again.

"Thay' . . ." I warned.

"What? I only want to scare him off."

"They don't do things the same as we do. He might not—"

The female sprang up, scattering water and globs of foam. The male fell off her back. She grabbed him by the neck and clamped her jaws until he squealed. They rolled through the surf, getting coated in foam. When they stopped rolling, the female sat on top, pushing the male's head under the water.

"She's going to suffocate him."

He struggled on his back, flippers threshing. A red knob protruded from the soft flesh of his underside. She slid over him, using her weight to hold him down, and then . . . stopped. The soft parts in her stomach did a weird pulsing thing. She arched her neck and honked. It lasted only a short time, and then she slid back to the sand. Red bloomed on the male's lower stomach.

She jumped back into deeper water, staining the foam with blood-coloured sperm.

Thayu and I looked at each other. Then we both burst into laughter.

"I would like to think that we are a little bit more graceful and less noisy about our reproductive activities," I said.

"Definitely less messy." Thayu looked over the foam-covered bay.

The male scrambled up from the undignified experience and followed his mate into deeper water. His head was covered in foam.

Veyada walked down the beach in our direction.

"I think we should be able to get the boat out later today," Veyada said.

"We'll take Melissa to the hospital as soon as I pick up the chargers and panels from the other beach," Thayu said.

"Do you want me to come?" I asked.

"Sure."

We shook the water off the solar sails on top of the wings. Veyada helped us drag the plane to the far end of the beach, from where it was a short slide down to the water before taking off. We flew in an arc over the point at the southern end of the island.

"Can you see the three boats?" Thayu asked.

"Nope. I don't see them at all." I scanned the silvery calm water.

"Damn it. I never liked having those Pengali along. So many of them are just plain unreliable. Yeah, before you say anything, I know it's a culture thing and they have different priorities, but I think that since we're paying them, they should learn our priorities and not demand that we fit their schedule instead of them fitting ours."

"Thay'—"

"What? I've been saying this all the time. I've been going along with their weird fishing trips and disgusting diets. You know, I can live with that, *if* they meet us halfway and show some loyalty towards us. But I'm fed up with them."

"Just land the plane. All right?"

"How are we going to get back without the boats?"

"The boats are on the other beach. See? There they are."

They lay lined up under the trees. Only there was no sign of the three Pengali. Neither was there any sign of the solar charger.

"Oh, fuck it." I rarely heard Thayu swear. "You know what those things cost?"

I did. And I wasn't prepared to say anything else until we were on the ground and could see what the situation was, but to be honest, part of me was as unimpressed as she was. If the Pengali needed to have sought safe anchorage during the storm, they could have let us know. The transmitter was still working when the storm hit.

The plane glided onto the beach and came to a halt. I opened the door.

Behind me, Thayu said, "Wait."

She grabbed my shoulder and pushed me down with one hand while taking the gun from her arm bracket with the other.

"What is it?" The cabin had leaked during the storm and the ground where I sat was wet. Just when I thought I couldn't get any more disgusting.

Thayu had ducked behind the other side of the exit. I unclicked my gun from its bracket.

"What did you see?"

"Someone here."

"Wouldn't that be our three Pengali?"

"They would have come out to greet us."

"Maybe. Maybe they're asleep. Maybe they're afraid of planes."

"Look, this is why we shouldn't have taken them. We don't know what they're going to do."

"I was actually thinking we may need to go the other way: I wanted to employ some Pengali in the office."

Thayu snorted. I couldn't see her face, but I imagined that she rolled her eyes.

"It's my job to try to make sense of different people and find some sort of compromise."

"That was between the Coldi and Aghyrians, and the Aghyrians are gone now."

"There is a lot more to understand about different people. I'd like to understand Tamerians, too, but Pengali would be a good place to start, because I don't understand them either. Do you see anything yet?"

"Nope. You might want to stop talking." She slowly shuffled into the door opening and let herself drop to the sand.

I followed her example.

For a while we stood still, scanning the edge of the forest, listening for the tiniest sound over the crashing of waves.

Then she slowly walked sideways to the spot where the solar charger had been. Deep drag marks showed where it had been taken away, in the direction of the forest.

One thing I didn't understand: there were no boats other than the ones we had brought. If there were other people here, how would they have gotten here?

Robert?

Or other accomplices of his who had been in hiding on the island?

We followed the drag marks to the forest, all the while scanning dark places under the trees and vantage points. If they were Pengali, we wouldn't see them.

After last night's storm, it was so humid and pressing that I was soon sweating. Not a leaf moved.

We came to the forest's edge, where the drag marks simply stopped. I couldn't see any footsteps either.

Thayu looked up, and there was our charger, hanging in a tree. What the hell?

"Should we get it down?" I asked.

But she motioned me to be quiet. She pushed into the forest very slowly without making a sound. On the forest floor, half-hidden under loose leaves, lay four Pengali, asleep. None of them were our drivers. These ones wore leather gear. A couple of guns lay on a piece of leather. They also had armour: vests made from metal threads with tiny resin beads. Their shoulders and upper arms were marked with large pentagonal grey-brown patches.

Thousand Islands tribe.

I didn't know what I had expected. I knew that the Thousand Islands tribe had a town along the south coast, and that they traded manufactured goods in their own, strange, Pengali way. These were goods that Pengali made, from local materials. I knew that the only Pengali who still lived traditional tribal lives did so by choice and only for a short period, but I hadn't expected sophisticated clothing and weapons either. No, I was wrong, I hadn't expected them to *produce* sophisticated clothing and weapons.

We backed away very quietly.

"Where are our drivers?" I whispered once we were back on the beach. I realised that when we had come here before, I'd forgotten to ask the Pengali drivers about the currents and the campfire we had found. Had that been a Thousand Islands tribe camp, too? With the storage jar? Had someone perhaps lost a whole container of these jars and were they distributed all over these islands?

But Thayu looked over my shoulder, and said, "Shit."

I turned around. At the far end of the beach, another group had come out of the shadows—five Pengali, Thousand Islanders, pushing Langga, Maray and Della in front. Their hands were bound behind their backs and their tails were tied together.

Langga's eyes widened when he saw us.

One of their captors yelled out, and more Pengali came out of the forest, including the ones we had just seen asleep. There were at least twenty. They surrounded us, a wall of small people armed with guns the likes of which I had never seen before: they looked like they were made of resin and wood, but their shapes were sleek and modern and whatever went inside, whether they were charge guns or projectile, I had no doubt that these weapons were deadly. That's what people always said about Pengali: do not, under any circumstance, underestimate them.

We had assumed that by staying away from the tribe's settlement, the tribe would cause us no trouble. We had been wrong.

"What are you doing on our land?" the leader said.

She was a middle-aged woman, with greying hair at her temples. She wore a singlet made from a rubbery black material and leather trousers and vest. A leather band around her head held her hair out of her eyes and contained the usual adornments of coloured glass beads and eel teeth. But it also contained a little device with a lens.

Thayu raised her gun, but I put mine away. I had no illusion that we could fight this many people. I would have to solve this in the best way I knew: with my mouth.

I stepped forward and knelt in the sand. "I'm sorry about trespassing on your land. We came to look for people who have been causing trouble for everyone in the region. I have employed the

Pengali you hold captive. It is my fault that they are on your land." I didn't know if I used the right words and right noun inflections. Keihu was not my strong point, but I supposed I should be happy she *did* speak keihu, because my knowledge of Pengali was less than rudimentary.

The woman snorted.

I continued, "I offer my sincere apologies. If you ask the Pengali Office in Barresh, they will confirm that I did attempt to ask for permission to travel here."

"They cannot give it." Her keihu was harshly accented.

"She told me that. I didn't know where else to get it. She said she didn't know where to find people from your tribe in Barresh."

"Did they tell you that, eh?" She said something in Pengali to her companions, and they all made snorting piggy noises of laughter.

"They did, and honestly, that's all I can say. I am not proud that I know nothing about your ways. I came here to find a man, because I had been ordered to find him. I have since learned that he did not want to be found, or at least not by us."

She snorted again. She flicked her tail, and her armed companions backed off a little.

She sat in the sand. "You talk much."

"I'm sorry. I'm afraid talking is my thing. My name is Cory Wilson. I am a representative of *gamra*."

Judging by her face, that didn't hold much sway by her, not that I could blame her.

"My talking name is Abri. Are you a friend of the sky stone men?"

"You mean Robert?"

"We call him hairy face. There is another one we call red face. They are ones with the hair on their face and half-blind little eyes that see nothing in the dark. You look like them, but . . . ." She eyed my face, but these days my beard regrowth was limited to a few hairs here and there.

"I am from the same world. But I am interested in what you just said: there is more than one man? The man you are talking about, hairy face, is he the one who was on the other beach yesterday?"

"He's been there for a few days. The other one I haven't seen for a while. They come for the same reason. They buy sky stones and cut them. They give our young people easy money that they will go and spend in the city on things they do not need. They will not take their vile business off this island and every time we come and someone is here, they will shoot at us. They should leave and we told them so. This is our island."

"Do they come often?"

"Not often. But we do not want them. We do not understand why these stones are worth so much to them. When they are not seen as a part of the land where they grew, they have no value."

"How long has this been going on?"

"Red face first came here ten seasons ago. He was alone, and he watched us fish, and some of our people spoke to him. We had some young people who wanted to go to the city, and he told us he'd help them. He did. It was all right. Then he came back later with two other people. They did fishing and he took more young people. And he came back a few times. Then he brought hairy face, and we knew he was different, because he had evil in his eyes. He did not go fishing, but he went digging in our streams. He came back the next dry season and took machines to makes holes in rock. And then the next time red face came back with some people, they all started making holes in rock. They collected sky stones. We told them that we didn't like it, but they made threats to us. So we told our young not to go to the city anymore. They ignored us, so we said that if they didn't stop taking sky stones, they would not be allowed back. Next they brought Kasamo."

Gusamo? My heart was thudding.

"He is not like the others. He is a friend. He comes to us to learn our ways. He teaches the youngsters to ride on waves on pieces of wood. Then something happened. He ran away from the other men. He made a camp here. Then hairy face discovered him and killed him. But beisili are his friend. The beisili took him to us, even if he was already dead, and we followed the trail. We found his camp. We found evidence of hairy face's evil."

"What evidence?"

She rose suddenly. "Come. You will not like to see this, but I think you must."

The circle of armed tribespeople parted for her, and Thayu and I followed her to the very far end of the beach, where we had not been before. She preceded us into the forest.

We had only gone a few steps when I became aware of a vile stench. I looked over my shoulder at Thayu, who had a much more sensitive nose than I did, and she had fallen back, covering her nose with her hand. She held her other hand close to her gun.

Abri pushed aside some vegetation and exposed a little clearing. The ground had been disturbed, and at first it was hard to see what I was looking at.

"They think they can get away with killing Pengali because they think no one cares about Pengali."

The dirt-covered body half-buried in the ground was Pengali, I thought. It was hard to tell, and I didn't want to get one step closer.

"Who is this?"

"I do not know. Someone from the Washing Stones tribe. Hairy face does not like prisoners. He brings them here, shoots them and buries them in the sand. We have seen him do it. Kasamo ran away, but hairy face found him anyway. He killed Kasamo and buried him like this, but the beisili took him out."

"Are you sure?"

"We can see the hole, back there." She waved towards the other end of the beach. "We can see his footsteps. We can smell his scent. We can see beisili tracks. We know that beisili brought him to us."

Damn it, so that was what we had seen.

We retreated from the site back to the beach, where it was easier to breathe and Thayu uncovered her nose.

"I'm reasonably certain that I know who wrote the note in the jar," I said to Thayu.

"I thought we already knew that."

"No, it wasn't Robert. It was the second man on the trip. I think they came to the island for the supposed surfing holiday, and there was a disagreement. Clovis left and Gusamo fled to this beach. Robert found him and shot him. I have no idea why the disagreement happened, but we won't know the exact truth before we find Robert."

The Pengali were looking at us with suspicion. Maybe some of them had never heard Coldi spoken.

"We need to go back to our people on the other beach," I said to them. "We have a person who is injured and she needs to go to the hospital. We came here to retrieve our equipment that's hanging up there in the tree. We need to find Robert so that we can take him back to our world." Meanwhile, I wondered how many other bodies lay buried in the sand. This pristine island had a dark secret. We'd found no trace of Melissa's crew or her Kedrasi partner.

Abri's face was very serious. "Hairy face went to the city. We are ready to track him and fight the Washing Stones tribe for letting this evil man onto their land. It's through them that these men came here."

Langga snorted and said something sharp in Pengali. A few others protested.

Before an argument broke out, I said, "If you release our boat drivers, we will take everyone back to the city and leave you alone."

She snorted, but flicked her tail. One of the other Pengali extracted a glittering glass-stone knife and sliced through Della's bonds, and then Maray and Langga's. The three huddled together. Langga took his knife from his belt and cut through the rope that held their three tails together. He snorted, his nostrils flaring. Holding or tying down a Pengali's tail was a serious insult.

He made a sharp remark in Pengali. Abri snapped something back.

I stepped between them. "Look, I'm sorry about coming here with these people. I hired these Pengali and I wish to have no part in your disagreements. We'll leave now, and we are going to find this man."

"And we will come." Abri snapped her tail.

"We will be there, too," Langga said.

20

———————

I **HAD NOT** imagined that we would return to Barresh in the company of two warring tribes, yet that seemed exactly what was happening. The Thousand Islands Pengali insisted on coming with us to make their displeasure of the situation clear. And if I'd doubted Langga's assessment that Thousand Islands Pengali would have occupied the beach with a lot more people, a whole bunch of other Pengali came out of the forest. I'd heard people say that you could visit a place and think you were alone, but all the while hundreds of Pengali could be watching you.

Abri ordered a couple of them to lower our solar charger from the tree, while most of them congregated around Langga, Maray and Della on the beach. I kept an eye out for hostilities, holding my arms crossed so I could grab my gun from its bracket the moment trouble erupted. I assumed that the contract of employment for boat drivers included returning the boat intact and the driver alive.

A lot of shouting and tail snapping went on, and the argument was still going by the time Thayu and I climbed back into the plane.

Thayu shook her head. "Those two tribes have had their petty disagreements for many thousands of years. I don't think you'll be successful in getting them to accept each other's existence."

"Well, I can only try."

"Because your mouth is your biggest weapon." She grinned. "They will keep fighting and won't bother us."

"But we need the boats."

"They will come. They like money more than bickering."

She was right, because the last glimpse I had of the beach before the rocky ridge of the island blocked my view showed that our three boats had just cleared the surf. If anything, Pengali understood the concept of completing a task for payment.

That they were leaving the Thousand Islands people on the beach with no means of transport, I couldn't feel terribly sad about. On second thoughts, the Thousand Islands people probably had some boats hidden around the corner. Or maybe they rode beisili now that those all seemed to have finished their reproductive activities and were heading back out to sea in small groups.

Thayu and I returned to the other beach and while the Pengali were still motoring around the point, we brought Melissa out of the shelter to the plane. She lay on a stretcher, was awake, delirious and incoherent. Telaris reported that the wound looked infected and that if she couldn't be taken home today, he would have to try to get the bullet out.

I told him no, thanks, and we removed some seats from the back of the plane to make room for her.

Thayu set up the charger and contacted the hospital. We also contacted the Barresh guards to be on the look out for Robert, as well as the Exchange not to allow him to leave. I hoped that would work, because he had obviously come into town under a false identity, and appearances were easily changed. Also, how did one describe the concept of a beard to someone not familiar with beards or the fact that they were easily removed?

The Exchange informed me that there was a raft of urgent messages for me. I briefly spoke to Devlin, who informed me that a good number of those messages were from the medico who was upset that I had ignored her directives not to do anything too strenuous.

It seemed medical people had this air of self-importance all over the universe.

There was also some news that he'd discuss with me when I got back. I didn't like the sound of that, but I could do nothing about it until I got home.

When everything was packed and secured and the plane charged, we set off. The plane rose quickly in the bright morning sunshine. The bad weather was gone and the day bright and clear. The islands floated like little green dots in the turquoise sea, like the jewels that Robert sold.

"Isn't this just the most beautiful sight ever?" I said to Thayu.

"It's nice. Not as pretty as sunrise over Athyl."

And that was the measure by which a Coldi compared everything. "That's very pretty, too. But I'm thinking we should come back here, ask for the proper permissions and learn about the Pengali life. I would like to visit the Thousand Islands settlements." If anything, I owed it to Gusamo, whose business I had used, who had respected the Pengali and who would never return home.

Maybe I should start a surf school for bored and directionless youths. It was all very well concentrating on the big picture things that happened at *gamra*, but it was no good treating the city where I lived as something quaint to be viewed from the window of a moving train. I needed Pengali in my household, no matter how much Thayu would hate it. Eirani, too, probably.

The weather had calmed, and the trip was easy and without drama. Thayu notified the hospital of Melissa's arrival and they said they would send people to pick her up.

They were waiting outside the terminal when we landed, a couple of people in purple uniforms. With all the noise from aircraft, roaring engines and cargo being loaded and unloaded, it felt like it was so *busy* here. All these people were just annoying.

We accompanied Melissa to the hospital, since she had no relatives in Barresh to do this for her. I would have to try and contact her parents later. I seemed to remember that her mother lived in Germany and had remarried a Coldi man who went by the Earth name Ludo Chan. He might be able to come here to keep her company.

There was going to be some fallout from this case. I was still hitting myself on the head that I had sent Melissa out there. It was a sign of how addled I had been while I was sick, and how focused on Robert as innocent victim.

There wasn't much for us to do at the hospital while she went into surgery. The medico told me that the bullet might have missed a lot of vital organs, but it would still be tricky to remove. And yes, the wound was infected, which made recovery dicier. They would have to keep her sedated for a while. They let us know that they would contact us as soon as she woke up. Her story, when it finally could be told, would be an interesting one. I also realised that her experience brought Melissa in the firing line if there was some sort of court procedure resulting from this. Damn it, I'd probably have to cover some of her job while she was recuperating.

"How far off are the others?" I asked Thayu, who was doing something on her reader.

"They've just passed the sand bar. Nicha says that a good number of boats are following them, which are probably Thousand Islands tribe people."

Damn it. I'd hoped to avoid that. "I know you want to go home, but would you come with me to do one more thing?"

She gave me a surprised look. "Why do you ask?"

"Because last time I didn't, and you got angry. And because it's important that we make this visit while we still have the element of surprise. And because we're already quite close to our destination."

"You planned this, right?"

I grinned. I loved that woman.

We left the hospital quickly and vanished in the backstreets of the new rich part of the city. We arrived at Clovis and Juanita's house via a detour, again to make sure no one followed us.

The house looked the same as during my previous visit. The garden was neat and the doors to the veranda stood open to let in fresh air.

Thayu and I went through the gate, making sure to shut it quietly, and walked through the garden to the front door.

"Hello," I called at the screen door.

I could hear a noise inside the house, a rustling of paper or something like that. I waited, but after a while no one had come to the door.

I called again, "Hello, is anyone there?"

Again I waited, but no one came.

Meanwhile, Thayu had walked to the side of the veranda. She looked inside the windows and then around the corner of the house.

"Someone is here," she said. "I can see them."

Yes, I thought she was right. I tested the screen door, but it was locked. That was interesting. It looked like he didn't want to see us.

Thayu went down the veranda and walked around the corner of the house. From there, the garden sloped to the water's edge. After the rain, the water had risen and inundated the reed beds. Someone had brought a boat up to the bottom end of the garden, one of the flat-bottomed ones that people used in the delta. Did this mean he had visitors?

Thayu stopped and looked around. She took the gun from its bracket on her arm. She listened.

A second boat came around the point, heading for the garden, but when the driver, a keihu youth, saw us, he changed course and continued past us, without looking in our direction.

"Do you get the feeling that was heading in this direction?" I asked.

"I know for certain," she said.

"So, what's Clovis' game? He's trying to flee? Trying to hide?"

We walked along the side of the house and up the back veranda. The chairs were out and there was a teapot on the table; it was hot, too. The door into the house was open. Sloppy.

Thayu went in first. She walked carefully, trying to be as quiet as possible. There was no one in the kitchen, but a cutting board and a knife had been abandoned on the table, as well as a half-cut fruit.

I called, "Is anyone there? Clovis? Juanita?"

There was no reply. It was all very strange. I followed Thayu further into the house, into rooms where I hadn't been, like the bedroom, a study, the bathroom—which looked very Earthly, with a porcelain wash basin and toilet—and the guest room, where someone had dumped a couple of sturdy travel bags on the floor. They looked well used, of high quality material. There were brand logos on them, a distinctly Earthly thing.

That was interesting.

I went into the room, and as I crouched to check the bags and their content, someone appeared in the doorway. It was Clovis. He carried a hunting rifle. One of Robert's? He noticed Thayu and was sensible enough not to raise the gun.

"What are you doing here?" he said. "This is my private house." He was breathing fast.

"I knocked and called several times but no one opened," I said. "I have to talk to you. It's important."

"And you have to break into my house for that?"

"The back door was open."

He snorted. "Well, ask your question then."

"Whose bags are these?"

"What does that have to do with anything? You were going to ask a question."

"That was part of the question."

"It's none of your business whose bags those are."

"I think it is. We're looking for a fugitive, a man who has killed several people."

"Do I look like I would have someone like that in my house? I have no idea what you're talking about. Two weeks ago you came to me with this infantile note in a bottle, and now you're talking about murderers."

"I have since found out that the person who wrote that note is dead. His name was Gusamo Sahardjo and he was a businessman from Earth. Apparently, he came on a trip that advertised 'surfing with plesiosaurs', and apparently it was also not the first time he has been here. The Exchange has no records of him, nor of a man called Robert Davidson, visiting Barresh, so they came under a false identity as part of a well-planned scheme. I have seen an ad for these 'exclusive' trips for very rich people."

I let a silence lapse to study his reaction. His face remained blank.

"When I found that note in the jar, I assumed it was either a hoax of some kind, or child's play, but I persisted because the note was written in Isla; and few people, and none of the children, in this town can write Isla. It seems that Robert Davidson and Gusamo Sahardjo went on this surfing trip, but that Robert had a different agenda, and that maybe the organiser of this trip had a different agenda as well. At any rate, there was a falling out of some kind, the organiser took off, or was killed, Gusamo fled and wrote the note, before he, too, was killed. I found the note, but because I was ill, sent Melissa Heyworth out to investigate, because at the time I genuinely thought someone was in danger."

Was that a flinch, a look of distaste, or worry even?

"We arrived at the place where Robert was stranded, and he shot at us. He shot Melissa. We've found no trace of the other people on Melissa's team."

I had to stop to draw breath. "There will be quite a bit of fuss once people on Earth find out what has happened. Gusamo was well-known and well liked, an A-list businessman with a high profile in the graphic design world. He ran a lot of charity projects, had a lot of contacts, and there will be a lot of questions asked. So it would be helpful if you came forward with what you know about this business of running illegal tourist trips."

"Why do you assume I am involved?"

"I don't assume. I know you were. But let's add up the facts, shall we? I don't have to tell you about the continued boat wars in Barresh. Learning about those has been very educational for me. What would be more lucrative than hiring out boats for the very rich to visit a place where you have almost exclusive access: the territory of the Thousand Islands tribe. Or should I say: used to have, because the Thousand Islands elder Abri has told us that she no longer approves of your activities on their land."

"Abri is an old crone. The youth holds the future."

A seed of victory grew in me. He was talking. "I don't think most of the tribe will agree with you on that. They're on their way to Barresh as we speak. They can testify that Robert killed Gusamo."

His eyes widened briefly.

"They aren't too impressed that you used the trips as a cover for a diamond smuggling business—"

"That whole business was *his* idea. He's a mining person."

"Still, he came on a trip *you* organised. Illegally."

He snorted. "You may not believe me, but we, Juanita and I, have always been about educating young Pengali. We use the trips for that purpose."

"The hideous fees you charged the participants were just a side issue, I suppose?"

His mouth twitched. I knew I had him.

"At any rate, whatever happened, you were told by the tribe that you were no longer welcome because of the sky stone business. And this is my speculation: you are a half-decent person and wanted to pull out, but your partner, Robert Davidson, did not. Because Robert has a thing about guns and survival and is capable of defending himself against savages, he decided to dig in."

"That man is an idiot. I should have seen that much earlier."

I looked at the bags on the floor between us. "So these are not his things?"

"I have no idea why you would think so. If you really must know, I'm packing to take Juanita on a trip to Miran. She wants to go to the baths and spend some time in the fresh mountain air. As you can imagine, this climate is very hard on her. She hates the wet season."

"So, it has nothing to do with the fact that a man, who used to be a partner of yours but has become a dangerous enemy, is on the loose?"

He looked at me, blinked a few times, but said nothing. He looked old and tired and I felt sorry for him.

I continued, "I am also guessing that you are not going to help me find Robert, because you're afraid that any investigation will bring your own illegal activities to light, such as giving your rich customers false identification and bribing members of *gamra* and the council in order to get favours from them."

"You have no proof to make any accusations like that."

"Yes, we do. That box of documents we retrieved from the channel was very illuminating, and worth me spending a few days in hospital for."

He stared at me. Drops of sweat pearled on his upper lip. Behind his eyes, I could see him fighting not to show his disturbed feelings. But he remained silent.

"Well," I said, "I wish you a nice trip to Miran then. I'll continue to look for Robert. My next visit will probably be to Jasper Carlson. He's the only person who has voluntarily come forward with any information."

He continued to stare at me. The light filtering in through the window highlighted the deep crevices on his face.

"All right then. If there's anything you want to tell me later, you know where I am."

I went into the hallway. Thayu followed me like a silent shadow, and Clovis hobbled after her. We walked through the kitchen and Thayu and I went out on the veranda.

We were about to leave when he said, "Be careful of what Jasper says. He'll try to get you to contradict yourself in a way that incriminates you. Then he'll string you up with your own argument."

"I guess he'd have an easy job doing that with you."

"Oh, man, fuck off. You're an arrogant piece of work. I can see why Danziger ditched you. I'm helping you, giving you a warning. Jasper Carlson is an agent of some kind. What you tell him goes into places you don't want it to go and comes back to bite you."

"Don't worry. We know."

He snorted. "Worry? Don't know why you think I haven't got better things to do than worry about *you*."

Thayu and I walked back to the gate through the garden. It was early afternoon, the heat pressing as hell; the air vibrated with the absolute fucking racket of the ringgit in the reeds on the other side of Robert's yard, and even a couple of meili squabbled in the trees that lined the street.

Something was on the verge of breaking, and not just the thunderstorm building over the escarpment.

21

"**WELL, THAT WAS** interesting," Thayu said when we were in the street. At times I wondered how much Isla she understood; and at other times, like this, I was sure that through a combination of knowledge and translation software, she had understood every single word in the room.

"I think we've got the basic gist of it. There's more, but I don't think Clovis is a major partner, so I'm not sure how much he's worth bothering with at the moment. He's merely a man who owns boats, and is opportunistic to the point of criminality. I think he does care about the Pengali, in his own, misguided way. I feel sorry for Juanita. I also think Clovis knows where Robert is. He is possibly inside that house, threatening Clovis. Unfortunately, a hunch is not going to be strong enough to make a case with the guards or to get them to do anything. Also, I don't think that the guards are going to care much about protecting Clovis from Robert, or the other way around. I don't think they even care much about people going illegally *to* Earth. That would be for Athens to sort out. And we all know how much *they* care." Probably a little unfair to Amarru, but Earthly crime was very low on her list of priorities, even if the criminals travelled off world to do it.

Margarethe cared, that was for sure.

"We'll keep an eye on the house," she said.

I met her eyes. Hesitated. I so badly wanted to say, *No, leave it.* This mess had taken far too much of our resources already, and caused too much pain, to myself and my association, and Melissa and her people.

"Yes, we can," Thayu said, picking up on my feelings through the feeder.

"We've got stuff to do. It's Nations of Earth trouble. Clovis is right. Nations of Earth didn't want me. How high should I still jump for them?" I guessed the whole issue could be boiled down to how loyal I still felt to Earth, a question I had been avoiding for years.

"Would Margarethe be in contact with Jasper?"

"I don't think so. She would have mentioned it to me." At least I hoped so, because at the moment, nothing seemed certain anymore. "At the end of the day, I don't know what Jasper is doing here or who he works for. He seems like a nasty piece of work, and I don't want him involved."

She dug in the pocket of her jacket. "Well, isn't it good then that we can use these."

She held her hand out. In her outstretched palm lay a little spy camera. I didn't often get to see all the devices she hid in various places, but I had seen these things before: little sticky pads that could look like an unevenness in the wall, a fallen leaf or something else unremarkable. This one looked like a smudge of mud. "I'll stick this to the inside of one of these fence posts," she said.

She walked a few steps back along the wall where there was a little decorative opening with metal latticework, a common design feature in houses in Barresh. She stuck her hand through the opening and slapped the bug on the inside of the wall.

"That's the last one," she said, oh so casually. "It can form a nice network with all the other ones in the house and let us know if anyone is moving."

I stared at her. "You didn't!"

But oh, yes, that was just the thing Thayu would do.

"Have I ever told you I love you?"

She gave me a rare, lopsided smile.

I took her hand, which she even held until we came to the corner of the street where there were other people. We were a team. We figured out the best way of doing things and, occasionally, we were sneaky. But we worked so well together because we loved and respected each other. And, damn, if Lilona said she could change my genes but I needed to spend a month in hospital and would never be able to return to Earth, I'd still do it.

We walked back to the station and caught the train to the airport. In the middle of the day, most of the passengers were servants going to market or people going shopping. We got a few strange glances, dirty as we were.

On the way, we visited the guard station to notify them of a fugitive in town and possible action by us, but as I had predicted, I had trouble finding a supervisor who would listen to my story. Why didn't I ask *gamra* guards, they said, and I said they wouldn't be interested because it concerned a non-*gamra* world. The people I could prove Robert had injured or killed were all from Earth, or were Pengali, and of the latter they said, "They don't want us to interfere with their tribal law, so we don't, unless they specifically ask us to."

Which was fair enough. I hadn't seen evidence that anyone cared much about the Pengali, or that the Pengali thought that other people *should* care about them. But I thought that maybe it was time someone did. It was no good having a shadow society in town of people living their own lives in their own way in places where the normal processes of law broke down. Because criminals would take refuge in those places, and that, in turn, reflected badly on the Pengali.

After we left the guard station, we paid a visit to the Exchange, where I made sure that the security employees would check all passengers boarding transport to Earth against a description of Robert. I left them images and contact information in case they found him.

They nodded and took my descriptions and pictures of Robert, but I wasn't sure they took me seriously.

The net I was trying to cast for Robert had so many weak links. I couldn't imagine that the Exchange would want to slow their schedule in order to do the checks necessary to make sure that he didn't escape. I still had no idea what identity he was travelling under. Security at the airport was not particularly tight and there were many ways of getting into the building.

It was not the first time that I'd found the bureaucracy and lethargy of the Barresh authorities frustrating to deal with.

We were tired and filthy and the best thing we could do was to go home, have a bath and rest and wait until the others arrived. Maybe it would be a good idea if I looked at those urgent messages that Devlin said had come in for me.

There wouldn't be a flight to Athens until after dinner.

So we took the solar plane back to the *gamra* island because, fortunately, that was where it belonged, and just the thought of having to catch the train made me tired.

The tiny service airstrip was on the eastern side of the island, already half-covered by the lengthening shadows of the buildings along its western side.

The island's operations and maintenance manager seemed relieved that the plane was back in one piece. I wondered what powers of persuasion Thayu had used to borrow it.

We walked home across the leafy avenues without saying much. No doubt the madness would start again as soon as I opened the door to the apartment.

Indeed, when we came home, Devlin had already picked up though the signal of my reader that I was in the building, and he met us in the hallway.

"I'm so glad that you're back," he said. "The news just keeps piling up. The messages, too." He did not usually get flustered any more, so I knew that the situation was worse than normal. Then his cheeks coloured. "I'm so very sorry, Muri. You must be tired." He was looking at my trousers which bore splatters of mud and beisili sperm and green smudges from climbing over mossy boulders.

"I am tired, but it's urgent, so I'll have a look."

"Do you need me?" Thayu asked.

"Not immediately. I'll join you in the bath soon."

She went into the hallway and I followed him into the hub where he opened a considerable list of messages. All of them were marked urgent. I scanned the names of the senders. Most of them were from Margarethe Ollund. There was a single message from Jasper. It said, *Need to see you urgently*. I wondered if that invitation still stood. Actually, the more I thought about it, the more convinced I became that if

Jasper wanted to see me, it might be best to play hard to get for a while, even if only to see how desperate he got.

Margarethe mostly asked for details about Robert. I replied to her with a single message asking why she was so keen to have him back, which I knew she wouldn't answer.

I was afraid that I was going to have to visit in order to find out. Not only that, but if and when we caught Robert, I would probably have to escort him to Rotterdam. Until this had happened, I hadn't realised how much I'd avoided Rotterdam since the incident where vice president Danziger had almost wiped my citizenship, after I'd let Asha solve a non-Earthly problem on Earth in the best way the Coldi military could: by nuking it from orbit. In the few years since then, I'd dodged the questions, the legal implications and the politics associated with that attack by not going there. I didn't work for Nations of Earth anymore.

The moment I set foot inside the compound gates, the sharks would be waiting for me, ready to blame me for everything that was wrong with the Earth-*gamra* relationship.

Damn, I really didn't want to go to Nations of Earth and face a grilling over who I worked for and how I'd betrayed Earth and worked for the enemy.

Ezhya was not the enemy. I didn't understand why they couldn't see that.

Arguing was a lost cause, because they only saw *Help! Aliens!* and their opinions never grew any more nuanced than that. I'd tried to explain. I'd failed miserably.

Damn and crap.

I was about to shut down the inbox when I noticed Devlin hovering around.

"Yes? Is anything else the matter?"

"Well," he said, and hesitated. "I know you're really busy, and this isn't the highest priority, but while you were away I discovered something that I think you might like to see."

My heart sank. Devlin always had a wonderful way of understating a problem.

"All right, then, let's have it." I wondered if Thayu was in the bath yet and if I should call her so she could hear this, too.

Devlin sat next to me. He opened up a projection with lines of text. "Do you recognise this, Muri?"

I frowned at it. "That looks like a message I sent to Amarru before we left. At least the main part of it. I'm not sure what all the bits of code at the beginning are."

"I wasn't sure either. These little messages showed up in the directory that you left intact in the office account that was compromised."

"But the office doesn't send my messages."

"No, but somehow, the bug that you received in that message about archiving managed to use the office to break into your *gamra* account and captured this."

"They could skim the Exchange feed and read this anyway."

"They could, but what makes this unique is that it captures the message before it leaves the house and therefore captures all your passcodes."

Shit. "You said earlier that the code opened an outside link?"

"Yes, that's where it send these bits. We've traced it." He showed the map to me. I knew the location on the southern side of the island. Jasper Carlson's warehouse.

I stared at the dot, heart thudding. Jasper Carlson had lived in town for a long time. He'd been here longer than I had, since before Seymour Kershaw, my ill-fated predecessor. I thought back to that strange visit of his to the hospital, when he'd come to tell me about Clovis' smuggling, which was essentially true but not really, since the diamond business seemed to be Robert's contribution that Jasper was keen to pin on Clovis. He'd given Thayu enough information to trust him so that she would leave me with him alone with no listening devices. He could have strangled me during that time. But he hadn't. He'd saved my life by letting me use his pet Tamerian. Then he'd offered more information and another meeting.

He had a high status with the Trader Guild, and worked for the Courier's Guild, which—wait. That data-selling business that was skimming low-grade information off my office account had an account at the Courier's Guild.

Shit.

Shit, shit, shit.

"Muri?" Devlin asked.

"He's the one who sent me the message with the bug," And I was almost certain that the skimmed information would be going back to Earth.

I went into the hall. "Thayu, can you come here?"

There was no reply.

The living room was empty; the bathroom was empty. I found her in the bedroom, face down on the bed, still in her dirty clothes. She was fast asleep.

I backed away quietly, but I hadn't been quiet when I came in, and those rolling doors made a lot of noise. She stirred and opened her eyes.

"What? Did you say something?" Her voice sounded slurred.

"No. It can wait. I didn't know you were so tired."

"I forgot to bring my supplements on the trip."

Her red-coded poisons. Did that mean she had been without the entire trip? "You could have asked the others."

"Yes, but I used to do without all the time, and I used to be fine."

"I think maybe you didn't realise before that you weren't fine."

"Maybe I'm just getting older." She met my eyes. She said nothing else, but I sensed what she meant with this remark.

"I absolutely promise that when this is over, we will see Lilona." And then I remembered I'd vowed not to ask favours from the candidate's partner before the election. Damn.

She was right. It was getting ridiculous. If one looked for an excuse not to do something, there was always an excuse.

She asked, "Did you want to talk to me?"

"I did, but . . ."

I was tired, too. I decided to let both Jasper and Robert wait until the others had arrived back home and we could formulate a plan. My whole life was crashing down around me, and I had no energy to repeat the whole story twice, and have the same discussion twice. We went in to the bathroom, washed quickly and went back to the bedroom, where we curled up against each other and slept.

I was wakened what seemed barely five minutes later by someone coming into the room.

"Cory."

It was Nicha, silhouetted by the light in the hall. It was almost dark outside. He retreated. "Oh, I'm sorry."

I sat up. "No, it's all right. We should get up anyway. When did you come back?"

There was a lot of noise in the hall: rattling of wheels on the tiles, thuds of items hitting the ground, footsteps, the echoing of voices. Ayshada babbling.

"Just now. We're just dumping all our stuff in the hall. Eirani says there will be tea soon."

Tea was always good. It might even involve cakes and bread.

Nicha left, and I sat on the edge of the bed, rubbing my face. Damn it. What was the time?

I went to the window and peeked between the curtains. The sky was darker than it should be for the time of day. The thunderclouds that had built during the day had spilled over the city.

I sat on the bed and watched Thayu sleep. She was strong and formidable, but not indestructible. I decided to leave her. The others would be equally tired. They would have a quick snack and go and clean up before we came back for dinner followed by a strategy meeting.

As quietly as I could, I found clean clothes and sneaked out of the room.

As I should have known, *tea* was an understatement to describe the variety and quantity of food on the table.

Everyone was in the living room. Eirani bustled around with the teapot and for once didn't complain about getting the floor dirty.

"I'm so glad that you're back," she said. "It gets so terribly quiet when all of you are gone."

The nanny was also there with Ayshada and he lapped up the attention. Outside, it started raining, punctuated with the occasional flashes of thunder.

Between us, we talked a bit about business anyway. I asked Nicha where the three Pengali were, and he said they had to return the boats to their owner.

"Did the Thousand Islands people give you any trouble?"

"They hung back once we were close to the city. I suspect they're going to wait until after dark."

I wasn't sure if that was a good or a bad thing. But at least I'd let the Barresh city guards know about this impending invasion.

"Any sign of our man?" Nicha said.

"No, but I visited Clovis again. I think I have a pretty good idea of what happened between those two." I told him about the things Clovis had told me and the things I had worked out between the lines.

Nicha sucked in a breath.

"I need to discuss a few other things before we go to bed. There's a shuttle tonight. I really hope that if Robert tries to get on it, the Exchange security check will recognise him and stop him." I hated that we couldn't be involved with this. "Most importantly, Nich', we're going to have to escort Robert to Rotterdam when we catch him."

He listened quietly to my thoughts about this, nodding every now and then.

Then a voice at the door said, "Why is everyone in here without me?"

Thayu.

She looked sleepy, mussed up and confused.

"You didn't wake up when Nicha came in to call us, and I thought it best to let you sleep. We were going to start with the meeting after dinner."

She sat down next to me. Then she had to be filled in about the events since we'd come home, and the gathering turned into a rolling meeting anyway, where Eirani and the kitchen staff kept up the supplies of food and tea and people would take turns to duck out quickly to freshen up and get changed.

Devlin came in as well, and talked about the link going to Jasper's warehouse. We debated whether or not we needed to take any action, whether we thought that Jasper could be hiding Robert. I told them about how Jasper had come into the hospital and alerted me about the smuggling.

I still didn't understand the relationship between those men. We discussed the possibility that Jasper was some sort of secret police. No one knew. I was supposed to be the expert on that front.

Sheydu said it wasn't our business, and she was right about that. I apologised for getting them all involved, and in the same breath said I couldn't have done things differently.

Nicha agreed with me that we'd invested too much time in it to waste all our acquired knowledge.

We *did* have so many other things to do. And we had to cover part of Melissa's job—

Thayu checked her reader. Her eyes widened. "You were right. He was hiding in Clovis' house."

She showed me the screen, where two men made their way along the veranda of the house. Robert, sans beard, was carrying his bags.

I got up. "Everyone, to the airport now."

22

———————

W E ALL JUMPED UP. We'd been lazing and relaxing, and suddenly everyone was awake.

I started organising my team.

Thayu was coming. Nicha was coming. Both had bathed and looked reasonably rested. Veyada had needed to deal with some legal issue upon his return and hadn't had time to clean himself. He looked exhausted, but would not be left behind.

"This could be dangerous," he said. "We all need to go."

He was right. And I was glad of Veyada's continued contribution to my team. He had become very dear to me.

I went into the bedroom and donned the horrible armour again, strapping on my gun. Thayu had three guns, all visible and charged. Two on her arms, one at her hip. She'd have a selection of zappers, stunners and knives in her pockets. Her belt bristled with listening, code-breaking, viewing and spying equipment.

We waited in the hall for the others to get ready, while Thayu arranged for the plane again. Then I asked Devlin to get us a water taxi.

He frowned. "But I thought you were using the plane."

"We are, but the water taxi company is Clovis'. I want him to think that we're falling into his trap. The driver that will turn up will have orders to deliver us somewhere other than the airport, or delay us until the craft has left."

Comprehension dawned on his face.

"When the driver calls that the taxi is ready, tell him we're coming. Then do nothing for a while. When I give you go ahead that we're in the city, go downstairs and pay him and tell him we changed our minds."

We left the apartment not much later, a quiet, stealthy group armed to the teeth.

For a group this size, of course, we needed two planes.

As added problem, the thunderstorm still hadn't cleared. In fact it looked like a second front was about to hit us. Squalls of wind tore at the small craft as they took to the air. The outside was made from sturdy fabric, and at times I could feel it being pushed inwards by the wind.

I sat in the co-pilot's seat next to Thayu, and she had trouble keeping us on course. The other craft was somewhere behind us, but I could only see them on the radar. Ahead of us, the lights of the city shone through a thick veil of rain.

Then the rain hit us, and I saw nothing anymore. Thayu was flying purely on instruments until we were almost on the ground, and the glow of the floodlit tarmac appeared underneath us, much closer than I had expected. The landing was a bit rough, but nothing like when we landed on the beach.

The parking spots at the area near the terminal each contained a couple of rings embedded in the concrete. As soon as Evi opened the door—letting in a cloud of drops and humidity—Thayu threw out the tie-down straps which we used to secure the plane to the ground by the eyelets in the wings and tail so it wouldn't be blown over.

Then we made our way towards the building. Rain came down in sheets, reducing visibility to barely a couple of steps in front of us. Judging by the noise, a fairly large aircraft was going through engine tests. A cloud of mist and drops thrown up by its downward jets lashed into our faces, whipped up by the wind. There was a second shuttle, too, with a lot of activity from vehicles and people surrounding it.

"That's the one," Nicha said, pointing at the closest craft.

It was hard to see through the driving rain. I didn't think they were up to letting passengers board, but they had definitely turned on the engines.

"We better be quick," Thayu said.

We ran the last part of the way to the terminal.

The large hall was packed full of people, the windows fogged up with the humidity. A shuttle from Kedras was due as well as the regular service from Miran that came in a few times a day. Passengers and families and friends alike were all waiting. Everyone was wet and a couple of cleaners with mops were wiping the floor.

We spread out in teams, keeping in contact with each other through our feeders. I went with Thayu, while Deyu and Evi were going to check the passenger records. Not surprisingly, Robert's name did not come up.

Any names that look suspicious? I asked.

How do names alone look suspicious? Deyu said. *There are over one hundred and fifty people listed. Some of them are waiting here, but some will be over in the main hall. I can't check the names before I know which face belongs to it.*

And we had no access to that part of the job. Not only that, I didn't trust that the Exchange security checks were anywhere near adequate.

We went to the public waiting area, where people sat on every available seat and on the ground, and stood waiting between the seats. It was hard to see who would be passengers on the craft and who would travel on other flights or who were there to see off friends and family.

There are too many people here, I said to Thayu behind me.

Telaris and Nicha had gone to the business area, but reported that they couldn't see a sign of either Robert or Clovis.

There were just too many people here.

Let's go up there, Thayu said.

"Up there" turned out to be the viewing platform, from where you could see over the heads of the crowd and out through the large window over the tarmac. Thayu and I went halfway up the stairs. I was afraid that being up there would make us visible, but there was no way we would be able to find Clovis and Robert in this crowd otherwise.

Thunder boomed overhead and predictably all the departure signs started flashing delayed. People complained loudly about missing other flights and having to wait even longer. The rain lashed against the large window on the tarmac side of the building. Lightning showed up silhouettes of all the craft out there, tied down by the wings and tail like ours. A single person ran between the aircraft, holding a shirt over his head.

Thayu was scanning the crowd with her reader, using the face recognition program.

"It's not easy," she said. "Everyone is moving too much and I can't get a good view of most people." This was not helped by the long-veiled rain hats that functioned as umbrellas.

Then Sheydu said, *Jasper is here.*

Now that was interesting.

She and Veyada had gone to the ticketing area in the foyer of the building. We ran to the side of the viewing platform that looked out in that direction. Sheydu and Veyada were standing near one of the pillars that supported the stairway that came up to the platform.

He went that way, Sheydu said, gesturing with her eyes in the direction of the large window. I looked, but couldn't see him in the crowd.

Is Jasper Carlson on the flight? I asked Deyu.

Not that we have seen.

Unless Jasper, too, was flying under a false ID.

The flight notifications had gone back to showing scheduled times. Two airport crew were outside, about to open the double doors for people to walk to the aircraft. Most of the passengers on the flight were Coldi, a couple with their hair died dull black, who clearly lived and worked outside the Exchange.

We're going to have to go there and keep people from getting on the flight, I said.

We're onto it, Sheydu said. She and Veyada started making their way to the waiting area. Deyu and Evi said that they were moving outside from the business lounge. Nicha and Reida had been at the far end of the hall where luggage was being collected. I could see them push their way towards the boarding exit along the window.

Telaris just came up the stairs to the viewing platform from the other side. He had most of the equipment to communicate with Devlin at home. He was going to coordinate us.

Let's go down, I said to Thayu.

The Exchange security people had opened the doors. A long line of people waited to have their passes checked and one by one, they left the building.

Sheydu and Veyada were pushing past the queue, drawing annoyed looks in the process. They intended to push past the checkpoint, too, and go out to the craft.

The trouble was that we had no authority to do so.

Then I saw them: Jasper and Robert. They stood near the giant pillars that supported the roof. Jasper wore his hair loose, black and hanging over his shoulders. He was digging in the pocket of his trousers.

There. Thayu said.

Sheydu and Veyada were the closest. They changed direction, wormed themselves through the line of waiting people—drawing more annoyed looks—jumped over a row of seats and crossed the hall in giant strides. Both had taken guns from their arm brackets. People pushed out of their way, watching them go past.

Jasper was giving Robert something that looked like a document.

Then he turned sharply in Sheydu and Veyada's direction.

I think he's seen you! I said.

At the same time Thayu warned, *Action!* Jasper drew a gun and shot . . . at Telaris up on the platform.

Telaris, however, had seen it coming and had ducked safely behind the balustrade.

Shit, shit, shit.

Veyada and Sheydu had moved sideways. People were screaming and running away. The smart ones cowered under or between the seats.

Thayu and I crawl-walked down the stairs so that they couldn't see us over the railing. Nicha and Reida came running in our direction. Deyu and Evi hurried along the outside of the window.

The security guards shut the door just as they arrived. They wanted to keep Evi and Deyu outside. Evi loomed over one guard and said something to him, while Deyu forced the door open. Evi pushed the guard away. The man reeled back against the glass. His colleague was on his comm. More trouble.

Deyu and Evi came into the hall, both carrying guns in their hands. Thayu and I reached the bottom of the stairs. Thayu unclipped her favourite weapon.

Someone yelled, "Stop!"

Deyu sprang into action a split second before Evi did. Both ran across the hall to where Robert was. Thayu ran off as well. I had no hope of keeping up with her.

When I reached them, they had Robert on the ground in the darkness under the stairs. Sheydu sat on him, and Veyada pushed his head down with his knee while trying up his hands. Robert was kicking and cursing but was absolutely no match for two of the best and most experienced fighters in my team.

I walked around so that I could see his face. He calmed down when his eyes met time.

"Mr Davidson," I said, keeping my voice cool.

He snorted. His face was red and sunburnt, skin peeling from his nose.

"You're accused of murder, attempted murder, smuggling, illegal entry and evading quarantine. We arrest you in the name of Nations of Earth."

He spat. "You have no authority to do this. I'll get my lawyer onto you."

"Sure. He can deal with my lawyer, who is currently sitting on your head."

Robert glanced aside to where Veyada's knee blocked his view.

Sheydu had tied up his ankles and Veyada was done with his wrists. He rose, dragging Robert to his feet by the back of his shirt.

A wide circle of curious onlookers had gathered around us, including several unarmed security personnel. Those were soon joined by armed guards.

"What's going on?" a man asked.

"This man is an illegal visitor. We'll be returning him to his world."

"What authority do you have to carry those weapons?"

"This is Cory Wilson. He is a delegate in *gamra*'s special projects division."

The guard gave me a wide-eyed look. He seemed not sure whether to back away or persist. I thought his orders would tell him to persist. He knew we were outside our authority. Hell, we knew it. But then he would have to take our accusations of murder seriously.

He jerked his head. "Take him out of here, before I see this happening."

So we crossed the terminal with our prisoner, who appeared to have resolved to say nothing.

Telaris watched from above.

"Did anyone see where Jasper went?" I asked.

"No, but look," Thayu said.

Outside the window, a long string of small figures crossed the tarmac. In the driving rain, they all looked dark, but I didn't miss their tails.

The Thousand Islands Pengali had arrived.

The guards opened the door for us, letting us out onto the tarmac. The rain belted down and we were soaked in no time. Thunder rumbled in the distance.

The Pengali had stopped to watch us.

A figure came forward. It was Abri. In her hand she held a fearsome glass-stone knife.

Robert started struggling.

"Hold still," I ordered him. Veyada and Sheydu tightened their grip on him.

His eyes were wide. "You're not going to allow her to do it, right? You're a decent person."

"Yes, and you are not."

"Hey. Humans don't do that to each other."

"You didn't kill Gusamo Sahardjo?"

His mouth twitched. Water was running down his face into his neck. I gave Abri the *back off* sign and she did. "He will face our laws. I may need to come to you for evidence." It would be the very first cross-world court case for Earth. I'd put Veyada in contact with the Nations of Earth lawyers, and if those people were smart, they'd use him.

"All right, let's go," I said.

The Pengali didn't protest, but as Veyada and Sheydu dragged Robert past the group of Pengali, Abri lashed out with her tail. The tip snapped like a whip, right in Robert's face.

He yelled, "Ow!"

He struggled against Sheydu and Veyada's grip. Blood ran out of his nose.

"That is what we think of him," Abri said, lifting her chin. "It will be told to the entire tribe. Now we will go and sink a certain person's boats."

And they all ran off to the side of the tarmac, where they disappeared in the darkness, and would probably climb the fence.

"Oh boy, I would not like to be Clovis tonight," I said.

We arrived at the two aircraft. Nicha opened the door, and Veyada and Thayu manhandled Robert inside. They tied him to the seat in the very back.

We all piled in. I sat next to Thayu, and Veyada next to Robert.

"I swear, if he does any funny business, I'll kill him," Thayu muttered.

Robert remained quiet for the trip.

We came home where Thayu and Sheydu took Robert to the downstairs storeroom for the night. I told Eirani not to open the door under any circumstances. It had no windows. Upstairs, I asked Devlin to book a flight for the next day, and I informed Margarethe that we had the man.

She replied, *His wife will be overjoyed.*

Wouldn't she, ever.

Initially, I had thought that Thayu, Nicha and I would have a quick trip to Rotterdam, maybe take Evi and Telaris, but that was it. But the more I thought about it, the more I realised this was going to be about me as much as it was about returning Robert. Margarethe might ask me to speak at the Nations of Earth assembly. We would definitely spend time in her office and in the official buildings. I was no longer a junior delegate. I couldn't rock up in casual clothing with a few companions. I represented *gamra* and Ezhya. I needed to go with my full association in full colours.

I said, "Devlin, I'm sorry to dump this on you after you already made the booking, but I want you to book places on the shuttle for everyone else, too."

"Including the young ones?"

"Everyone, including Evi and Telaris. They can be Robert's personal guards."

"I don't know if there will still be room."

"Try it."

He did, and there was room, so I asked everyone to come into the hub and explained what we were doing. There were nods all around, except for Reida and Deyu, who were both so excited that they could barely keep their composure.

I sent them to pack all their official gear, a set of casual clothing and their temperature retaining suits, because—I checked—it was February.

Then, when they were all gone, I asked for a line to Ezhya. I had only been in contact with him through messages since we defeated the Aghyrian ship, and it was good to see his face again.

I asked him how the new baby was, because I was in a position that I could ask him things like that.

"She's starting to be a handful," he said.

I explained to him that I needed to go to Rotterdam and why. I told him why I was taking everyone, essentially to explain the giant hole this would blow in the budget.

He nodded, his face grave.

"I'd have wanted you to visit there and check what was actually going on. I've heard some disturbing noises."

I forgot that he still seemed to have a special relationship with Margarethe, ever since the two of them had been forced to spend a few weeks together on Kedras when the Exchange went down. Neither of them had ever elaborated on that time, but there was definitely a relationship.

"I have the chance to check it out now. Anything in particular you want me to ask or look at?"

"Observe, don't ask too much. Don't forget that they are the non-*gamra* world with the largest population by far. If they were to join, they'd be second only to Asto, and that's only when you count Asto's offworld population." Like the vast military stations. "It seems that some people on Earth have realised this and are starting to do something with that fact. Margarethe is going to have to move on joining, or risk fracturing *gamra* forever, if these people start setting up their own systems."

That was definitely a serious matter. I promised him I'd find out as much as possible of the things that the Exchange didn't report and that Amarru might interpret wrongly.

I signed off with a cold feeling in the pit of my stomach. This was not about Robert, not about a single criminal act. It wasn't even about the fact that he had ruthlessly murdered people. It was much bigger than the crimes of a single man.

We were still in the hub, eating from a platter of biscuits that Eirani had brought, when a message came in for me. It was from the hospital. Melissa was awake.

I met Thayu's eyes. It had been a long day and I was tired, and we'd been into town twice already, but we were going to Athens tomorrow, and I needed to know what she had to say.

She sighed. "All right. I guess a boat is out. Do we catch the train?"

I hated asking anyone in my association to go back into town. By the look of things, most of them were either packing or had gone to bed early, or at least retired to their rooms.

Evi and Telaris were still at the door and said they'd come, so the four of us walked to the station, as we used to do before my household expanded. It was quite late, and few people still went into town.

The rain had calmed a lot of normal outdoor activity in the city. The streets were much quieter than usual, since no one had yet set up the wet season tents that would spring up everywhere.

The trip was uneventful.

Melissa sat in bed, propped up against a pile of pillows. Her arm and shoulder had been bandaged up, and she was still attached to various machines.

"Oh, Cory!"

I sat down on the bed.

Her eyes were red, and her cheeks wet with tears.

"I'm sorry for sending you out there."

"He killed Taysin. We got out of the boat at the island and he just started shooting. He killed her, and the driver and the other Pengali I brought and he dragged me into this cave. I thought I was going to die—" She burst into tears.

"I'm sorry, I'm sorry." I hugged her. She felt thin and weak and smelled of hospital. Her body shook with her cries.

Thayu had retreated to the door, unsure what to do. Most *gamra* societies didn't approve of the display of this kind of emotion in public.

I waited until Melissa had calmed down somewhat. "We caught Robert today. I'm going to deliver him to Nations of Earth tomorrow.

Can I take a statement from you about what happened when you went to what you thought was a rescue?"

She nodded and wiped her cheeks. "Do you want to do that now?"

Underneath her grief, I knew she was a professional. Thayu came into the room with the recording equipment.

Melissa described how she, Taysin and the Pengali she had hired had set out for the island.

"You didn't bring any guards?"

"It was a rescue. I had a number of Pengali who were good at survival in the wild, I had a boat, Taysin is . . ." Her eyes filled with tears. She continued in a lower voice. "Taysin was trained in medical emergencies. There was no reason for him to just start shooting at us. No reason."

She described how they arrived, saw his boat and called out to him, and he opened fire, pretty much in the same way he had done with us.

"Sorry about asking this, but what did he do with the bodies?"

Melissa's lip trembled. "He . . . he took them away in the boat. I don't know where to."

I thought I knew. "Did you see the lab and the diamonds inside the cave?"

She shook her head. "He tied me to a post in that shelter outside. He . . ." Her eyes filled with tears again. "He threatened to kill me several times."

"Did he give a reason why he didn't?"

Melissa blinked away tears. Her short hair lay plastered against her head, making her look smaller than she did in her normal pixie-style, spiked-up hairdo.

"I think . . ." she said. Her voice was hoarse. "I hoped that he had a bit of decency. I don't think he could kill a woman. Not a *white*, human woman at least. Someone who looks like his wife."

Fiona Davidson was similar in build.

Melissa wiped her eyes again. The skin at the top of her cheeks was red from wiping it.

"Did he say anything to you about why he was there?"

"He said . . ." She tried very hard to keep her composure. "He said that we would find out. He was never really coherent about it. He said that Nations of Earth were stupid, and that they were missing a lot of opportunities, and that he didn't need all that bureaucracy. I don't know what he was talking about and what alternative there would be to either Nations of Earth and *gamra* but those are the things he said."

I nodded. Damn it. Echoes of Renkati. Their agenda had been to set up a second Exchange so that a secondary society could operate independently of the Exchange which they said was too tightly controlled by the Coldi. Were they setting up something like this, and was it controlled this time by rich business people on Earth?

I asked Melissa for precise details about the people Robert had shot, as much as she remembered of what he had said to her. And if she knew how he had travelled to Barresh.

She didn't, but she had already let it come through that this was not a random idea by a single random man. This was a highly organised group. A rich group, which had the resources to buy what they needed, legally or illegally. Robert had bought Clovis. And poor Clovis, with his penchant for wanting to grab easy money, had fallen for it, and had then tried to extract himself. He'd probably panicked when he found out more about the group's aims, and had abandoned Robert on the island.

Poor Gusamo had been caught in the middle. Melissa hadn't seen him at all so maybe he was already dead by that time. Maybe Robert had found Gusamo camping on the other beach when he came to dump the bodies. No one would ever know.

I asked her whether Robert had spoken of Jasper. Melissa said no, and she was surprised about my question. Why did I think Robert and Jasper had anything to do with each other? I guessed that we were dealing with two men who were utter professionals.

The interview stressed her, and when I thought I had exhausted her memory I asked Thayu to stop recording. I felt terrible about leaving her without anyone to visit her.

"Do you want me to contact your family?" I asked.

"I already contacted them. My father said he'd come . . . stepfather," she amended.

"Does he still have permission to go to Asto?"

She shook her head. "His family has lived in southern Germany for a long time."

"What clan are they?"

She glanced at my Domiri earrings. "German."

"Fair enough."

I let a silence lapse. Just like not every human wanted to return to Earth, not every Coldi wanted to return to Asto. Me and my big mouth.

"Do you have any other family? Brothers? Sisters?"

"I have a brother-in-law. He says he's met you."

"Has he?"

"A few years ago."

"He has a better memory than I do—wait, is he Coldi?"

"No. He's German."

I stared at her. "You're not telling me that Klaus Messner is your brother-in-law?"

She smiled. "You have a better memory than you think."

And then I remembered the things she had told me when I first visited her with the note in the jar. She'd been worried about a conspiracy listening in on us. To her, the security breach had been a bigger story than me and my jar. If Klaus was her brother-in-law, then maybe there was a reason for that. And maybe I, with my stupid attitude that I know better, should start listening to her.

23

KLAUS MESSNER, I explained to Thayu on the way back, was a top-level spy for the Exchange. We had met him briefly, when travelling in the hidden freight train from Rotterdam to Athens after the attack on us at the airport.

"He was the man who showed us onto the hidden carriage?" she asked.

"Yes, that one. I keep meaning to have a chat with him. His story will be interesting."

"I'm wondering if he is the one . . ." She fingered her upper lip. Like Thayu usually did, she would not say any more until she could verify her suspicion. Yes, if we went back to Earth, scheduling a talk with Klaus might be beneficial. I now had the excuse: to let him know about Melissa.

We came home not much later, were informed by Devlin that everything had been quiet and everyone had packed.

"The young ones are very excited," he said. "They have never travelled outside the system."

"They deserve to come. They've been very valuable."

Thayu and I finally retired to the bedroom. It had been an extremely long and tiring day, but we still found some energy for each other before falling into a deep sleep.

The various members of my association started rummaging around long before I was ready to wake up. It wasn't even light yet, but Nicha

came into the room, Thayu started going through the cupboard in our
room looking for something that he'd come to ask about, and there
were scuffles and voices in the hall.

Urgh.

I sat on the edge of the bed, rubbing sleep out of my eyes. Thayu
opened the door to the hall. A smell of freshly baked bread drifted in,
together with sounds of people talking and laughing. Better go and
have breakfast then.

I got dressed in my house clothes—no need to risk getting food
stains on my *gamra* blues. Most of my association were already at the
breakfast table. Deyu and Reida in their blacks, Veyada in the grey
suit that he wore under his white lawyer's gown. I grabbed a quick
bite before submitting to Eirani's ministrations: doing my hair,
helping me into my blues and brushing the hair off my back.

"I won't have anyone to do this while I'm gone."

"First impressions count," she said. "And I can't count on those
people having any sense of sophistication that they will tell if something is not right. But I've done my best."

"Thank you, Eirani."

She squeezed my shoulder. "If I had a son, I would have wanted
him to be like you. You make me proud."

I had an insane idea to take Eirani to my father's farmhouse one
day. She was like a favourite aunt, always fussing, but only happy when
there was something or someone to fuss about. It would be my thank
you to her, and she would like being introduced to the concept of
scones and jam. Rephrase that: she would go nuts over them.

I went back into the hall, where everyone was ready.

Overnight, Evi and Telaris appeared to have sourced proper hand-
cuffs and manacles, which they had put on Robert. He looked pale,
unshaven, only slightly cleaner than before, still badly sunburnt and
worn out. Evi and Telaris were a head taller than their charge, very,
very black and very imposing. They wore their blacks, with blue *gamra*
bands around their upper arms, hard armour of the type that went
over the top of clothing and a variety of weapons and devices.

People shouldered bags and weapons and the column started
moving towards the door, watched by Devlin and Eirani and the
nanny with Ayshada, who was waving and yelling "Bye! Bye!" at the
top of his voice. His hair was getting a bit long, but I would hate

Nicha to cut it. It was elfin-like, sleek, fine and iridescent purple. I'd never seen that before, and it amazed me. In places I frequented one rarely saw Coldi babies. It turned out they sometimes had purple hair.

Then we were out on the gallery and on our way.

It was still very early, many delegates were still away, and only a few people saw us walking to the station. The train, too, was virtually empty. It grew a lot busier at the airport, where we waited in the business lounge. During the trip here, or indeed at home, Robert had not said a single word. He seemed to have resigned himself to the fact that we were going to hand him over to Nations of Earth.

But while we were waiting, and he was sitting in between Evi and Telaris, I asked him, "What name *did* you travel under?"

He snorted. "Fuck off."

All right. I'd find out soon enough anyway.

———

The trip was uneventful. The Exchange process messed with time, so I had no idea how much real time had passed when the shuttle floated down into the giant maw in the ground that was the entrance to the departure hall of the Athens Exchange. To me, it always felt like the trip took the best part of a day, but even on occasions when I'd taken an old wind-up watch, it would say 4 o'clock when going into the jump and it would say 12 o'clock coming out, for a process that felt like five minutes.

It was dark in Athens, because the Exchange and regular air traffic control had long ago come to agreements about air traffic and not getting in each other's way. The Moon was out and the sky clear.

During the flight a lot of other passengers had given us curious looks. Most of them were Coldi, although I spotted one keihu woman who, when the craft was manoeuvring into its landing bay, donned a veil and changed into an attractive middle-eastern woman.

If nothing else, that brought home to me how necessary it was to have a formal structure for travel and access to different societies, or every place would be rife with hidden identities of people who were someone else on another world, and the whole mess would become impossible to keep track of.

The door opened. Passengers started gathering their bags.

"All passengers, please remain seated," one of the crew announced.

That was unusual. People craned their neck to look at the door in the back of the cabin. A couple of heavily-armed guards came in. For us.

"Delegate, come with us please."

I glanced at Thayu. She gestured, *go*. They were *gamra* guards, wearing black with thin blue stripes.

I took my bags and we followed them out the door and down the gangplank. They didn't stop to explain what was going on, but led us across the gallery, past the other craft that stood there. It looked like the Exchange had just opened for the day, because there was a lot of activity on all levels of the hall. The noise of departing craft was deafening.

The guards led us out a side door into a long corridor.

"Phew," Deyu said behind me. "A lot of noise in there."

Nicha explained to her about how the Exchange worked and a bit of its history.

"Really, did they make a separate entity just for the bit of land that surrounds it?" Deyu's eyes widened.

"And the city it's in," I said. "Which is a local city, where Coldi have lived for almost two hundred years."

Both she and Reida drank in the information. Sheydu and Veyada would have been here before, maybe once or twice with Ezhya, although their exposure to local people would have been fairly limited. Evi and Telaris were veterans, but it was the first time that neither had bothered with any kind of disguise. No sunglasses, no coloured lenses to turn their moss-green eyes black, no hair dye in their copper-coloured curls.

In fact, none of us pretended to be anyone other than ourselves.

We had gone quite a way before I realised that the guards were taking us to the main public foyer. I had wanted to talk to Amarru, but I guessed it would have to wait.

Indeed they used their passes to open the large double door that led into the foyer, the door that was normally only used by people coming in.

The huge hall on the other side had changed little since I last came there. It was still full of people. There were still giant news screens on the walls, and the windows still looked out over the stately, date-palm-lined driveway.

A military vehicle stood outside the main entrance, with a handful of soldiers. *Nations of Earth* soldiers. Special Operations. Uh-oh.

Yes, indeed, they were waiting for us. The *gamra* guards handed our group over to them under the overhang of the entrance. Some of them looked like they had been ordered to take charge of Robert, but backed off when they saw Evi and Telaris.

"Mr Wilson?" The highest-ranking officer searched around the group, and it was a while before his gaze met mine. Certainly I wasn't that hard to recognise?

He nodded a very cold and very formal greeting. His gaze went down my full *gamra* blues, the non-Earthly gun in the bracket on my arm. Disapproving, I thought. "Come with us. An aircraft is waiting." He hesitated, looking at the others.

"They're with me." I kept my voice equally cold.

And so we were back playing the *Oh, I hadn't expected that you were travelling with such a large group, and they look like they're all aliens* game. In all the years that I'd worked for *gamra* no one had gotten over this shit yet.

It did not bode well for the rest of the trip.

We got into the passenger compartment of the vehicle. I gave my association the *careful* sign. Only talk about innocent things. The scenery, the weather.

We went to the airport, of course. Like the previous and last time I'd had anything to do with Nations of Earth, the president had sent a private craft.

As we boarded, I didn't miss the usual *Do we have to take all of them?* and *Yes, he says they should travel with him* discussion that went on between the military guards and the craft's crew.

This had always annoyed me, but right now it annoyed me even more than usual.

As I sat down and belted up, I also wondered why Amarru hadn't yet been in contact with me. Thayu sat next to me, but I didn't want to ask her, because we'd be monitored. Deyu, across the aisle, was looking around with wide eyes. She had been very good and not asked a single sensitive question and not said anything about sensitive subjects. On the way through the city, the simple sight of a girl walking a dog had set her and Thayu off into a discussion about dogs and what they were and what they were for. Thayu explained that Fred, my father's dog, liked to fetch things and Deyu went, "Really?" Then she noticed pigeons and wanted to know if they were useful for anything. And then cats, to which Thayu said they weren't useful, except to keep you warm. I could only imagine Deyu's delight at the concept of a horse.

The plane took off and made an uneventful trip to Rotterdam. It was night, of course, but that did not keep Deyu from looking out the window and asking us what all these lights were.

It was still pitch black when we arrived in Rotterdam. Not only that, there was a rare blanket of snow on the ground.

Deyu did her very best to contain her excitement, because things were getting serious now. A contingent of Nations of Earth guards were waiting for us to take care of Robert. One man grabbed him by the arm and dragged him across so that he almost fell. Robert cursed and the soldier belted him on the ear. The men then pushed him into the highly secured back of a waiting truck. He'd been quiet and sullen but obedient during the trip, and I saw no reason for the rough treatment those guards gave him. It made me feel uneasy.

Much more luxurious transport waited for us: the Nations of Earth VIP train carriage that would transport dignitaries to and from the compound to the airport. The carriage came with more guards. A short train ride later we were at the little station which was open only to this particular train.

The clock on the platform said 2:13 am. It was pitch dark. The Moon was out—another source of wonder to Deyu and Reida because neither Asto nor Ceren had moons worth mentioning. It was full, big and fat, and its blue light made the snow glitter. It was also cold. I spotted Reida blowing out breath and waving his hand through the resulting steam—and Coldi with their high body temperature made even more steam than other people—but as soon as he noticed I was looking, he straightened up and put on a serious expression. It would have been funny if I hadn't been getting worried about what we would find at the end of this trip. If Margarethe needed to see us at this time of the day, then there had to be some problem, right?

We walked the short distance from the station to the president's office. The three guards who accompanied us seemed nervous. No one said much. Thayu hid deep inside her jacket. I pretended not to notice how Sheydu slipped in the snow and almost fell.

We went up the broad marble staircase to the foyer that once, what seemed ages ago, I'd seen full of police and other security personnel on the day that President Sirkonen was murdered. There was no one in the hall now; the lights in the chandelier were off and the stairs dark, even if a light was on in the upstairs foyer.

The guards exchanged a few words. I was ashamed to say that I didn't understand them. Maybe once I had been familiar with some of the codes they used, but no longer.

It was protocol that I go in to see the president alone.

My association had seen Margarethe. They trusted her, so they had no problem with having to wait in the secretary's office. The secretary was not at his desk, of course. Everyone sat on the couches and the floor between the couches and the table. They were most fascinated by the screen tabletop that displayed the news, and even more intrigued when the screen revealed itself to be sensitive to touch. Thayu would soon show them how to use their feeder to control it, but by that time I had gone into the president's office.

Margarethe sat behind the familiar desk. It no longer stood in the position where both Sirkonen and Danziger had put it, underneath the portrait of the current president on the wall, but to the side, in the darker corner of the room where the library used to be. The old shelves with their old books were gone. The walls had been repainted and the lighting adapted to modern design. The room looked less stuffy, more airy and modern.

"Cory." Margarethe rose.

She wore a stylish dark purple suit. Her hair was, as usual, piled in a bun at the top of her head. In Barresh, the style had seemed a little quaint, but here, while she crossed the room, all the memories came back of Eva and her penchant for Victorian-style dinner parties.

She took both my hands. Her hands were cold, and indeed it was none too warm in this office.

"Sit down," she said. "Do you want tea?"

I had no idea who would be drummed out of bed to provide this tea, but I couldn't say no to that.

Silly me: a machine made the tea, in the corner of the room.

Margarethe took two cups and carried them to the table. We sat on the armchairs.

"Why are you still at work?" I asked.

"I was working late, and then I heard you were coming in, so I stayed." She sounded casual. I didn't think she was so relaxed.

"I brought Robert Davidson back. He was quiet and well behaved on the trip."

"Thank you for that."

Then she let an uneasy silence lapse. It was one thing to meet her in an informal capacity in my apartment, but another entirely to see her here.

"What is so important about this man?"

Margarethe sighed. "Have you heard of the Pretoria Cartel?"

I hadn't.

"It's a group of influential people who don't want Earth to join *gamra*—"

"Has Nations of Earth ever made any progress on that subject?"

"There are many issues associated with joining and we're talking about all of them."

"Just talking? Because I haven't heard anyone at *gamra* as much as mention Earth for quite some time."

"Yes, Cory, just talking. Melissa observes, she reports to us and she answers questions for the assembly. The committees advise us on a final decision."

"This has been going on for how many years?" Were these all still the same issues that Sirkonen and I had discussed when I first started to work for him?

"It's not a fast process, no." She sounded a bit annoyed. "Tell me where you're going with this."

"We don't *have* years. People are impatient to have a decision made either way."

"You don't need to tell me that. It's my platform for the upcoming election."

Wait, there was an election coming up here as well? Yes, I should have known that. The assembly, including the position of president, was up for re-election every four years. Had it been that long already? It didn't seem that long—because Ceren years were much longer than Earth years.

"So, I guess *gamra* membership has finally become an important issue. What are the camps?"

"I was just telling you that. One is a large group of people who don't care particularly much either way. They've seen enough of various *gamra* people not to be afraid of them—I mean, some of the inner city of London is virtually ninety percent Coldi—and they are never going to afford to travel off world. They may be slightly in favour if it means they'll be able to buy interesting gadgets as a result of opening imports. They could be swayed the other way by a big scandal."

Oh. I saw where this was going now.

"Most of the authorities are in favour. Most industrialised countries are tired of dealing with these groups of people that fall outside their laws."

She let a silence lapse.

"And the ones against?" I prompted.

She sighed. "The Pretoria Cartel. They're a hotchpotch of powerful groups with strong interests. Countries in war zones who have seen offworld weaponry and fighters get hired by various parties. Countries with natural resources, who see the potential for competition. Industry groups. As you will appreciate, these are powerful lobby groups, and they're not political activists. They will act in silence, use powerful resources and have very good lawyers. They have a very smart, down-to-earth, figurehead candidate. I suspect you even know her." Her grey eyes met mine. She looked tired. "Fiona Davidson."

"What?" I burst out. "Her husband is a criminal."

"A gun-crazy, too-rich-to-care company executive. None of what he's done is technically illegal."

"Travelling on false identities isn't illegal?"

"They're not false identities. They are created identities, and yes, there is a big difference. Aliases is perhaps a better word, except it's not always easy to find out who the alias belongs to. We have, for a long time, allowed people like Nixie Chan to practice law under her assumed name, because no one would recognise her Coldi name. She has a European travel pass that says Nixie Chan that she can legally use everywhere. Her law degree says Nixie Chan, and I bet so does all her legal documentation. Most of the older Coldi residents have an assumed name that is legal on Earth, while their Coldi names have become legal only much later. Even so, it is still common practice for a Coldi child born on Earth to be given two identities at birth. The rule was always: as long as you can prove that both identities are the same person, this was allowed. The cartel took the precedent set by these cases and twisted it around. They created offworld identities for people from Earth."

"But Amarru would have known—"

"They didn't use the Athens Exchange. They knew that every day, many new people are registered with the *gamra* citizen register in Damarq. They knew that you only need to prove that you're a real person and that either you conduct business or that you have work, own property or have a family on a particular *gamra* world. Searches for their names did not come up because we are not a *gamra* world. They put together this data based on the prospective traveller's real identity, spiced up a bit with some local details. They have vast data mining operations."

Shit. Data mining. Jasper Carlson.

"They acquire citizenship cards that allow the owner to travel off world without revealing an Earth name. They sell those cards at high cost."

"Certainly that's not legal."

"No, but getting a ruling on that requires Earth and *gamra* lawyers to put their heads together and what is the likelihood of that happening?"

She was right.

"They also target high-value imports. The diamond trade is one of the most lucrative examples. These people know how to manipulate the market. They created the demand for blue diamonds through clever advertising and they also hold the monopoly on the supply of blue diamonds. No one on the source world cares much about these stones—"

"Not entirely true."

"Well, maybe they never thought that anyone might, or judged the objections insubstantial. This is a harsh, money-driven group of people who don't let a few bad cases of exploitation stand in their way. They sell dirty money, they sell dirty energy to marginalised groups." I remembered the ancient diesel trucks I had seen in Ethiopia. "They don't want *gamra* membership because it would take away all their means of income. They package it as fear. What if aliens take over our governments? What if they invade? What if they take all the world's water? And if *something* bad happens, this group is going to become vocal, say 'I told you so' and will push their candidates forward. If there is a scandal, there is a good chance they will win."

Shit.

"But certainly *murder* isn't legal anywhere?"

"Again proving it and getting a conviction is the hard part. No lawyer is going to be able to get a conviction for the killing of some local person in Barresh."

"I'm not talking about some local person. I'm talking about Gusamo Sahardjo."

She met my eyes and said nothing for a while. "Do you have absolute proof that Robertson killed him?"

"Yes."

"Any that would stand up in court, given by verifiable individuals?"

Well, maybe not. I could see despair in her eyes. She wanted a thread of hope.

She continued to look at me. "Mr Sahardjo's partner, his parents and sister are in hiding. They asked questions that the group didn't like. This is how far the tentacles of power of this group stretch."

"Shit, Margarethe."

She nodded. "Yes. Shit." She sighed. "These are not dumb people. They are smart, very rich people. Their budget is bigger than ours, their influence is greater. Of course they hide behind many layers. They use innocent people to carry their political message, like Fiona Davidson. They use faceless mercenary squads to carry out their dirty work, men who, when they are killed, we can't even identify."

My heart jumped. *Please don't tell me there are Tamerians here.*

But Jasper used Tamerians. One had even saved my life.

"So, thank you for bringing back Robert Davidson and handing him into custody, even though that won't solve everything. It's satisfying that we have a few things we can pin on him that will take him off the street for a while."

"Can his wife even stand against you while he is under investigation, or if he's convicted?"

"They'll use another puppet candidate if they think she can't. At the election, the issue is going to be that big mass of people in the middle, the people who don't care if Earth joins or not and who are, come August going to vote one way or another. The only way we will win is if we can appeal to them, while the powerful cartel does their best to discredit us or, at the very least, show that our ideas are not in the interest of the people of Earth. We have to win this, Cory."

24

——————

I T WAS CLEAR to me: strong collaboration, legal and otherwise, was going to be required to get a murder conviction. We needed to act quickly. Gather the evidence, bring it to court, call witnesses, wherever they needed to come from. Had any Pengali ever travelled to Earth? If not, Abri would be the first.

Since it didn't seem appropriate to invite my association into the president's office, I asked Margarethe to come outside to meet them.

She had seen most of them before, of course, but only as inhabitants of my apartment. They sat on the couches or, in case of Deyu and Reida, on the floor, for the lack of seats.

When I finished the introductions, she said, "That is certainly an impressive team."

I explained to her that we could, given the right access and permits, unleash Thayu, Deyu and Devlin on the Nations of Earth systems to rat out spy systems. Veyada could liaise with legal experts. He was reasonably certain that the charge of murder could be made to stick *somewhere*, especially since it looked like both Robert and Gusamo had used *gamra* identities. We should find out which were the created identities and persecute them in their own jurisdiction. Having recently qualified as *gamra* lawyer, Veyada could do that.

"Mind you," I added. "It may not be possible to make sure that he actually does time in jail, but we can at least prevent him using the Exchange."

"Oh, when we get a conviction, he will spend time in jail," Veyada said. "He might even have the choice of facing a jail term here or in Barresh."

If he was sane, he would choose Earth, because the Barresh jail was notorious for never releasing murderers. They tended to die in jail.

I had to translate that for Margarethe, and she smiled at him. "I think I like this guy."

"I like him, too. Very much."

"I also like the idea of getting spying routines out of our systems."

"That would require my assistants to have access to them. Can you make this happen?" That was a slightly self-centred question. I wanted access to the Earth news again.

"It's not easy, but I think I can. Let me investigate."

"We have a bit of time, depending on how long you can hold Robert for. We have an election coming up in a few weeks, and I need to support the candidate I'm sponsoring."

"It's an election year for you, too, huh?"

"It certainly is. And you know the candidate. Marin Federza. He has a really good chance of getting the position. Hopefully, *gamra* will be a bit more stable then."

"That's good, because I fear the opposite for us. Our election is in August. *Gamra* membership is a very volatile issue, and public opinion could easily switch either way."

I nodded. I knew. I had lived on that line between Nations of Earth and *gamra* for years, until I went to work for Ezhya. It was a finely balanced and at times hostile environment.

"There are a number of hot-button topics that we have to deal with."

"Religion," I said.

She nodded. There were no more words necessary. People still believed that *gamra* would have an antireligious agenda. That argument was just not going away, no matter how much I tried to disprove it.

"If there is anything I can do . . ."

"Yes, while you're here, I'd like you to address the plenary session of the assembly," she said.

My heart jumped. This was something I'd signed up to do when I first accepted my position: give a report of my six-month tenure to the assembly. Because of the events that had transpired back then, and because Ezhya had taken over my contract, that had never happened.

I'd always wondered how my speech, had I gotten the opportunity to make one, would have been received.

"Is there anything in particular you'd like me to address?"

"Just your perspective on the reasons for joining and what it will mean for ordinary people."

"I can do the first. In all honesty, I haven't lived as an ordinary person on Earth since I was ten. I don't think my contribution on that front will be valuable."

"Fair enough. Stick with your perspective then. I'll schedule you for this Wednesday."

"Uh, what day is it now?" That was my alienation from Earth speaking right there.

"Monday. I'll schedule you for a voice coach, too."

I frowned at her. "Voice coach?"

"In this speech, I don't want to hear any of that Coldi accent you've got."

I was going to protest with *Me? Coldi accent?* But I realised she was probably right.

I rarely spoke Isla anymore. I thought in Coldi, I dreamed in Coldi. I was looking into a procedure that would turn me effectively Coldi. This shouldn't come as such a surprise to me.

But ouch, it was certainly sobering.

I said that I'd be there at whatever time she required me, and then an employee came in to tell us that he would take us to our accommodation.

This accommodation was a unit inside the compound, not terribly far from where I used to live as a boy with my father and Erith. Since it was morning in New Zealand, I rang him.

He was not entirely surprised that I was in Rotterdam.

"There have been rumours of the blue diamonds coming from Barresh for many years. It doesn't surprise me at all, and I doubt it's the only such scheme."

Sadly, I agreed with him.

The line was probably bugged, so I asked him about the horses and the camels. They were fine, he informed me, but they were in the midst of a rabbit explosion. Erith had taken to making rabbit pies.

I told him we'd visit soon, and I meant it. I wanted to tell him in person of my decision to go ahead with gene treatment if it became available.

When I went upstairs to where everyone was asleep, I looked out the window in the stairwell. Outside in the snow stood a guard.

Thayu woke up when I wormed myself into the unfamiliar bed, after having tripped over a chair.

"Things have changed a lot here," she said.

"How?" I agreed, but was unable to put my finger on why.

"Everyone is nervous. Everyone is trying to protect their little patch of ground. Everyone thinks that everyone else is an enemy."

"Yeah. We've brought Robert, but there are a lot more like him. This is only a small part of the problem."

"As is always the case."

We were silent for a while. I tried to get comfortable on the strange pillow with a strong smell of soap. The blanket was quite thin, I thought. Thayu wasn't cold because she was wearing her temperature retaining suit.

"Did you hear what Margarethe said about me?"

"I think I missed that."

"She said that I have a Coldi accent."

Thayu chuckled, but she said no more. I was sure she understood my dilemma, and I knew she would give me the time to work it out.

We were silent for a bit, and then I said, "I'm going to have to get out of bed again. This blanket is too thin. I'm cold."

"We all know how to solve that."

"Haha." I did get out of bed. I had to turn on the light, found a thick blanket and put that over the bed. Thayu took off her suit and it got very warm under the blanket.

Fortunately, it gets light very late in Europe in early February.

———

Addressing the assembly at Nations of Earth involved just as much preparation as it did at *gamra*, if not more, due to my unfamiliarity with the process.

I saw Margarethe's voice coach the next day, a middle-aged lady who told me that my accent had acquired a lot of Coldi intonation and made me repeat sentences until I sounded like one of the Nations of Earth high society set. It reminded me of Eva and her dinner parties, and other things I didn't want to be reminded of.

I came back to lunch in the accommodation.

"You're grumpy," Thayu said. "Why are you grumpy?"

"This woman is trying to turn me into some kind of high-class stodgy delegate. Why should I speak like all of them? Why should I take my earring out? Why should I cut my hair?"

"Is that what she told you?"

"Yes."

"Because that is the way *they* want to see you. They're happy for you to wear the blues, but everything else needs to look as if you're one of them."

She was right. I went to stand by the window. That guard was still outside, standing in the snow that didn't look half as pristine during the day as it looked at night under the light of the moon.

Was that man there because we needed protection, or was he there so that we didn't go anywhere and contact anyone that Nations of Earth might not like?

Both, probably.

Or maybe I was seeing ghosts everywhere.

I sighed. "Well, screw them. When I walk in there, I will do so as someone who was born in New Zealand, who spent most of his life off-Earth, who is fluent in Coldi and spends more time speaking that than Isla, someone who is a member of the Domiri clan, and someone who cares about peace and cooperation. If they don't like that . . ." I spread my hands. I didn't know what would happen if they didn't like that. They probably didn't.

I couldn't help that. I didn't want to pretend to be what I was not.

Veyada said, "Whatever happens, we will be there."

And that was the bottom line. They were my association and they supported me, unconditionally.

———

I didn't just decide to ignore the voice coaching; I went a step further.

I decided that I would go into the assembly hall with my full association in full regalia. I'd have Nicha and Thayu on either side of the speaker's dais if they could get that far. I wanted the others, too. Veyada in his white lawyer's gown and Sheydu in black, as well as Reida and Deyu in *gamra* colours.

On the morning of the speech I told them all to prepare and look their very best. I caught Deyu and Reida in the bathroom slicking each other's hair down so not single strand escaped their ponytails. Veyada performed Eirani's task for me. He combed and plaited my hair, brushed hair and dust off my shoulders and arranged my jewellery. Then I did the same for him, combing and tying up his thick hair with its typical metallic sheen.

I was probably more agitated and nervous than any of them, but I tried very hard not to let it show. If anything, I had never expected my first-ever address to the assembly to be like this, from the outside looking in.

We walked through the compound, past the school, across the lawn where I used to play and that seemed to have become much smaller. We went up the ramp to the hall's forecourt, where driverless cars queued up to deliver assembly delegates to the meeting. Some of the trees in front of the assembly hall were no longer there. Others had grown much bigger. We followed the stream inside. The guard at the door looked on with wide eyes as our party came up to the door.

Predictably, he needed to check with his supervisor whether we could all get through. Was I a member? No. Did I fall under visiting dignitaries? If so, what was the status of my companions?

Eventually, the matter went up to Margarethe and she had to send someone to rescue us from the bureaucrats. Had I not been at the place that used to be my home and had I been less familiar with the situation, an altercation might well have taken place. I was so fed up with this rubbish.

As we followed the guard into the big assembly hall, I remembered Veyada's words back when we were in Taysha's apartment in Athyl and we'd spoken about Coldi protocol in the case of writs. Veyada had explained the whole legal process, and then I'd asked if that was what he and Sheydu would do if Taysha insulted them as he had insulted me, and he'd said, "No, we'd just have gone to his quarters and shot him."

I'd come to appreciate Veyada's down-to-earth view on matters, but it was a strange memory to come to my mind as I was walking through the hall, on the main floor where I had never set foot, watching the various delegations in all tiers of seating around me. The hall was not unlike the *gamra* assembly hall—and, to be honest, how many more ways were there to organise two thousand people in a conference hall? The inner council, including Margarethe, sat on the circular arrangement of tables on the main floor, each section backed up by countless technicians and interpreters who read over the computer translations and corrected as necessary.

It occurred to me that I could have appealed to give my address in Coldi. That would have annoyed the living daylights out of them.

I ignored the people who whispered and pointed at me. Thayu and Nicha walked on either side of me, Veyada and Sheydu in front of us and Deyu and Reida behind us. It was a classic defensive formation. I didn't think too many people would pick up on the fact that a Coldi leader feeling comfortable would walk at the head of his association. Margarethe looked up at me. She might know some of the very subtle messages Coldi used by altering their appearance or stance. Her eyes widened briefly. If she had assumed that my submitting to her voice coach meant that I was going to behave like her woman wanted, she knew me poorly.

My association reached the dais intact.

There were some guards on the floor who looked uncertain of this alien invasion of their domain. Margarethe had probably let them know that we were allowed through, but happy about it, they were not.

I stepped up to the dais, and an employee came to turn on the light. Thayu and Nicha remained on the floor in front of me, the others took up position behind me.

I looked into the darkness of the hall, at all those thousands of largely hostile faces, and started speaking.

It was not the best speech I'd ever written. Margarethe had let her speechwriter read over it and he had removed a good number of statements he considered too controversial or too strongly worded.

In addition, Isla was a poor language in which to deliver a speech. At *gamra*, when holding a speech in Coldi, your most powerful weapons were pronouns. Isla only had one version of you we, I, he, she. So my speech amounted to little more than a simple recount of what had happened, what I had done and what my conclusions were. I could not poke any faction by using a polemic pronoun, or mollify another faction by using a friendly pronoun. To be honest, I was unfamiliar with the factions and where they sat. Margarethe had given me a rundown of the politics, but as I stood there, I had never felt more out of my depth or more alien.

I didn't belong here anymore. Possibly, I had never belonged here and it had taken me this long to see it.

There were lots of questions when I finished. Some of them were legal, and I referred them to Veyada. Some were in relation to security and I gave them to Sheydu. Others related to spies and I let Thayu deal with those.

I translated for them.

Some questions related specifically to Robert's case, some were about Gusamo, but many were about *gamra* in general. I was happy that the questions were not so much about the technicalities as they were about the politics of *gamra*, how membership would be received and what mutual benefits could be.

Some people wanted to stir up controversial topics, but I was well-versed in deflecting these questions.

But it seemed that the cogs of the huge bureaucratic machine were turning and that people here were starting to see potential benefits of joining.

———

I saw Margarethe in her office after the meeting ended.

"That was a very good speech," she said. "Thank you for doing that."

"These people have no idea what a good speech is," I said, sitting down. "Next time, I'll give the speech in Coldi." Although that wouldn't change the fact that Isla only had one pronoun form with which to please, annoy or insult someone.

"You and your assistants looked very impressive. You are really more Coldi than human."

"We're all human," I said.

But I knew what she meant, and I would have to accept that she was right.

We spoke about the impending court case. Lawyers had charged Robert with some sort of bureaucratic offence with the aim of keeping him locked up until we had gathered enough evidence and witnesses for the murder case. Margarethe was going to relax visiting rules for offworld people for the purpose of the case. I guessed that if and when Abri was called to testify I'd have to come with her to coach her and avert disasters.

It would be interesting.

I walked next to Thayu on the way back to our accommodation. We'd stay for a few more days to organise and prepare, but then we needed to go back to Barresh for the election there.

"Is your father hanging around in orbit somewhere?" I asked her.

"I truly have no idea where he is," she said. "Why are you asking?"

"I'd like to accept his invitation to have a ceremony to accept me into the Domiri clan. I'm also going to see Lilona as soon as we're back. And I need to speak to Amarru. I'm going to officially ask for a Coldi identity."

She stared at me. "Are you sure? I thought you were still thinking about it."

"I've thought about it far too long already. I'm done with thinking."

"Well . . ." she said, and then she said nothing for a long time. But she took my hand as we walked through the snow.

A Word of Thanks

THANK YOU very much for reading *Blue Diamond Sky*.

In book 6 of the Ambassador series, *The Enemy Within*, Abri and the Pengali witnesses are called to testify at Nations of Earth. The court case reveals a deep political divide in the Nations of Earth assembly.

Be a champ and get The Enemy Within direct from the author in ebook, print or audio.

ABOUT THE AUTHOR

Patty Jansen lives in Sydney, Australia, where she spends most of her time writing Science Fiction and Fantasy.

Her career started in earnest when her story *This Peaceful State of War* placed first in the second quarter of the Writers of the Future contest and was published in their 27th anthology. She has also sold fiction to genre magazines such as Analog Science Fiction and Fact, Redstone SF and Aurealis, before making the move to independent publishing.

Patty has written over fifty novels in both Science Fiction and Fantasy, including the *Icefire Trilogy* and the *Ambassador* series.

pattyjansen.com

BOOKS BY PATTY JANSEN

MORE INFORMATION:

PATTYJANSEN.COM

For a complete list of books, scan the image below with your phone.